THE LAKE DISTRICT MURDER

JOHN BUDE

With an Introduction by Martin Edwards

THE BRITISH LIBRARY

This edition published in 2014 by

The British Library
96 Euston Road
London NW1 2DB

Originally published in London in 1935 by Skeffington & Son

Introduction © Martin Edwards 2014
Cataloguing in Publication Data
A catalogue record for this book is available from The British Library

ISBN 978 0 7123 5716 6

Typeset by IDSUK (DataConnection) Ltd
Printed and bound by CPI Group (UK) Ltd, Croydon, CR0 4YY

CONTENTS

INTRODUCTION

MARTIN EDWARDS

John Bude was quick to follow up his enjoyable debut mystery novel, *The Cornish Coast Murder*. In the very same year, 1935, Skeffington also published *The Lake District Murder*. The titles of his first two books indicate that Bude had hit on the idea of setting stories in attractive areas of Britain, in the hope that the background would appeal to readers as well as the murder mystery plots. This is a shrewd marketing ploy, but has no chance of success if the author lacks a genuine feel for the location. Fortunately, Bude not only knew but clearly loved his Lake District.

The story opens one March evening, with a farmer finding a man's body in a car outside the Derwent garage on an isolated road in the Northern Lakes. The macabre discovery is reported to Inspector Meredith, and at first glance, the evidence at the crime scene suggests that Jack Clayton has committed suicide. The seasoned mystery fan does not, of course, need to rely on the giveaway clue in the book's title to realise that all is not as it seems. It soon emerges that Clayton had no reason to do away with himself. He had been in good spirits, and was engaged to be married to an attractive and likeable young woman called Lily Reade. When Meredith discovers that Clayton was planning to move abroad, and that he had much more money in his bank account than would be generated by a half-share in the profits of a wayside garage, the plot begins to thicken. But if Clayton has been murdered, what could be the motive?

In his first novel, Bude had counterpointed the police investigation with some amateur sleuthing, but here the focus is from start to finish on Meredith's patient and relentless quest to uncover the truth: 'Whatever faults may be attributed to the British police force by the American or continental critics, a lack of thoroughness is not one of them'.

The emphasis is not on whodunit, but on how to prove it. Today, because of the phenomenal success of Agatha Christie, there is a widespread assumption that Thirties detective fiction was invariably set in country houses or picturesque villages like Jane Marple's St Mary Mead. In fact, crime novelists of the time adopted a range of approaches, and Bude's method here is firmly in the school of Freeman Wills Crofts.

Crofts (1879–1957) was, at the height of his fame, regarded by many as Christie's equal or superior, and T. S. Eliot, a detective-story fan and occasional critic, was among those who extolled his virtues. Starting with the hugely popular and highly influential *The Cask* in 1920, Crofts specialised in meticulous accounts of painstaking police work, in which the plot often pivoted on the detective's attempts to destroy an apparently unbreakable alibi. The care which Crofts lavished on story construction impressed readers and fellow authors alike, and he had a number of notable disciples, including Henry Wade and G. D. H. Cole. Here, John Bude produces a book of which Crofts would have been proud.

Meredith is neither an eccentric genius nor any sort of maverick. He is tactful and a team player, an ordinary, hard-working professional, with a long-suffering wife and eager teenage son. After the inquest on Clayton records a verdict of murder by person or persons unknown, piece by piece, Meredith puts together a case against the guilty. The clues are slight, but prove significant – pleasingly, they even include an Adolf Hitler-style moustache.

Despite using the Lake District as a 'hook' to attract interest, Bude wisely avoids falling into the trap of turning the book into a travelogue. We see the Lake District where people live and work, rather than the tourist trap. Bude's Lakeland is an often sombre place of quiet pubs and lonely filling stations, with towns and villages inhabited by affable bank managers, burly tanker drivers, and women who 'shopped, cooked, cleaned, darned, mended, washed, and ironed, and all for a matter of ten shillings a week'.

Instead of more familiar spots such as Ambleside and Windermere, Bude's storyline features relatively unglamorous coastal towns such as Whitehaven and Maryport, and is all the more credible because of it. This book may be a product of the Golden Age of detective fiction, but it is a world away from the unreality of bodies in the library and cunningly contrived killings in transcontinental trains. Meredith earns a well-deserved promotion at the end of the book, and he proceeded to appear in most of Bude's murder stories, which numbered thirty in all by the time of his death in 1957.

Three years after *The Lake District Murder* was published, Muna Lee and Maurice Guinness – who, under the pen-name Newton Gayle, wrote a quintet of acclaimed detective novels in a short-lived burst of creative energy – produced *Sinister Crag*, a climbing mystery set among the Lakeland fells. But theirs is essentially the perspective of outsiders; Bude's book conveys a broader and perhaps more authentic picture of life – and death – in this beautiful part of the world.

Bude, whose real name was Ernest Carpenter Elmore, was born in Kent in 1901, and his literary career began with a couple of weird and fantastic tales, *The Steel Grubs* appearing in 1928 and *The Siren Song* two years later. Although he is now best known for his crime novels, he worked in the theatre as a producer and director, and in 1953 he became one of the founding members of the Crime Writers' Association. The British Library editions of his first two novels, both rare and sought after by collectors, bring him at last to the attention of a new generation of readers. Those who like a soundly crafted and unpretentious mystery will surely agree that John Bude deserves to be better known.

THE LAKE DISTRICT MURDER

CHAPTER I

THE BODY IN THE CAR

WHEN the northbound road leaves Keswick, it skirts the head of Derwentwater, curves into the picturesque village of Portinscale and then runs more or less straight up a broad and level valley until it arrives at the little, mountain-shadowed hamlet of Braithwaite. There is a fair amount of traffic up this valley, particularly in the summer; tourists wending their way into the Buttermere valley are bound to take this road, for the very simple reason that there's no other road to take. It also links up the inland Cumbrian towns with the coastal towns of Whitehaven, Workington and Maryport.

About half-way between Portinscale and Braithwaite, on a very bleak and uninhabited stretch of road, stands a newish stone-and-cement garage on the rim of a spacious meadow. There are a few petrol pumps between the road and a broad concrete draw-in, where cars can fill up without checking the main traffic. The garage itself is a plain, rectangular building with a flat roof, on one side of which is a brick lean-to with a corrugated iron roof. About ten paces from the Braithwaite side of the garage there is a small, stone, slate-roofed cottage. It is not flush with the road, but set back about fifty feet or more, fronted with an unkempt garden which boasts a few wind-stunted crab-apple trees. Altogether this small desolate group of buildings is not exactly prepossessing. One feels that only the necessity of earning a livelihood would drive a man to dwell in such a spot.

One wet and windy night, toward the end of March, a dilapidated T-model Ford was rattling through the deserted street of Portinscale. At the wheel sat a red-faced, bluff-looking farmer of about sixty. He was returning from a Farmers' Union dinner in Keswick. He felt pleased and at peace with the world, for he had that inside him which sufficed to keep out the cold, and the engine of the Ford, for all its years, was running as smooth as silk. Another twenty minutes, he reckoned, would see him in Braithwaite, roasting his toes at a roaring fire, with a "night-cap" at his elbow to round off a very convivial evening.

But it is precisely at those moments when the glass seems to be "set fair" that Fate invariably decides to take a hand.

And Fate had decided that Farmer Perryman was to make a late night of it.

He had, in fact, only just cleared the last outlying cottages of the village when the Ford engine broke into a series of spluttering coughs and finally petered out. Drawing into the side of the road, Luke, cursing under his breath, buttoned up the collar of his coat, pulled an electric-torch out of his pocket and proceeded to investigate the trouble. He didn't have to look far. His first diagnosis proved correct. He was out of petrol.

Luckily Luke knew every inch of the route and, although he could not actually see it, he knew that the Derwent garage lay just round a slight bend about a quarter of a mile up the road. Realizing that there was nothing else to be done, since he carried no spare can, he shoved his head down into the wind and rain and trudged off surlily in the direction of Braithwaite.

Soon the row of lighted petrol pumps hove in sight and in a few minutes Luke Perryman drew abreast of the garage. Although a light was burning in the main shed, the place seemed curiously deserted. Nor did Luke's raucous demands for service do anything to disturb this illusion. Noticing a push-bell, obviously connected with the cottage, he pressed it and waited. But again without result. He was just on the point of investigating a light which he had noticed burning in the window of the cottage, when he stopped dead and listened. Faintly above the bluster of the wind he heard the sound of a car engine. At first he thought it must be a car approaching up the road, but suddenly he realized that the sound was coming from the lean-to shed on the Portinscale side of the garage.

Luke was puzzled. There was evidently no light burning in the shed, for although the doors were closed it would have been natural for a glimmer of light to show through the cracks. His first thought was that either young Clayton or his partner, Higgins, had started a car, been called away on another job, and forgotten to return and switch off the engine.

He tried the handle of the doors, therefore, and finding them unlocked, opened them and shone his torch into the interior. His first impression was of an acrid and obnoxious odour cooped up in the sealed shed. An odour which made him catch his breath and cough. Then, as the air freshened, the circle of light from his torch travelled slowly over the back of the car and came to rest on a figure, seated, facing away from him, at the driving-wheel. Something about the set of the man's shoulders convinced him that it was Clayton.

He called out, therefore: "Hi, Clayton! I couldn't make anybody hear. I've run short of petrol and have had to leave my car way back up the road."

But to his profound surprise the man made no answer. A trifle alarmed, Luke thrust his way round to the front of the car and flung the light of his torch full on to the face of the immobile figure. Then he had the shock of his life. The man had no face! Where his face should have been was a sort of inhuman, uniform blank!

It took old Perryman some few seconds to right this illusion and when he did he was horrified. Although somewhat slow of mind, he realized, at once, that he was face to face with tragedy and, what was more, tragedy in its starkest and most nerve-racking guise!

The man's head was hooded in an oil-grimed mackintosh, which had been gathered in round the neck with a piece of twine. From the back Luke had mistaken this cowl for an ordinary leather driving-helmet. Frightened, bewildered, wasting no time on speculation, he laid his torch on the front seat and shot out a pair of shaking hands. Clumsily he undid the twine and drew aside the hood. Then, with an exclamation of horror, he started back and stared at the terrible apparition which confronted him. It was Clayton all right! Clayton with a fearfully distorted, blue-lipped, sightless face! He felt his heart. There was no movement! The man's hand was cold!

In the stress of the moment he had not fully realized what it was which had slipped from under the mackintosh when he had loosened the twine. He had heard something thump on to the upholstery of the other front seat. Now he took a quick look and, in a flash, he knew *why* Clayton was dead.

Hastily closing the doors, he remained undecided for a moment, unable to make up his mind whether it was worthwhile finding out if the cottage was really deserted. Then convinced that his violent rings on the service bell would have brought somebody forward if indeed there was anybody there, he lumbered back into the main garage, found a can of petrol and set off at a smart trot toward his car. In less than five minutes he was speeding as fast as the T-model would allow in the direction of the Keswick police station.

It was striking ten as the Ford drew up outside the station. As luck would have it, Inspector Meredith was still in the building.

Arrears of routine work had kept him working late. When the constable showed the farmer into the office, Meredith looked up and grinned.

"Good heavens, sir," he said in his pleasingly resonant voice, "you haven't come here to tell me your car's been stolen, surely? You won't get me to believe *that*!"

Old Luke, who was sadly out of breath and shaken by his discovery, dropped into a chair. His first words took the smile off the Inspector's face.

"I wish it was that. But it's something serious, Inspector. It's young Clayton out at the Derwent garage."

"Well?"

"Suicide, I reckon."

"Suicide, eh!" The Inspector was already reaching for his cap. "Your car's outside, Mr. Perryman?"

Luke nodded.

"Then perhaps you'll give me details on the way over."

As they passed through the outer office, Meredith turned to the constable. "Phone Doctor Burney, Railton, and ask him to meet me at the Derwent garage on the Braithwaite road as soon as possible. Then get out the combination and join us there."

As the old Ford rattled off again through the rain-wet streets, Meredith gathered in the details of Luke Perryman's discovery. When the old man had finished his recital the Inspector grunted:

"Not a very pleasant wind-up to your evening, Mr. Perryman? Looks like a late night for me, too. Do you know anything about this young chap?"

Old Luke considered a moment.

"Well, I do, and then again, I don't. I've heard he's engaged to Tom Reade's eldest daughter. He's the Braithwaite storekeeper, as you may know. But beyond a few words with Clayton in a business sort of way, I can't rightly say I know him."

"The girl lives at the shop, I suppose?"

"Ay."

"And what about this partner of Clayton's? Know anything about him?"

Luke shook his head and then declared: "Though from all accounts it's Clayton who's got the business head. I've heard—mind you, I don't know—that Higgins is a bit too fond of lifting his elbow."

Meredith registered this piece of information. Wasn't it possible that Higgins was drinking away the profits of the concern? It might turn out to be the reason for Clayton's suicide.

He had no more time for theorizing, however, for with a wild screeching of brakes the old Ford drew up on the concrete beside the petrol pumps. Immediately Meredith sprang out, whilst Luke shut off the engine of the car. Faintly above the wind the Inspector heard the sound which had previously drawn the farmer to the tragic spot. Striding over to the shed, he opened the double doors and flashed his lamp into the interior.

"No switch in here?" he asked.

Luke confessed that he had been so upset by his discovery that he hadn't troubled to look. Meredith, however, soon found what he was looking for just inside the door. The next instant the shed was flooded with electric light.

"You didn't move the body, I take it?"

"No. Just the mackintosh that was over the poor fellow's head and the bit of string tied round his neck. You see, Inspector, I wasn't sure at first that he was dead."

"Well, that's all right."

Meredith leaned over the dash-board and switched off the engine.

"Now, then—let's see exactly how he did it."

A brief examination soon made this clear. The fish-tail end of the silencer had been removed from the exhaust-pipe at the rear of the car. Over the end of this pipe had been fitted a length of ordinary, flexible garden-hose. This in turn led over the back-seat of the car, an old open tourer, and thus up under the mackintosh which Clayton had tied over his head. It was the end of this hose which had fallen on to the front seat when the farmer had removed the mackintosh.

"Neat!" was Meredith's blunt comment when he had completed his examination. Then: "Hullo! Who's this?" he added, as a car swung off the road and drew up behind the Ford.

A brisk, well-set-up young man in a belted overcoat crossed into the radius of the light.

"Evening, Inspector. I was just putting away the car when I got your call. What's the trouble here?"

Meredith in a few words outlined Luke's discovery to Dr. Burney, who without delay made a thorough external examination of the body. At the end of a few minutes he reported:

"No doubt as to the cause of death, Meredith. Asphyxiation due to the inhalation of exhaust fumes. One of the chief products of petrol combustion, as you probably know, is carbon monoxide. Looks as if he's taken a pretty big dose of the stuff."

"How long do you think he's been dead?"

"Difficult to say exactly. Probably two to three hours. It depends, of course, on individual reaction."

As they were discussing the matter further, Railton arrived on the motor-cycle combination and Meredith sent him over to the cottage to investigate. He returned in a short time to say that although there was a light burning in the parlour, the place was deserted.

"Looks as if Higgins is away," commented the Inspector. "We shall have to get in touch with him as soon as possible. Now, suppose we move the body into the cottage—less public there, eh, Doctor?"

The doctor agreed and Meredith and Railton between them carried their burden down the garden path and laid it out on a horsehair sofa in the little sitting-room. There Doctor Burney made a second examination, which did nothing to modify his first opinion. In the meantime Meredith was gazing round the room with a great deal of interest and surprise.

The table was covered with a white cloth on which a meal had been laid, evidently a sort of high tea. The teapot itself had the lid off and a spoonful or so of tea had already been measured into it. There was also, Meredith was quick to note, a peculiar, metallic, burning smell in the room. Almost instinctively his eye wandered to the fireplace where, on an old-fashioned kitchen-range above a fire which had now died down to a handful of glowing embers, was a large black kettle. On picking it up he was not surprised to find that it had boiled dry and that the base of it had already begun to melt away.

Meredith was puzzled. It was curious that Clayton should have laid the meal, put tea into the teapot, the kettle on the range and then abruptly left the cottage with the idea of taking his own life. The method he had employed argued premed-itation—the mackintosh, the string, the hose-pipe—these objects suggested a carefully planned and cleverly executed suicide. That being the case, why had he made all these prepa-rations for a meal? Was it that a suitable opportunity suddenly presented itself and Clayton had seized the chance? But surely the early hours of the morning would have been better for his purpose than a time when there would almost certainly be cars on the road.

He turned to Railton.

"Do you know if Clayton and Higgins have a woman to look after them?"

Railton shook his head.

"No, sir. That is, not after two o'clock. I happen to know Mrs. Swinley who comes out from Portinscale to do for them. But they don't have anybody living in."

Meredith wondered if one of Mrs. Swinley's duties was to lay the evening meal before she went home. If so, that would account for a great deal. But not everything. The kettle, for example. She certainly wouldn't put the kettle on to boil at two o'clock for a meal that was to be eaten, say, at six. He drew the doctor's attention to the facts.

"It's strange, I admit," was Doctor Burney's comment. "But people who are contemplating suicide often do strange things."

"You've nothing further to report, Doctor?"

"Nothing. Except that it looks as if Clayton had taken a good stiff peg of whisky before attempting the job. I noticed a faint smell of spirits round the lips. But beyond the usual symptoms of asphyxia the young fellow appears to be in a normally healthy condition. I'll put in my official report, of course. You might give me a ring when the day of the inquest is fixed."

The Inspector crossed over to the door with Doctor Burney, shook hands and watched him drive off in his car. Then, still thinking hard, he turned back into the room to take an official statement from Luke Perryman.

CHAPTER II

MEREDITH GETS GOING

WHEN Luke Perryman, rather grey and shaken by his experience, had clattered off in the Ford, Meredith heaved a sigh of relief. He could now turn his full attention to the matter in hand. As it was already past eleven o'clock he did not feel justified in notifying Miss Reade about the tragedy. Time enough for that in the morning. On the other hand, where was Higgins? As he was in closer touch with Clayton than anybody, he ought to be found.

"It's a nuisance about this Higgins chap," he said to Railton. "He's probably away for the week-end. No chance of us finding out where he is, eh?"

Railton thought for a moment.

"Well, there's David Hogg at the Hare and Hounds in Braithwaite. Higgins is a regular customer of his. He might know. If you like, I could run the bike in and find out, sir."

Meredith at once fell in with the suggestion and Railton departed on his errand. Left alone with the body, Meredith's thoughts again drifted to the curious fact of the waiting meal and the burnt-out kettle. Somehow he could not dismiss the fact with the facile explanation given by Dr. Burney. Granted suicides are often the result of temporary mental aberration, but everything in this case showed that Clayton had not acted on the spur of the moment. There was the hose-pipe, for example. Meredith had noted that it fitted exactly over the exhaust-pipe of the car. It may have been pure chance; on the other hand, it was a strong argument in favour of premeditation.

Then there was another point. Why had Clayton left the light burning in the cottage? If his idea was to be safe from interruption, this seemed an idiotic thing to do. A customer, not being able to make anybody hear at the garage, would naturally investigate at the cottage if they saw a lighted window.

Then, finding nobody about, they would instinctively jump to the conclusion that something was wrong. And again—the time? There would be cars on the road, particularly as it was Saturday night. If anybody drawing up at the petrol-pumps shut off his engine he would be bound to hear the engine of the second car in the shed.

The more Meredith thought about it the less satisfied he was with the aspects of the case.

He searched round to see if Clayton had left any letter, either to the Coroner or to his fiancée, Miss Reade. But a cursory rummage round the room brought nothing to light. He then went methodically through the pockets of the dead man.

Clayton was dressed in buff dungarees, over a shiny, blue lounge suit. From the first Meredith extracted an adjustable spanner, a roll of insulating tape, one or two odd nuts and bolts and an oily piece of rag. These he placed on the table. From the pockets of the suit he obtained just those articles which a man of Clayton's type and calling would naturally carry around with him. Pocket-knife, a bunch of keys, a packet of Players, matches, and so on. But there was no sign of any letter.

Turning out the light, Meredith closed the door of the cottage and returned to the lean-to shed. This time he examined more closely the coupling of the hose with the exhaust-pipe. Then putting on a pair of leather gloves, after a lot of cautious twisting and tugging he succeeded in working the hose free. At once he was struck by a fresh detail. The end of the hose-pipe which had been fitted over the exhaust had been newly severed. The white rubber had been cut through, leaving a clean circle, whilst the end of the hose which had been thrust under the mackintosh was both frayed and soiled.

"One more detail in favour of premeditation," thought Meredith. "Obvious that the hose has been cut to an exact length."

He then picked up the fish-tail end of the silencer, which lay under the rear-axle. Noticing that there was a bolted clip to fix it to the exhaust, he tried to get it back into place. After a lot more twisting and easing he succeeded in doing so. Then satisfied that there was nothing further to occupy his attention in the garage, he switched out the light and returned to the cottage.

His investigations in the lean-to left him more puzzled than ever and it was with a feeling of dissatisfaction that he began to pace up and down the little room. Clayton had obviously cut off that piece of hose to some predetermined measurement, and yet, after all his detailed preparations, what had he apparently done? Walked casually out of the cottage, after laying his meal, and as casually taken his life! Surely there was something wrong somewhere? A man doesn't plan out a careful suicide and then, with a sudden reversion of tactics, put his plan so carelessly into execution.

Disturbed by these curious discrepancies in the affair, Meredith tugged off his gloves and flung them on to the white table-cloth. He was not the sort of man given to erratic flights of imagination. Reason, he always argued, was the common-sense basis on which to found a criminal investigation. And in this case what did his reason suggest? Did it mean that——?

Suddenly he broke off his meditations and uttered a sharp exclamation. His gaze was riveted on the table-cloth, now no longer white but sadly blackened by the contact of his gloves. An idea had flashed into his mind. The grime on his gloves had accrued from his fiddling with the fish-tail end of the exhaust. He realized, instantly, that it would be impossible for anybody to have unscrewed the fish-tail and to have replaced it with the hose without considerably blackening their hands. A fact which struck Meredith as extremely significant.

In two strides he was beside the body. With a quick action he caught hold of Clayton's right hand and turned it palm upward. *It was perfectly clean!* Then the left hand. Clean also! Although there was a certain amount of ingrained dirt, it was startlingly clear that Clayton had recently washed his hands with soap and water. Then how, in the name of thunder, had he removed the silencer and fitted on the hose to the exhaust without soiling his hands?

Two explanations at once occurred to Meredith. Either Clayton had worn gloves or else he had fitted the hose to the exhaust some time before the tragedy. But why should he wear gloves? It was unlike a car mechanic to be squeamish about soiling his hands. And why run the risk of fixing the hose to the exhaust some time before the fatal apparatus was needed? Higgins probably had a key to the smaller garage. A lot would depend, of course, on what time Higgins had left the place, but with Higgins about it seemed pretty certain that Clayton wouldn't be such a fool as to run the risk of his partner finding out about his intended suicide.

That being so—what did it mean? Was it within the bounds of possibility that somebody else, not Clayton, had coupled the hose with the pipe? If that were the case, all manner of unexpected suggestions opened out!

To begin with, it was quite natural that the tea should be laid and the kettle boiling. It was quite natural that the light should be burning in the parlour. Above all, it was quite natural that Clayton should have just washed his hands. If he was just about to sit down to his tea, wasn't it obvious that he would first remove the grime of his labours?

And if Clayton hadn't fixed the hose, then Clayton hadn't committed suicide. It meant—but at that point the Inspector drew himself up short. Where was all this theorizing leading him? Weren't his suspicions rather running away with his common sense? After all, the affair had every appearance of suicide and just because one or two extraordinary details of the case had intrigued him, he had no right to assume that it wasn't suicide. Still, there it was. He would have to incorporate his suspicions into the official report. After that—well, he couldn't do better than leave it to his superiors.

His meditations were cut short by Railton's return.

"It's all right, sir. I've traced him. He's staying at the Beacon Hotel in Penrith. I didn't wait to report first but got through on the 'phone from the Hare and Hounds."

"Good. And he's coming over?"

"Right away on his motor-bike. He should be here in under the hour, sir."

"How did he take it, Railton?"

"Well, he sounded pretty cut up, of course. Surprised, too. Said something about it being 'impossible'."

The Inspector nodded. It was not the first time he had heard that particular phrase.

The constable's prophecy proved correct, for in less than an hour a high-powered motor-bike roared up to the garage and a round-shouldered individual, encased in a leather coat and helmet, came quickly up the cottage path.

Without wasting time on preliminaries, Meredith introduced himself, uttered a few words of sympathy and got Mark Higgins formally to identify the body. Higgins was a thin, ferret-faced man of about thirty, and there was that about his speech which the Inspector immediately placed as Cockney. He seemed a highly strung sort of fellow, but Meredith was unable to say if this was normal or whether the shock of Clayton's death had temporarily unnerved him. After answering a few official questions, Higgins drew off his helmet and gloves, wiped his rain-wet face with a handkerchief and, dropping into an arm-chair, lit a cigarette.

"Rather spoilt your week-end, Mr. Higgins," observed Meredith casually. "When were you intending to return?"

"To-morrow afternoon. You see, I had business over in Penrith. I was meeting a customer of ours at eleven-thirty to-morrow morning. I hoped to fix him up with a second-hand car." Higgins made a grimace. "Rather looks as if the deal's off now, doesn't it? Poor old Jack! Can't think why he's been and done this, Inspector.

Never seemed that sort of chap to me. I can tell you, it's fairly cut me up!"

"What time did you set off to-day for Penrith?"

"About quarter to six, I should think. And I'll swear there was nothing strange about Jack when I left him. Mind you, I don't say he hasn't been a bit moody at times. It's a lonely spot this in the winter months. Trade's not been too brisk, neither."

"You think that Clayton might have been a bit worried over the affairs of the garage?"

"It's possible. Not that we're in a bad way, but things always slacken off a lot in the winter. It's the tourists we rely on to bring out the balance on the right side."

Meredith nodded. He was rather puzzled by Higgins's behaviour. He seemed shaken and genuinely upset about his partner's death, yet at the same time curiously matter-of-fact. Probably he was trying to cover up any signs of what he considered unmanly emotion. However, as there seemed little point in questioning Higgins any further at the moment, Meredith explained that his presence would be required at the inquest and arranged to let him know the time and date.

"We shall have to get in touch with Clayton's relatives, of course. Do you know anything about them?"

Higgins didn't. He had always understood that his partner was an orphan. He had never heard him speak of any relatives, and he had rather gathered that, being a bit of a rolling stone, Clayton had not been in touch with his home circle for fifteen years or so. The two men had met, shortly after the War, in a Manchester pub. They both had a little capital and they had soon decided to go into partnership in a garage business. They had opened first in a Manchester suburb and later bought their present business at a favourable price when the late owner had suddenly decided to go abroad. Now, of course, Higgins didn't know what was going to happen. He'd carry on, if he could, single-handed for a time and then, perhaps, look around for a new partner who was willing to put money into the concern.

Before he left, Meredith saw the body laid out on the bed in Clayton's own room and got Higgins to accompany him to the lean-to. There Higgins identified the mackintosh as one belonging to his partner. The hose he remembered had been hanging in a woodshed behind the cottage with a lot of other old junk. No—as far as he knew, there hadn't been any trouble between Jack and Lily Reade. Of course, she'd have to be told, wouldn't she? Higgins gave the Inspector to understand that it wasn't a job he particularly relished doing himself. Meredith reassured him on this point and promised to acquaint Miss Reade with the tragedy on the following day. Then after "Good nights" had been said, Railton motored the Inspector back to Keswick.

Early the next morning Meredith was in touch with the headquarters of the Cumberland County Constabulary at Carlisle. The result of his report was not long in coming to light. The Superintendent demanded his immediate presence at headquarters. Before coming over he was to see Miss Reade at Braithwaite and gather all particulars about her relationship with the dead man. From the trend of the conversation Meredith felt that headquarters were as dissatisfied with the superficial aspects of the case as he was.

At ten-thirty he was in Braithwaite, ringing the bell of the closed general store. The Reade family were just getting ready for church. In a few carefully chosen words the Inspector broke the news of the tragedy and when the unfortunate girl had, more or less, gained control of her emotions, Meredith signed for her parents to leave them alone in the overcrowded little front parlour.

"I quite realize how terrible this is for you," said Meredith in kindly tones. "But I'm afraid there are one or two rather personal questions that I must ask you. Firstly, Miss Reade, I understand that you were officially engaged to Mr. Clayton?"

The girl nodded. The significance of that "were" in the Inspector's sentence had not escaped her notice. The tears welled up into her eyes. In that one word lay the whole essence of tragedy for her.

"And I suppose that since your engagement there has been no quarrel of any sort? You haven't had any disagreement or anything like that?"

Again the girl shook her head.

"No! Never!" she exclaimed. Then fighting back her tears she went on brokenly: "It was all fixed up. Jack was over only last Wednesday to see mother about the wedding. We were going to be married in early April. Then after our honeymoon we were planning to stay here for a week before going to Canada. Jack had already fixed up about the tickets. He had a job waiting for him out there. And now——"

The girl quickly buried her face in her hands and broke into renewed sobs. For some minutes Meredith preserved a discreet silence. He knew from long experience that it was inadvisable when certain vital information was needed from a witness, to ride roughshod over the human element in a case. Later he went on in a quiet voice. "I suppose Mr. Higgins knew about this arrangement? About Canada, I mean?"

The unhappy girl glanced up and shook her head. Then, struggling to overcome her acute distress, she said jerkily:

"No, Jack hadn't told him when he was over on Wednesday. They haven't been getting on too well of late. Jack knew it would mean an upset and he didn't want to make things difficult along at the garage. He was going to wait until about six weeks before ... before our marriage—then he was going to tell Mark. He felt it would be better like that."

Meredith agreed that he quite saw Clayton's point of view.

"What was the trouble between them, Miss Reade?"

"Oh, one thing and another. I'm afraid Mark's too fond of the public house. It meant that poor Jack had to do all the work. Mark was always gallivanting off somewhere. But it didn't make any difference to the money. The agreement is, so Jack told me, that they share the profits. So you see how it is?"

The Inspector could see only too clearly. It meant that Clayton, who had the brains and energy, was being forced to carry Higgins like a dead weight on his back. Higgins was no better than a sleeping partner in the concern. He felt, however, that it would not be politic to question the unhappy girl any further until he had received more detailed instructions from Carlisle. So, after proffering his sympathies, he climbed into the side-car and instructed the constable to drive him to headquarters.

Superintendent Thompson was waiting in his office. The two men shook hands and settled down without delay to discuss the affair in hand. Whilst Meredith catalogued his suspicions, the Superintendent every now and then shot out a trenchant query. At the conclusion of Meredith's statement he was obviously impressed.

"It strikes me, Inspector, that there's a good deal that wants explaining away here. That matter of the waiting meal, for example, and the fact that Clayton's hands were so clean. My feeling is that the coroner's inquest should be adjourned, pending further inquiries. At first glance, I grant you, it *looks* like suicide. Probably it was meant to. If it's not suicide, then the little scene staged in the garage was obviously a blind. That's my idea, anyway."

"And behind the blind, sir?" asked Meredith, meaningly.

"There is only one alternative. Murder. One can rule out accident, of course. A man with Clayton's knowledge of engineering wouldn't be such a fool as to experiment with exhaust fumes."

"So what do you suggest, sir?"

"That you go ahead and find out who called at the garage after Higgins left for Penrith at 5.45. Anybody passing the place may also be able to give you information. The Chief's over at Whitehaven to-day, but I'll get in touch with him directly he's back. In the meantime consider it your pigeon, Meredith. You started the hare and it's for you to follow it up."

Meredith left the office very well pleased with the interview. This *carte blanche* was just what he wanted. He felt more and more certain that there was some mystery behind Clayton's death. More so since he had interviewed Lily Reade. If there had been a quarrel between the engaged couple, there would have been the motive for the suicide. But there hadn't been a tiff. Clayton in fact had planned out his future with an exactitude which pretty nearly precluded the idea of contemplated suicide. There was the matter of the Canadian bookings, the plans for the wedding, the fixing of the date. Meredith decided that one of the first things to do was to verify from the steamship company the booking of the two berths. That, at any rate, would decide whether Clayton was playing square with Lily Reade.

Then there was Higgins. Suppose Higgins had learnt that Clayton had intended to sail for Canada and suppose that there was some existing arrangement that in the event of Clayton's death, the money invested in the garage business was to go to Higgins? It would be doubly profitable for Higgins to get Clayton out of the way. Firstly Clayton's capital in the concern would not be withdrawn, as would be the case if he sailed for Canada. Secondly that capital, in the event of his death, would go to Higgins. The thing was to get a glimpse of Clayton's will, if such a document existed. If it had not been altered in favour of Lily Reade, here was a motive for Higgins's desire to do away with his partner.

With these thoughts running round in his head, Meredith got Railton to draw up at the Beacon Hotel in Penrith, which was luckily on the route from Carlisle to Keswick.

The manager, who knew the Inspector, showed him at once into his private office.

"I won't take up much of your time," said Meredith. "But I want you to give me some information about a man called Mark Higgins."

The manager, a fat, comfortable sort of soul, chuckled.

"Mark! What the devil's he been up to?"

"Nothing—as far as I know. He says he intended to stay here last night."

"Quite right, Inspector. He did book a room, but about 11 o'clock he had a 'phone-call from Braithwaite and he left in a hurry."

"What time did he turn up here?"

"About six-thirty. And after a bit of supper he spent the rest of the evening in the bar. After closing-time he sat in the lounge until the 'phone call came. I didn't charge him for booking the room because he's a good customer of mine. He often pops over here for the week-ends."

"Any idea why?"

"Company for the most part, I reckon. He's what you might call a good mixer, is Mr. Higgins. He's got a lot of pals here in Penrith, and I guess he finds the bar of the Beacon a bit more lively than a village ale-house."

"I see. No other reasons for the visits as far as you know?"

"Well, I'm not so sure about that! If you keep your eyes and ears open you can often do a nice little bit of business over a pint of bitter. As a matter of fact, Higgins told me that he'd got a chap coming this morning to see him about a car. In the lounge here at 11.30, if I remember rightly. I've been half-expecting Mark to turn up and keep the appointment!"

Meredith glanced up at the clock. It was 11.25.

"Look here, Mr. Dawson—I want you to do me a favour. When this gentleman turns up, explain that Higgins was called away last night, and then get the fellow's name and address.

Tell him that Higgins had spoken about sending through a message but forgot to tell you where to forward it. Understand?"

The manager winked.

"Righto! I'll do my best." He glanced out through the glass door of his little office. "As a matter of fact this looks like our man now, Inspector. Shan't be a jiffy!"

In less than a minute the manager was back in his office, beaming all over his amiable face.

"Got it!" he exclaimed. "Mr. William Rose, 32 Patterdale Road."

"Good!"

"As it happens," added the manager, "I know the chap quite well. He's often in here. He's the manager, or whatever they call it, of the Nonock petrol depot here. Daresay you know the place? Lies out about a quarter of a mile or more along the Keswick road."

"Thanks, Mr. Dawson. No need to tell you, of course, to keep your mouth shut about all this?"

The manager winked again.

"That's O.K., Inspector. Mum's the word."

"So far so good," thought Meredith, as the combination purred off along the undulating Keswick road. "Higgins has got his alibi all right. That appointment looks genuine, too. It looks as if I can rule Mr. Higgins out of my suspect list right from the start."

On the other hand, who but Higgins could have known about that length of hose-pipe? And who could have had time to fit up that lethal apparatus in the lean-to shed without rousing Clayton's suspicion? It argued somebody with a good local knowledge. And who was gifted in this direction *save* Higgins?

CHAPTER III

THE PUZZLE OF THE HOSE-PIPE

ON Monday morning it was still raining—a steady, whispering downpour which blurred the massive contours of the mountains. The wind had dropped over the week-end, but it was still intensely cold. For all that Inspector Meredith was early abroad. There was a great deal to be done and he realized that the inquest on Clayton could not be postponed indefinitely. It would mean three or four crowded days of investigation if he was to establish his theory before the coroner sat. The burial of the body could not be held up, anyway, for much longer than a week.

At nine o'clock, therefore, he was already closeted with Mark Higgins in the garage office.

"I'm sorry to tell you, Mr. Higgins, that owing to one thing and another there will have to be a slight delay in the holding of the inquest. With your permission I'm going to suggest that we have the body moved to the mortuary for the time being."

Higgins looked surprised, but after one or two questions, which Meredith cleverly parried, he offered no objection to the body's removal. It was thereupon arranged that a police ambulance was to call that morning and convey the body to the Keswick mortuary.

"Now as to Mr. Clayton's will," went on the Inspector. "I suppose you can't give me any details of this, provided, of course, such a document exists?"

"As a matter of fact I can, Inspector. Clayton's will was drawn up some years back with Messrs. Harben, Wilshin and Harben, the Penrith solicitors. I was one of the witnesses and as far as I know the will still stands. The main proviso was that the capital which Clayton had invested in this concern was to remain in the business in the event of his death."

"In other words, the money was, in a sense, to come to you?"

"That's about it, I reckon."

"Were there any other beneficiaries?"

"Not as far as I remember, there weren't. Of course there may have been a codicil. If so, I didn't witness it. I shall be getting in touch with Harben as soon as possible. After all I shall be properly in the soup here if the original will has been altered. You see, I couldn't afford to run this business off my own bat."

"Exactly," said Meredith. "By the way, did you know that after his marriage to Miss Reade, Clayton was planning to settle in Canada?"

A look of incredulity came over Higgins's ferrety features.

"Canada? What, Clayton? That's the first I've ever heard about that, Inspector. What was the idea, anyway? I always understood that after he was married, Jack intended to set up house with Lily in Braithwaite. He never told me that he was going to back out of the concern like that. Straight, he didn't."

"Oh, well, it's probably just a rumour," observed Meredith, lightly dismissing the subject. "Now can I have a look at that wood-shed you spoke about?"

Higgins, though puzzled and seemingly disturbed by the Inspector's inquiries, proved quite ready to do all he could to help. He conducted the Inspector through the garden and led him round to the rear of the cottage, where a wooden shack had been erected at the end of a vegetable patch. The place was dark and damp, cluttered up with all manner of odds and ends. Hanging from a rusty hook on the wall was a coil of white rubber hosing. Meredith examined this closely. It was just as he expected. One end of the pipe had been recently severed. There was no doubt that the 9 ft. length attached to the exhaust had come from the wood-shed. But that being the case, how did the murderer know that the hose *was* in the wood-shed? And how did he succeed in cutting off an exact length and fixing it to the exhaust without previous knowledge of the required dimensions? The length and diameter of the hose were exactly right. The Inspector remembered the difficulty he had had in easing the hose off the end of the exhaust-pipe. Again his mind concentrated on Higgins. He alone would have the opportunity to take the necessary measurements and fix up the apparatus with any degree of safety. But at the time of the supposed murder, Higgins was in the bar of the Beacon. So much for that!

His next call was at the Braithwaite general stores. Lily Reade was sitting, white and distraught, over a late breakfast, in the room behind the shop. Her mother was hovering round solicitously, trying to make her daughter eat. When Meredith entered, the girl looked across at him with sleepless eyes and tried to summon up the ghost of a smile.

"I'm sorry to bother you again, Miss Reade, but it's a little matter of routine. It's about those steamship bookings. You don't happen to know what line Mr. Clayton was intending to sail by?"

The girl shook her head listlessly. She barely seemed to understand what the Inspector was talking about. It was Mrs. Reade who came to the rescue and gave Meredith the desired information.

"I don't rightly know what line it was, sir—but I know that Jack was getting the tickets through one of them travel agencies in Penrith. Maybe they'll be able to tell you."

The Inspector thanked the woman and after a few enheartening observations to the grief-stricken girl, he left the general stores for the village post office. In a few seconds he was through to the Penrith police station.

"This is Meredith speaking. I want you to go round the travel agencies over there and find out if they have issued two tickets for the Canadian crossing to a fellow named Clayton. Yes, J. D. Clayton. Got it? What's that? Oh, second class, I imagine. Probably for about the end of April. Shove the report into Keswick when it comes through, will you? Thanks."

As Meredith closed the door of the telephone cabinet, the village postman came into the office and hung his empty mail-bag behind the counter. On seeing the Inspector, who was a familiar figure in the district, he gave him a knowing look.

"Bad business about young Clayton, eh, Mr. Meredith?"

The Inspector agreed.

"Strange too, to my way of thinking," went on the postman, obviously trying to inveigle the Inspector into giving his opinion of the case. "Very strange. There's a rumour going round that things aren't all they look to be—if you take my manner of meaning?"

"Really?" Meredith smiled blandly.

"Not that I'm the one to listen to tittle-tattle. But I thought it strange myself, seeing that when I returned from my afternoon round on Saturday young Jack seemed as merry as a cricket. Yes—stopped and had a chat with him I did, same as I might be chatting to you now."

For the first time Meredith's eye showed a spark of interest.

"You spoke to him? What time was that?"

The postman considered this question for a moment.

"Well now, let me see. I finished up at the Manor at about a quarter to six. I reckon it takes me a good fifteen minutes on my bicycle to get from Colonel Howard's to the garage. So that makes it about six, don't it?"

"And Clayton didn't give you any hint of what was in his mind, I suppose?"

"Not him!" answered the postman vehemently. "Right as rain he seemed. Joking about his wedding, we were. Maybe you know that he and Ted Reade's girl were to be hitched up in a month or so. I were pulling his leg about it. But he gave me back as good as I gave, did young Jack. Come as a bit of a shock to me when I heard as he had done away with himself."

"I can quite see that. Nice chap, from all accounts."

"He was that. Better than that ferret-faced partner of his."

"What, Higgins? By the way, was he about when you were chatting to Clayton?"

"No. But I see him pass me on that there noisy motor-bicycle of his as I was turning out of the Colonel's drive-gate."

Meredith's interest increased. This was another spoke in the wheel of Higgins's alibi. Higgins had said that he had left the garage at about quarter to six, a fact which fitted in with the postman's information. At all events, Clayton was alive and, apparently, in a normal frame of mind, when Higgins left for Penrith.

"Strikes me," observed the Inspector, "that you must have been the last man to see Clayton alive."

"That I weren't!" exclaimed the postman with something approaching triumph. "You know young Freddie Hogg—the publican's son?—well, he saw Jack Clayton a good hour and a half later on. We was discussing the case down at the Hare and Hounds last night, when young Freddie told us about him seeing Clayton in the garage on his way back from Keswick on his bicycle. He didn't stop—but he see him right enough."

"He was quite certain that it was Clayton?"

"Course he was. He and Clayton was pretty friendly, you see. I reckon Fred made no mistake about it."

"That's interesting," observed Meredith, concealing his pleasure at the news. "I should like to have a word with Mr. Hogg. Where can I find him?"

"Down at the pub. He helps his father behind the bar."

Freeing himself from the coils of the postman's everlasting chatter, Meredith directed Railton to drive him down to the Hare and Hounds. As luck would have it, Hogg was alone in the bar, polishing up the handles of the beer-engine.

"Mr. Fred Hogg?" asked Meredith.

"That's me, sir. Anything I can do for you?"

Meredith smiled. "I hope so, Mr. Hogg. It's about young Clayton. I believe you saw something of him on Saturday night?"

"That's right. I'd been over to the pictures at Keswick and as I passed the garage on my way back, I saw Jack Clayton standing in the entrance. I called out 'Good night' to him and he waved his hand in reply. As it was raining I didn't stop for a chat. But it was Jack right enough."

"You're dead sure?"

"I'd swear to it in a court of law if needs be," answered Hogg solemnly.

"Well, I hope there *won't* be any need," countered the Inspector. "What time was it when you saw him?"

"Seven-thirty or thereabouts. Perhaps a bit later."

"You can't fix it more definitely than that, I suppose? For example, do you remember what time it was when you got home?"

"Yes, I can tell you that. The bar clock was striking eight when I first came behind the counter. Say five minutes to put my bike in the shed and take off my hat and coat. That makes it five to eight."

"And how long would it take you to cycle from the garage to here?"

"Well, there was a head wind, of course, but I'm pretty sure I could do the distance in twenty minutes."

Meredith nodded and made a few rapid notes of these all-important facts. He looked up after a second and observed: "So you think it's pretty safe to say that you saw Clayton at 7.35 on Saturday night?"

"That's it."

"When you said 'Good night', did he answer?"

"He didn't say anything. Just gave me a sort of 'Cheerio' with his hand, if you see how I mean."

"You didn't notice if there was anybody else hanging around when you passed the garage?"

"I didn't notice anybody—no."

This terminated Meredith's visit to the Hare and Hounds and a few minutes later he and the constable were speeding through the misty rain towards Keswick. On their way they passed the local ambulance returning from the garage to the mortuary and Meredith could not help thinking that the inanimate object inside that vehicle had set him a problem that might prove extremely difficult to solve.

Back in his office he lit his pipe, stretched out his feet to the stove, and ran over the results of his morning's investigations.

One thing now appeared certain—at 7.30 on Saturday night Clayton was still alive. Old Luke Perryman had discovered the tragedy about half-past nine, which meant that Clayton had lost his life sometime between 7.30 and 9.30. Meredith deliberately employed the phrase, "lost his life", because he realized that it was still impossible to rule out the theory of suicide. On the other hand at six o'clock, according to the Braithwaite postman, Clayton was as "merry as a cricket", joking about his forthcoming marriage, in fact. Did that suggest suicide? And again at 7.30 when Fred Hogg cycled past, Clayton was to all accounts standing about idly in the entrance to the garage. Then what about the waiting meal? Surely with the tea already in the pot and the kettle on the boil, Clayton would slip off at the first slack moment to have his meal? Then there was the matter of the hose-pipe. At first sight that favoured the suicide theory because Clayton was one of two people who knew that the hose was there and that it would fit exactly over the exhaust-pipe of his car. But to counteract this there was the puzzling fact that his hands were clean. This seemed to suggest that it was Higgins who had fitted the hose on to the exhaust, but Higgins had already left for Penrith on his motor-cycle.

One thing obtruded in Meredith's mind—the complete absence of motive. Not only for the murder, if such it was, but for the suicide. Clayton was enjoying perfect health. He was free from money worries, as far as the Inspector had been able to ascertain, and about to marry the girl of his choice. Why then had he put an end to his life? The motive was equally indeterminate if it was a case of murder. Higgins might have committed the crime for the sake of the money which would come to him, but, once again, Meredith found himself up against that unassailable alibi.

Yet he now felt pretty certain in his mind that there had been foul play. His next move, therefore, was to try to reconstruct the crime from the meagre data available. Firstly, Clayton must have been overpowered in some way, dragged or carried to the car, placed in the driving-seat with the mackintosh over his head. The hose was then fixed and the car started. The murderer, probably in a car, then made himself scarce. That Clayton was still alive when sitting at the wheel of his car was certain. The cause of death, according to Dr. Burney, was asphyxia, due to the inhalation of carbon monoxide—that is to say, exhaust fumes. How then had Clayton been overpowered? Three methods occurred to Meredith. He could have been stunned, given an anæsthetic or drugged. The first could be ruled out on Dr. Burney's evidence. It is impossible to stun a man without leaving some form of bruise or abrasion. An anæsthetic, on the other hand, was possible, though rather improbable. All anæsthetics have powerful and characteristic odours, which are inclined to impregnate the clothes of a victim. Neither he nor Dr. Burney had noticed any smell of chloroform or ether clinging about Clayton's person. Not that this precluded the use of anæsthetics—it merely suggested that if Clayton's death had been arranged to look like suicide, the slightest hint of anæsthetic would defeat the whole cleverly thought-out scheme. Meredith's inclination was toward drugs. They are easily administered and certain in result. Clayton might have been persuaded to take a drink with the murderer and——

Meredith suddenly clicked his fingers and let out an exclamation of pleasure. Clayton *had* taken a drink! Hadn't Dr. Burney said that the man's lips smelt of whisky? Well, here, thank heaven, was *something* fitting in with his theory! And if Clayton had been drugged it would be a perfectly simple matter to come to a decision over this point. It would merely mean official permission to have an autopsy. And if traces of a drug were found in the stomach or intestines, that would settle all doubts as to whether Clayton had taken his own life or not!

Meredith felt elated. Here was daylight at last. It might be difficult to persuade the Chief Constable that his suspicions warranted an autopsy, but he was determined to go all out to get it.

He had just reached this point in his ruminations when the 'phone bell rang on his desk. He took up the receiver.

"Penrith station—Sergeant Matthews speaking. About those tickets. I've traced the bookings all right. Clayton had reserved two second-class berths on the *Ontario*—sailing Liverpool on April 7th. The tickets were paid for on the 20th of this month—by cheque, signed J. D. Clayton. Any good to you, sir?"

"Excellent. That's just what I wanted."

Meredith rang off.

"So that clears up that loose end," he thought. "Clayton must have been playing square with the girl. No doubt now that he did intend to sail for Canada. Otherwise he wouldn't have paid for the tickets. The 20th—let's see?—that's three days before his death. Looks to me as if the suicide idea hadn't crossed his mind then."

With an energetic stride the Inspector crossed into the outer office.

"I want you to get this notice into all the usual local rags," he said to the Sergeant on duty. The Sergeant took up his pencil.

"Will anybody who called at or passed the Derwent garage between the hours of 7.30 and 9.30 on the night of Saturday, March 23rd, kindly communicate with the Keswick police station at the earliest possible moment. Got it? Good. By the way, what about the Portinscale and Braithwaite constables? Anything to report?"

"Nothing, I'm afraid, sir. Usual number of private cars and lorries on the road, but nothing of any suspicious nature to report. I've been in touch with the A.A. people, but without any result either."

"Well, let's hope that appeal of mine will bring somebody forward. It's a curse that it was raining. It keeps people indoors."

"Any luck so far, sir?" asked the Sergeant, respectfully.

The Inspector shook his head.

"Nairy a bite, I'm afraid, Sergeant—a few nibbles perhaps, but that's all. It's a puzzling business, take it all round."

CHAPTER IV

CLUE AT THE BANK?

WITH his usual routine work to be tackled and a number of other commonplace little jobs to be attended to, Meredith had to shelve his investigations for that afternoon. But all the time his mind kept on straying back to the Clayton affair. One word continually reoccurred in his thoughts; a word which to him constituted the crux of the problem. *Motive.*

He now felt certain that the suicide theory could be abandoned. Clayton, for some reason, had been murdered and the murderer or murderers had so arranged the scene as to suggest suicide. But why had Clayton been killed? Several ordinary reasons for murder occurred to Meredith—jealousy, financial gain, revenge. He couldn't credit that it was a *crime passionnel*. The whole affair had been too cleverly thought out for that. What then about jealousy? Had there been another aspirant to the hand of Lily Reade? That must be one line of inquiry. Another line to be followed up was the real state of the dead man's finances—quite apart from the rather scrappy information already obtained from Higgins. Meredith felt that this was a matter which it might pay him to investigate as soon as he was finished at his desk.

At five o'clock, therefore, he rang through to the Pickford's branch in Penrith and asked for information about the cheque they had received from Clayton for the Canadian tickets. As far as the clerk could remember, the cheque had been drawn on the Keswick branch of Barclays. This was a bit of luck, Meredith realized, as the manager, Burton, was rather a friend of his. Anxious to waste no time he put on his cap and strolled round to the bank in the hope of catching Burton before he left for tea. The manager was still in the building and a few minutes later Meredith had obtained exactly what he was after—a confidential report as to the state of Clayton's finances.

The result astounded him. Clayton's account, a current account, showed a credit balance of something over £2,000! His pass-book gave no clue as to the source of this unexpected affluence. Amounts, varying from £50 to £100, had been paid in at odd intervals during the last seven years, but in every case they had been paid in in ordinary £1 treasury notes. Burton was certain that the money had not come from the profits in the garage—in the first place he felt certain that Clayton's share in the profits would not amount to £300 a year. If it did, it meant that the concern was showing a clear profit of some £600 a year, a possibility which the manager flatly refused to accept. In the second place, Burton knew that the garage account was in the hands of the Westminster bank. Clayton's account at his own bank was purely a *personal* account.

A further examination of the books showed that Clayton had first opened his account at the Keswick branch some eight years previously with a balance, transferred from Manchester, of £40 odd. For the first year only small amounts had been paid in and then, suddenly, the £50 and £100 entries began to appear. This fact seemed significant to the Inspector.

How, and from whom, had Clayton obtained the money?

"Do you happen to know the manager of the Westminster?" Meredith asked of Burton. "If so it would be doing me a favour if you could get his permission for me to run my eye over the garage account."

Burton knew him well, as they were members of the same golf club, and after a short phone conversation, the Inspector, puzzled and excited, left for the Westminster. Goreleston proved to be a little more reticent over his client's affairs than Burton, but after Meredith had briefly outlined the facts of Clayton's death, he seemed willing to do all he could to help. But this time Meredith drew a blank. The garage showed a fluctuating profit of about £6 a week. In the summer months the amounts paid in by the proprietors of the Derwent rose to as much as £12 to £14 a week, then gradually declined to as little as £2 or £3 a week in January and February.

"I suppose you couldn't tell me how the partners draw their money out?" asked Meredith.

"Nothing simpler," replied Goreleston. "Once a month Clayton presented a cheque for £16 and it was paid out to him in £1 notes. There was an arrangement, as a matter of fact, that not more than £16 could be drawn out by either of the partners in any one month. Both Mr. Clayton and Mr. Higgins of course, had an equal right to examine the dual-account whenever they wanted to. To tell you the truth, I don't ever remember seeing Mr. Higgins in the bank. He certainly never drew a cheque on his own signature, though there was nothing to prevent him from doing so, provided he kept to the conditions I've just mentioned. I suppose the monthly withdrawal of £16 was divided equally between the partners."

"I see." Meredith rose and extended his hand. "Thank you, Mr. Goreleston. You may rest assured that I shall make no mention of this interview and I trust you'll be equally reticent over what I've told you."

Wasting no time, Meredith hurried off through the wintry streets to his office, where he had soon put through a call to Messrs. Harben, Wilshin and Harben, the Penrith solicitors. Mr. Harben, the senior partner of the firm, flatly refused to divulge the nature of Clayton's will.

"After all, Inspector, it will be public property in a few days. I really can't see why I should disclose the terms of the will before it is formally declared!"

To this Meredith had no reply. He realized that he was treading on delicate ground and even if he had strong suspicions that Clayton had been murdered, a solicitor was the last person in whom to confide these suspicions. Rather nettled, he rang off and put himself to thinking about that astonishing nest-egg of £2,000. The first thought that entered his mind was theft. Was it possible that Clayton was a professional thief, whose activities spreading over some seven years had been attended with singular good fortune? But the record of local burglaries was disappointingly small. Besides, the amounts seemed to have been paid in fairly regularly about four times a year, and in every case in notes. Meredith could not conceive a clever thief being such a fool as to pay in the proceeds of his thefts in notes. Notes are numbered and often, when suspicion is aroused, easily traceable. Clayton would have to work in conjunction with a receiver and if any of the notes could have been traced back to a receiver the fat would have been properly in the fire.

Blackmail was a more feasible explanation. But if so, who was the victim? Surely not Higgins? That, at any rate, would supply a motive for the murder. Driven to desperation by Clayton's continual threats of exposure Higgins might have decided that the only way to regain peace of mind was to get rid of his partner. But once again Meredith found himself up against that alibi. Thoroughly disheartened, he at length abandoned all attempts to solve the problem of Clayton's bank-balance and decided to concentrate on the major problem of his death. Rather nervously he took up the phone and got through to Superintendent Thompson at Carlisle.

"This is Meredith speaking, sir. I want to have a word with you about this Clayton affair."

At the breezy command of "Fire ahead" Meredith outlined the progress of his investigations, laying particular stress on his theory that Clayton had been drugged before being placed in the car. To his intense relief the Superintendent anticipated his request.

"And now I suppose you want permission for an autopsy? Is that it, Inspector?"

"That's about it, sir. Any chance?"

"Hang on a minute and I'll have a word with the Chief. Luckily he's in his office. Don't promise, mind you, but I'll do my best."

"Thanks."

Meredith waited apprehensively for the Chief's decision. So much he felt depended on the autopsy. He was quite certain that he could not persuade a coroner's jury to bring in a verdict of murder by putting forward his present suspicions; but once prove that Clayton had been drugged and the result of the inquest was a foregone conclusion. Not that Meredith was hankering after a sensational verdict. It was merely that he now felt certain that Clayton had not taken his own life.

The Superintendent's voice drew him sharply out of his reverie.

"You there, Meredith? I've seen the Chief. He was a bit dubious at first. Thought that the reasons you'd put forward for the *post mortem* were a trifle too thin. But I'm glad to say that I got him round in the end, so you can go ahead with a clear conscience."

"That's really good news, sir. I'll get Dr. Burney on the job straightaway and send through my report early to-morrow."

"Good. By the way the inquest is fixed for Wednesday next at 2.30. The body's at the mortuary isn't it?"

"Yes, sir."

"Then we'll arrange for the Coroner to sit in the court-room. You'd better subpoena all the witnesses you think necessary. I shall probably be over myself if I can spare the time."

Immensely pleased with the result of his phone call Meredith had soon fixed up with Dr. Burney, in conjunction with Dr. White, to perform the necessary *post mortem*. In less than an hour the two doctors were at their gruesome job in the little mortuary adjoining the station. When the Inspector returned from a hastily snatched meal he found the doctors waiting for him.

"Well, gentlemen?"

Dr. Burney smiled.

"You seem anxious, Inspector!"

Meredith laughed.

"I am. A negative report would make me look a tidy fool after airing my suspicions so strongly at H.Q."

"Well you won't lose your beauty sleep on that account. We've no reason to alter our opinion as to the cause of death. That's asphyxia all right. On the other hand we found about thirty grains of trional in the stomach and intestines. You know what that is I suppose?"

"A drug?" asked Meredith on tenterhooks.

Burney nodded. Dr. White, a short podgy little man, cut in wheezily.

"A powerful drug too. Thirty grains of the stuff would send a man off to sleep in a brace of shakes."

Burney grinned at the older man's expression.

"I know exactly what you're going to ask, Inspector. What *is* a 'brace of shakes'? Say, in this case anything from twenty minutes to half an hour. That so, White?"

"Twenty minutes in my opinion. Can't be certain of course. People react differently to drugs. But that's about it!"

As the doctors were shuffling themselves into their overcoats, Meredith observed:

"No need to tell you, gentlemen, what this means?"

Burney winked.

"It wasn't suicide—if that's what you're after. By the way, when's the inquest? Is it fixed yet?"

Meredith told them and the doctors drove off together in Burney's car to write up an official report of their findings.

Left alone the Inspector allowed himself a moment of self-congratulation, then tired out after his day's work he trudged off through the frost-rimed streets to spend the tail-end of the evening helping his seventeen-year-old son, Tony, to assemble a new five-valve wireless set. Tony was apprenticed to a local photographer, but like Meredith, he had a mechanical turn of mind. A fact which did a lot to further the happy relationship existing between father and son. Meredith was inordinately proud of his only child, a feeling which he secretly believed to be reciprocated, and if it hadn't been for Mrs. Meredith, Tony would have long ago been destined for the Force.

CHAPTER V

MOTIVE?

TUESDAY morning ushered in a spell of fine, frosty weather. For the first time since the Inspector had started to investigate the Clayton case, he could look up over the roofs of Keswick and see the snow-capped ridge of the Skiddaw range etched in detail against a hard, blue sky. His spirits responded to the invigorating nip in the early morning air and it was in an optimistic mood that he set off after breakfast to his office.

He felt more than pleased with the result of the overnight *post mortem*, and shortly after nine he was in touch with the Superintendent at Carlisle. He seemed as pleased as Meredith that the autopsy had produced a positive result.

"A feather in your cap, Inspector. There's absolutely no doubt now that Clayton was murdered. I mean there was no point in drugging himself before taking that dose of carbon monoxide, was there?"

Meredith agreed.

"So you may as well," went on the Superintendent, "go ahead with your investigations over there. I'll have to talk matters over with the Chief and see what he thinks about the future of the case. He may decide to apply to Scotland Yard for the loan of a C.I.D. man. If so I'll do my damnedest to see that you work in conjunction with him. You may possibly have to come over here yourself this evening for a conference. I'll let you know later."

"Very good, sir."

After he had dealt with the letters lying ready on his desk, Meredith sent for Railton.

"About this Mrs. Swinley you mentioned, Railton. Do you happen to know where she lives? You do? What time does she start her duties out at the garage cottage?"

"Ten, I think, sir. I expect she leaves about a quarter to."

Meredith glanced up at the clock.

"Good. If you get out the combination I shall be ready to start in five minutes. We ought to just catch her before she starts out."

When Meredith arrived at Rosemary Cottage, a stone's throw from the Portinscale post office, Mrs. Swinley was just putting on her hat. The sight of the Inspector sent her into a rare flutter, for she had already been considerably upset by Clayton's tragic death. She invited him into the prim, cheerful little parlour, however, and in an agitated voice asked if there was anything she could do.

"Well, it's like this, Mrs. Swinley—I understand from the constable that you look after the domestic affairs for Mr. Clayton and Mr. Higgins along at the Derwent garage."

"That's right, sir, and a shocking thing it is, too, about poor Mr. Clayton. He always seemed a bright young lad to me. Can't understand what made him do it. Really I can't!"

"That's what everybody is saying," agreed Meredith. "Now the point I want to get at is this—when you leave the cottage after lunch do you lay the evening meal?"

"Never!" exclaimed Mrs. Swinley. "Food gets that dry if it's left on the table, as I daresay you know, Inspector."

"Exactly. And you never put the kettle on, either?"

"No. I just bank up the fire, fill the kettle and leave it standing ready in the hearth."

"What *are* your duties exactly?"

Mrs. Swinley took a big breath and Meredith prepared himself for a voluble recital. It seemed that it was less a matter of what Mrs. Swinley *did* than what she did *not* do. But the gist of it was that Mrs. Swinley shopped, cooked, cleaned, darned, mended, washed, and ironed and all for a matter of ten shillings a week.

The Inspector tactfully let this spate of information run dry before slyly leading the conversation round to Mrs. Swinley's opinion of the relationship existing between the partners. It did not take Meredith long to see that she was quite out of sympathy with Higgins. According to her it was Clayton who did all the work, whilst Higgins seized the slightest opportunity to slink off to the Hare and Hounds. She didn't think the gentlemen got on very well together, though she had never actually heard them having a violent quarrel. They often seemed to argue over business matters and she believed that Mr. Clayton had been thinking about breaking up the partnership.

At this, Meredith pricked up his ears. Did it mean that Higgins had been prevaricating when he said he knew nothing of his partner's intention to clear off to Canada?

"What makes you think he wanted to back out of the business, Mrs. Swinley?"

"It was something I overheard, sir. About three days before the tragedy it would be. I was in my scullery and the young men was having their dinner. And the door not being properly closed I couldn't help but hear what they was a-talking about. First I heard Mr. Clayton say, 'It's all very well for you, but I tell you I've got to get out of the concern.' Then I heard Mr. 'Iggins reply something about it being the worse for him if he did! Rather nasty like. Then Mr. 'Iggins went on to say as how Mr. Clayton was doing well for himself and what was the sense of clearing out in a hurry. He said something, too, in a low sort of voice, about Mr. Clayton knowing well enough what it meant if he did back out. Then the garridge bell rang and Mr. 'Iggins cleared off."

"That sounds rather as if Higgins was threatening Mr. Clayton, doesn't it?" suggested Meredith.

"That's just what I thought at the time, sir. I tell you, the tone of 'is voice fair gave me the creeps. Menacing it were—though in a nasty quiet sort of way, if you take my meaning?"

"Have you ever taken any particular note of any of Mr. Clayton's or Mr. Higgins's friends?"

"Friends!" Mrs. Swinley looked puzzled and surprised. "Why, they never had any friends. Not to my knowledge they didn't. Leastways nobody ever called on 'em when I was in the 'ouse."

"You're sure you've never seen anybody about?"

"That I am!" But no sooner had Mrs. Swinley given vent to this emphatic statement, when a distant look came into her eye as if she were calling something to mind. Meredith leant forward eagerly.

"Well?" he demanded.

"When I come to think of it—I have seen a gentleman there. Twice that is, but not during the day. It struck me as curious, I remember, that the only times I have called along in the evening this same gentleman should have been at the cottage."

After one or two apt questions the Inspector elicited the following information from the housekeeper. It appeared that on two occasions, separated by a matter of about a month, Mrs. Swinley had cycled along to the cottage after dark to let her employers know that she would be unable to turn up on the following day. The first time she had received a wire to say that her sister was dangerously ill and the second she had been asked by a neighbour, whose husband had been involved in a lorry crash, to look after her children. On each occasion, when Clayton had opened the door to her, she had noticed a third man in the parlour. She was quite certain that it was the same man. For one thing he had a slight stutter and for another he wore tortoise-shell glasses with very thick lenses. Asked by the Inspector to give a fuller description of this individual, Mrs. Swinley replied that he was short, well-dressed, with thin, cleanshaven features and weak eyes. She had, unfortunately, no idea as to what the trio had been discussing.

"And you first saw this gentleman when?" asked Meredith.

"Let me see now—it was last November. That was when my sister was first taken ill. The second time was just before Christmas."

"And you haven't seen him since?"

"No."

Feeling that Mrs. Swinley could help him no further, the Inspector cautioned her to say nothing of the interview, and climbed back into the waiting side-car.

"The Derwent," he said to Railton.

"You won't find anybody there I'm afraid, sir," replied the constable.

"How's that?"

"Mr. Higgins passed by here on his motor-cycle not five minutes back. Making for Keswick by the look of it."

"Well, in that case we'll pay a visit to the Braithwaite stores instead. There are one or two questions I want to ask Miss Reade."

But again the Inspector's luck was out. Mr. Reade, looking very business-like and obliging in his white apron, informed Meredith across the counter that his wife and daughter had taken the early train into Penrith. A letter had arrived by the first post from Harben, Wilshin and Harben, requesting his daughter's immediate presence at their office. He did not expect her back till one-thirty.

"In that case, Mr. Reade, perhaps you can help me instead," said Meredith in affable tones. "Could we go into that back room of yours, then we shan't be interrupted?"

When the two men were seated in arm-chairs before a cheerful log fire, the Inspector said gravely:

"I want you to keep this to yourself for the moment, Mr. Reade. After the inquest on Clayton it will be public property, but until then I should value your silence. The fact is—"

Here Meredith lowered his voice to impress the shopkeeper with the gravity of his statement. "We have good reason to believe that young Clayton was murdered!"

"Murdered! Good gracious me! But surely——?"

"I can't tell you now the reasons for this belief, but you can take it from me that we're pretty certain that there's been foul play. But there's one important factor missing from our chain of evidence—motive. This is where you can help. I want you to cast your mind back and see if you can remember anybody, save Clayton, who has paid attentions to your daughter."

"You mean?"

"That it is just possible that the motive for Clayton's murder was jealousy. Well, Mr. Reade?"

The shopkeeper puffed at his pipe for a moment in meditative silence, then:

"No—I think you're on the wrong tack there, Inspector. Mind you, I'm not going to say there hasn't been anybody else, but if so I know nothing about it. There's the chance, of course, that Lily has kept quiet over the matter. On the other hand she's a frank sort of girl and if there'd been any trouble of that sort I think she would have confided in me."

"Quite. Now what about her friends. Has she any particular girl friend in whom she might have confided?"

"Well, there's Rose Bampton, of course. She and Lily have been pretty thick ever since they were kids. If anybody could tell you about it, she could."

"Where can I find her?"

"At the school, Inspector. She's the assistant mistress."

"In that case I think I'll just run round and have a word with Miss Bampton."

As they were passing through the shop however, the phone bell rang behind the ground-glass screen of Mr. Reade's desk.

"Just a moment," exclaimed the shopkeeper. "That may be Lily now. Perhaps they have got through their business earlier than they expected and are coming home by another train. If you care to wait a minute."

The Inspector did care and he could not suppress a smile of intense amusement as the phone call proceeded. First the shop-keeper let out an astonished whistle, followed by a few exclamations of incredulity, which soon gave way to crows of delight and jumbled words of congratulation. When at length he hung up, he popped a grinning countenance over the top of the screen and demanded:

"What do you think? Lily's had a rare bit of luck! You'll never believe! She's come into a matter of something over *two thousand pounds*!"

Meredith put up an excellent show of surprise.

"Really. I say, that's splendid!"

"It's young Clayton," went on the shopkeeper, bubbling over with excitement. "Left everything to her, so it seems. But, by heaven, Inspector, I never thought the lad was worth that much!"

Meredith said that the thought had never crossed his mind either and after a lengthy discussion on the crazy ways of providence, during which he continually edged toward the door, he ascertained that the womenfolk would not be back until 1.30, and finally succeeded in regaining the street. A minute or so later the combination drew up in front of the village school.

His interview with the sturdy, athletic Miss Bampton, however, proved abortive. She felt quite certain that her friend had never so much as looked at anybody save Jack Clayton. According to her, Lily was a retiring, sensible sort of girl, full of fun, but not given to flirtatious interludes. She had, in fact, got the name among the village *beaux* for being stand-offish and unapproachable. Miss

Bampton didn't agree with this, but she felt quite sure that Lily had never encouraged any man except Clayton.

"Just as I thought," muttered Meredith, more to himself than to the constable as they drove off. "We're barking up the wrong tree. Jealousy wasn't the motive. And as far as I can see Clayton wasn't murdered for his money either."

"You don't think——?" began the constable respectfully.

"Look out!" shouted Meredith with sudden vehemence.

The combination swerved violently to avoid the passage of a large petrol lorry, which was lumbering round the corner in the very centre of the road.

"Swines," muttered the constable under his breath. "Shall I turn and catch 'em, sir? I could do it easy in a minute or so."

Meredith shook his head. He couldn't waste time on motoring offences, but although he hadn't been able to register the number of the lorry, he had seen the words "Nonock Petroleum Co." painted in flaring red letters along the sides of the bright blue tank. He wondered why the name seemed familiar. Then he remembered. The man whom Mark Higgins was to have met on Sunday morning at the Beacon was the manager of the Nonock depot on the outskirts of Penrith. He registered a vow to look in one day on the gentleman and air his official views about his lorry-men. It was a small concern, he figured, and the drivers probably had to cover a large area in far too little time. There was far too much of this "time-table" driving about as it was.

Higgins had not returned to the garage as they passed, but just outside Portinscale his high-powered motor-cycle roared into view and at the Inspector's signal he drew up at the side of the road.

"Sorry to stop you, Mr. Higgins, but I wanted to let you know that the inquest is fixed for to-morrow at 2.30 in the police court-room. You will be needed to give evidence, of course."

"Righto, Inspector. I'll be there all right. Looks as if I'm booked for a dose of third degree, eh?"

Higgins laughed, prominently displaying his rodent-like teeth and generally heightening the ferrety cast of his features. Meredith was amazed at the change in the man. All his nervousness had vanished. He no longer seemed upset by the tragic death of his partner. Elation and satisfaction were written all over his rather unpleasing countenance. The Inspector wondered what had brought about this sudden change of mood. He did not have to wait long, however, before Higgins himself supplied the answer to this question.

"I'm glad to say that things have turned out as I hoped they would. Jack's little bit in the business has come my way all right. I've just seen the solicitors."

"So the will hadn't been altered?" asked the Inspector casually.

"Doesn't look like it, does it?" was the equivocal reply.

"I'm not so sure," went on Meredith, watching the man closely. "I've just heard that Clayton has left Miss Reade a cool two thousand or so! What do you make of that?"

Higgins's start of surprise was just too late to be really convincing. Meredith was certain that the man's first reaction to the news was fear tinged with suspicion.

"Are you sure about that?" asked Higgins, as Meredith thought with an undercurrent of anxiety.

"Quite sure. I've just had the news from Mr. Reade himself. Looks as if there must have been a codicil added which you knew nothing about. Had you any idea that your partner was such a man of means?"

"By Jove, I hadn't. He never mentioned it to me."

"So you've no idea where the money could have come from?"

"None. I swear that, Inspector."

The over-emphasis in Higgins's reply was not missed by the Inspector. He felt more and more certain that Higgins *did* know something about the money, and what's more, about the source from which it was obtained. Then why this evasion and secrecy? Surely it could mean only one thing? The money had accrued from some illegal business and Higgins was mixed up in it.

"There's another thing you should know before the inquest," went on the Inspector after a moment's awkward silence. "The police have every reason to believe that Clayton did not commit suicide. In their opinion he was murdered. The suicide was faked to cover the murder—understand? And fortunately we have managed to see through the fake."

"Murdered? But that's out of the question! Poor old Jack had no enemies, Inspector. He was popular with everyone. That's a damfool idea—that is! You can't get me to believe that!"

"Maybe," answered Meredith curtly. "But there it is. That's all I can say at the moment."

When they were once more on their way Meredith asked the constable: "Look here, Railton—what do you make of that man?"

"Shady, sir. That's my humble opinion. An out-and-out rotter."

Back at the Keswick police station a surprise awaited Meredith. Seated at his desk was the Chief Constable, Colonel Hardwick, in the company of Superintendent Thompson.

"Ah, Inspector! Gave you a bit of a shock I daresay. I don't know whether it's a case of Mahomet coming to the mountain or vice versa. At any rate here we are. Draw up that chair and light your pipe. We've got a lot to talk about. But first of all suppose you post us up to date with your investigations into this Clayton affair. Then when you've done we'll hold the deck for a bit."

Without wasting a single word on irrelevances, Meredith gave a succinct account of his doings since the night of the tragedy. He left nothing unsaid, stressing what was to his mind an important factor in the case, the large amount of money left by the deceased, touching on the complete absence of motive and airing his suspicions of Higgins's integrity. When he had completed his recital he did not fail to register a swift glance of approval which passed between the Chief and the Superintendent.

"So you've no theory, Inspector—so far?"

"None, sir."

"And I'm not surprised," went on the Chief, after a few meditative puffs at his excellent cigar. "It strikes me that we're up against a ticklish problem. I can't help feeling, however, that there's something more behind this case than a mere matter of personal vindication. You've already commented on the complete absence of motive, Inspector. Clayton does not appear to have been killed through motives of jealousy or financial gain. Revenge is a possibility that we can't, at present, dismiss. On the other hand there's one very commonplace motive for murder that you've overlooked, Inspector. Suppose I explain what I mean in this way. The Superintendent here and I are running some sort of illegal concern. In some way or other you blunder on our secret and swear to give us away to the police. If we were hardened criminals faced with that possibility, what d'you think we should do?"

"Kill me, sir," replied Meredith with a grin.

"Exactly—silence you. That's one suggestion. The other is this. Suppose the Superintendent and I have managed to get a hold over you and, because of that, forced you to come in hand and glove with us in our illegal business, and that later, for some personal reason, you want to back out of the concern. What then? Doesn't the same thing apply? Once you were out of our clutches it would be easy and safe for you to communicate with the police and give us away, wouldn't it?"

"Yes, I quite see that, sir."

"Well?"

"Well, what, sir?"

"Doesn't it suggest anything to you?"

Meredith looked utterly blank for a moment, then suddenly he slapped his thigh and let out a brisk exclamation.

"By Jove, sir! I see what you're driving at now! You think Clayton might have been mixed up with some sort of shady business and was trying to back out?"

"That's precisely what I *do* mean," replied Colonel Hardwick with a twinkle in his eye. "Clayton, as I see it, was just about to marry a decent girl, who probably knew nothing about the illegal business in the background. He wanted to make a clean break with the gang. So without telling anybody, except the girl and her parents, he books a couple of passages for Canada. Unfortunately, the gang get to hear about this, with the result that Clayton is found murdered."

At the conclusion of the Chief Constable's speech the Superintendent, who up to the moment had played the role of audience, now took it upon himself to add a few enlightening comments.

"To my way of thinking, the fact that Clayton didn't tell Higgins about his intended flit to Canada is pretty suggestive. You would imagine, since they lived together, and had done so apparently for some years, that Higgins would be his closest confidant. According to you, Inspector, this wasn't the case. I rather think Higgins gave himself away there. It was a case of over-caution. If Higgins is one of the gang, as I rather imagine he must be, he would have done better to have said that he *did* know about those steamship bookings. That would have looked as if Clayton had confided in him. But Higgins probably argued rather like this—the gang have decided to do away with Clayton because he is trying to make a get-away. If I say that I knew he was making for Canada, then I shall probably get incriminated in the murder. Therefore—mum's the word."

The Chief Constable assented.

"There's certainly something in that. We know, of course, that Higgins wasn't the actual murderer, but there's no reason why he shouldn't be an accessory both before and after the fact. Provided, of course, that our theory holds water. The question is, does it?"

"Well, sir," put in Meredith respectfully, "it would help to explain away that two thousand pounds, wouldn't it?"

"I never thought of that!" exclaimed the chief. "Naturally, it would."

"On the other hand," said the Superintendent with a wry smile, "we are not much nearer to finding out who *did* murder Clayton, are we? You agree, sir, that this is only theory and that theory is the devil's own way from fact."

"On the other hand, Thompson, what about the matter which you brought to my notice this morning? I think the Inspector should know about that. After all, it *may* have some bearing on this Clayton affair or it may be a simple matter of coincidence. Anyhow, let's run over the facts of that particular case again."

CHAPTER VI

SENSATIONAL VERDICT

THE Superintendent drew up another chair to the desk and took a tiny sheaf of press cuttings out of his wallet. These he spread out neatly before him, whilst the Inspector pulled out his note-book and pencil and settled himself to jot down anything of importance.

"Now," said the Chief Constable, leaning back in Meredith's bentwood chair and stretching out his legs.

"Well, first of all, Inspector, I'll give the facts of the case in my own words, then afterwards you can run your eye over these contemporary newspaper cuttings. I want you to bear the facts of Clayton's murder in your mind all the time. Understand?"

"Right, sir."

"To begin with, do you know a place called Hursthole Point?"

"I believe I do, sir. It's on the west side of Bassenthwaite, isn't it?"

"That's the idea. It's a little promontory that sticks out into the lake. Well, a little over three years ago the body of a middle-aged man was taken out of the water at this point. It was seen floating on the surface by a workman from a railway carriage. You probably know that the railway line runs close along the edge of the west bank. Beyond the railway runs the Keswick–Cockermouth road, an alternative route to going over the Whinlatter pass. Well, we made inquiries into the matter and as far as we could see it looked like a clear case of suicide. The body had been in the water about three days and there were no external signs of violence. A rope had been tied round the man's waist and attached, as far as we could gather, to a large stone or some other heavy object. Whatever it was, it had slipped from the rope, and the body had risen to the surface. Now, there was one point which puzzled me at the time. The man had all four fingers of his left hand missing. I don't mean that they had been recently severed. According to the doctor's evidence, the accident, or whatever it was, had probably happened some few years before. Now, the rope was tied securely round the waist with a perfectly executed double clove-hitch—a complicated knot at the best of times. The question I immediately asked myself was, 'How had this man with no left fingers managed to tie that knot?' The point, of course, was brought up at the inquest and a pretty lengthy argument ensued as to whether it was possible or not. The jury eventually came to the conclusion that it *was* possible and a verdict of suicide whilst of unsound mind was brought in.

"Now, the reason I've dragged this skeleton out of the police archives is this: Peterson—that was the man's name—was in partnership in a garage. He wasn't a mechanic, because of his mutilated left hand, but he served the petrol pumps, looked after the accounts and so on. His partner, a fellow called Wick, naturally came under my observation, and I don't mind confessing that I took an immediate dislike to the man. I had nothing positive against him. He was away at the time of the tragedy and we couldn't do anything to shake his alibi. But for all that, my instinct insisted that he was a wrong 'un. I can't say whether I was justified or not in my suspicions. As a matter of fact, Wick still runs the place—single-handed, I believe. I expect you've noticed the building on an isolated stretch of the road beside the lake?"

"The Lothwaite, sir?"

"That's the place, and those briefly are the facts of the case. You see the similarity between the two tragedies? In each case the men are partners in a garage business. In both cases the garages are isolated. Both Wick and Higgins impress themselves on us as suspicious characters. Whether there is anything in this or not I can't say. But you see how it supports the Chief's theory that there may be some sort of criminal gang behind these two mysteries?"

The Inspector nodded slowly. As he had not been attached to the district at the time, he had heard nothing about this previous case, but now that he knew the facts his brain was already working full speed ahead to further the link between the two crimes.

"There's just one point, sir. Do you remember if this man, Peterson, left any money? I mean, a decent little pile."

The Superintendent grinned.

"I guessed you were going to ask that, Inspector. And I've got the answer ready for you. He did! A considerable amount. Round about one thousand five hundred pounds, if I remember rightly." He turned to the Chief Constable. "You see, sir, I hadn't mentioned this point before because it was only a few moments back that the Inspector informed us about Clayton's little nest-egg."

"Well, it only goes to make the coincidence more remarkable," was the Chief Constable's observation. "I don't want to be unduly optimistic—it's a dangerous policy—but I'm inclined to believe that we've hit on something. And something pretty big by the look of it."

Meredith hastened to agree and for some few minutes the trio continued to discuss the strange similarity of the two cases. Finally, after glancing at his watch, the Chief Constable rose from his chair and intimated that it was time he was on his way.

"And the future of the case, sir?" asked the Inspector.

"I've already made up my mind on that point, Meredith. I don't think we are justified in applying to the Home Office for a Yard man. After all, you know the district and all the facts of the case are in your possession, so I see no reason why you shouldn't handle the case yourself."

"Thank you, sir."

"You have a certain amount to go on," continued the Chief Constable, "and I daresay that notice of yours in the local papers will bring somebody forward. In my opinion, you want to find out who exactly was in the vicinity of the garage between the hours of seven-thirty and, say, ten-thirty. Then run the tape over them. Let's see, the mid-weekly editions come out on Wednesday, don't they?"

"That's it, sir—to-morrow. And I shouldn't be surprised if we know something more inside another twenty-four hours."

"Quite. Well, I can't do more than wish you luck with the case, Meredith. Just one piece of advice—stick at it. It's the only way to get results."

As the little group moved toward the door the Superintendent added: "By the way, I've left those cuttings. You'll find them interesting. If I were you, I should take a look at the Lothwaite as soon as you can. I shall be over in time for the inquest to-morrow, Inspector."

As soon as the big, blue saloon had purred off in the direction of Carlisle, Meredith strode back energetically to his office and threw himself into the task of drawing up a clear and comprehensive report of his investigations. He was pleased and rather flattered by the confidence which the Chief had placed in his ability. More than ever he was determined to get to the root of the problem—not only the problem of Clayton's death but the mystery which surrounded the source of that £2,000. Already he was beginning to think that the two problems might be in some way connected. And further, that the tragedy at the Derwent was in some inexplicable way linked up with the two-year-old tragedy at the Lothwaite.

After a hurried lunch at his home in Greystoke Road, the Inspector returned to the police station. There he spent the afternoon making a methodical examination of every exhibit connected with the crime. He tested the nine-foot length of hose-pipe and the fish-tail end of the exhaust for finger-prints, also the mackintosh which had been placed over Clayton's head. But, as he had expected, without result. The modern criminal, profiting by the bitter experience of his predecessors, has a penchant for rubber-gloves when engaged in any nefarious business! But Meredith was leaving nothing to chance. He even re-examined every article which he had taken from the pockets of the dead man. But again his efforts proved fruitless, and at six o'clock he returned home a trifle depressed.

On Wednesday, after a morning's routine work, he lunched at Greystoke Road and hurried off to join the Superintendent in the crowded little court-room. Punctually at two-thirty the Coroner took his place at the head of the long table and, after the jury had been sworn in, the inquest began.

From beginning to end the proceedings followed a course which Meredith had anticipated. Mark Higgins identified the body. Luke Perryman, very stiff and formal in his black Sabbath suit, described how he had discovered the dead body of Clayton in the car. Meredith then explained how Perryman had driven, at once, to the police station and how he had returned with a witness to the scene of the tragedy. He then endorsed the farmer's statement as to the position of the body and enlarged on the apparatus by which the deceased had evidently met his death.

So far it was all stale news to the public, but then came the doctor's evidence.

"The cause of death, you say, was asphyxia due to the inhalation of carbon monoxide gas?" observed the Coroner. "From your examination of the body, did you infer that the deceased had put an end to his own life, Dr. Burney?"

"That certainly was my first impression."

"What do you mean by your 'first' impression? Had you any reason later on to alter your opinion as to the cause of death?"

"Not entirely. But I was asked, in conjunction with Dr. White here, to make an autopsy. It appears that the police were dissatisfied with the results of the external examination."

For the first time a shiver of anticipation ran over the crowd.

"But why were the police dissatisfied?" asked the Coroner, glaring with a puzzled expression through his horn-rimmed glasses. Inspector Meredith got quickly to his feet. "Well, Inspector?"

"I think I can explain that point, sir."

In a few words Meredith set out his evidence about the waiting meal, the melted kettle, the burning light and the unexpectedly clean hands of the deceased. He also stressed the entire absence of motive for suicide, making mention of Clayton's plans for the future, the fact that he was about to be married and his entire freedom from financial straits.

"With this evidence to hand, sir, we felt justified in demanding a *post mortem*."

"I see," mused the Coroner. "Very well, Inspector. You may stand down." He turned to the Doctor. "Now, Doctor Burney, will you be good enough to let us know the result of this autopsy?"

"Certainly. We found thirty grains of trional in the stomach and intestines."

The sensation in the court-room was profound. Although most of the audience hadn't the slightest idea as to the nature of trional, they judged that the proceedings were about to take an unexpected and exciting twist. The Coroner had to rap once or twice with his gavel before silence could be restored.

"And what did that suggest to you, Doctor?"

"It pointed to the fact that the deceased had been drugged and, according to our findings, only a short time before the tragedy was discovered."

"Would there be any point in the deceased taking the drug himself?"

"None, as far as I can see. He had to seat himself in the car and start up the engine *before* the drug took effect. He had also to place the mackintosh over his head and introduce the hose-pipe beneath it. The carbon monoxide fumes would have rendered him unconscious almost at once. So, in my opinion, there was absolutely no need for the drug to have been self-administered."

"You are suggesting, then," went on the Coroner in his thin, precise voice, "that the drug was administered by a second person?"

"Yes."

Again the Coroner's gavel came into play to silence the excited murmur which rose from the public end of the court.

"You realize, of course, what might be inferred from your statement?"

"Perfectly."

At that Dr. Burney sat down, and after Dr. White had corroborated his colleague's evidence, the Coroner asked if there were any further witnesses to call. The Superintendent, after an inquiring glance at Meredith, intimated that there were none and the Coroner forthwith proceeded to sum up. He pointed out that the jury had three questions to consider. First they had to find the cause of death. In his opinion they would have no difficulty about that. Dr. Burney had definitely stated that death was due to asphyxia caused by the inhalation of carbon monoxide, or, if they preferred it, exhaust fumes.

Secondly, they had to consider whether this asphyxia was caused accidentally or whether it was suicide or whether it was murder. With regard to this first point, they had heard the evidence of Mr. Perryman and Inspector Meredith—how the deceased was found sitting in an upright position at the wheel of his car with a mackintosh over his head, beneath which a length of hose-pipe, connected to the exhaust-pipe of the car, had been introduced. In his opinion, all these facts combined to suggest premeditation. If the jury were agreed that this was so, they would rule out the idea of accident. Had the deceased taken his own life? That this was a possibility, the jury could not ignore. All the outward facts of the case pointed to suicide.

On the other hand, there was the Inspector's evidence to consider, and further, the evidence of Dr. Burney and Dr. White.
They, at the request of the police, had performed an autopsy.
The jury were cognisant of the result of this autopsy. A powerful drug had been discovered in the stomach and intestines of
the deceased. In the opinion of Dr. Burney, an opinion which
he, the Coroner, endorsed, it would have been pointless for the
deceased to have taken the drug himself. The only alternative
to this suggestion was that the drug had been administered by
a second party. The jury had to ask themselves, "Why had this
drug been administered?" If, in their opinion, it was for the purpose of incapacitating the deceased, so that the body might be
placed in the driving-seat of the car, then it was clearly a case of
murder.

The third question which the jury had to consider would arise
only if they brought in such a verdict. If they found that murder
had been committed, then they must state, if they could, the
guilty party or parties. In his, the Coroner's opinion, there had
been no evidence forthcoming to warrant any such statement.
They must, however, be guided solely by their own judgment
and find accordingly.

As both Meredith and the Superintendent anticipated, the jury
elected to retire. At the end of thirty-five minutes they filed back
into the stuffy little courtroom. Then in tense silence the Coroner
put the usual question and a thrill of horror animated the public
benches when a verdict was brought in of wilful murder by some
person or persons unknown!

CHAPTER VII

THE PARKED PETROL LORRY

"MAJOR RICKSHAW has been on the phone, sir," said the Sergeant on duty as Meredith passed through the office on his way from the inquest. "Wants to have a word with you."

"Who the devil's Major Rickshaw? Never heard of him!"

"Retired Indian Army man, sir. Only just come to live in the district. He's rented that house near the Old Toll Gate on the Grasmere road."

"What's it about? Did he say?"

"The Clayton case, sir. Said he was unable to come down and see you as he was confined to his bed with a chill."

"I'll go up at once."

Railton being off duty, Meredith took the combination out of the garage and drove off in the direction of the Toll Gate. He had no difficulty in finding the house—a square, grey, weather-beaten edifice overlooking Derwentwater, standing back off the road in a fair-sized garden. The maid showed him at once into the Major's bedroom, where the patient, a mahogany-skinned, hatchet-faced man, was lying propped up in bed reading the *Cumberland News*.

"Come in! Sit down, Inspector," he croaked. "Excuse my voice, but I've got a chronic touch of throat. That's it—draw up that chair. The closer you are the better. I'm damned if I can manage much more than a whisper."

"That's all right, sir," said the Inspector heartily. "I understand you've got something to tell me about the Clayton case."

"Quite right. I have. Saw that notice of yours in the paper." He waved the *Cumberland News* in the air. "This paper. Mid-weekly edition only came out this morning—otherwise I'd have got in touch with you before. Are you ready to take down my statement? Good!"

In a series of fierce, staccato whispers Major Rickshaw described how he had visited the Derwent garage on Saturday night. He had been speaking at a Conservative meeting over at Cockermouth and was returning home with his wife in the car. At the Derwent he stopped for a couple of gallons of petrol, and was served, in his own words, "by the young chap with the Hitler moustache who was usually in charge of the pumps". He supposed he had reached the garage about twenty minutes past seven. Neither he nor his wife got out of the car and as he handed over the exact money for the petrol he had no cause to hang about the garage for any length of time.

"What happened to the money? Did you notice, sir?"

"Yes—the fellow shoved it into the pocket of his dungarees."

"Buff dungarees?"

"That's it, Inspector."

"What was the denomination of the coins you handed over, sir?"

"Just one coin, Inspector. A half-crown piece. I always swear by the cheaper forms of petrol. Never pay more than one and threepence a gallon. Though I don't quite see——?"

"Just a small point. Nothing of importance," returned Meredith quickly. "The really important question is this—did you notice anybody else hanging around the garage?"

"Not a soul! There was a light in the office, I remember. Couldn't see if anybody was inside. Frosted glass, you see. There was a petrol-lorry drawn up in front of one of the pumps——"

"A lorry! Then there must have been somebody about!"

"Possibly," snapped Major Rickshaw with some irritation. "But I've already told you, Inspector, that I didn't see them."

"Did you notice the name on the petrol-lorry?"

"Yes, I did! Nonock Petroleum Company. That's Ormsby-Wright's affair. Got shares in the concern. What's more, they actually pay a dividend!"

"You feel quite certain in your own mind that the man who served you with petrol was Clayton, I suppose?"

"Confound it all, Inspector—I know a face when I see it." With an irascible gesture the Major smoothed out the newspaper and jerked his finger at a photograph reproduced at the bottom of the column dealing with the tragedy. Where the Press had unearthed it Meredith could not imagine. Probably from the Reades.

"That's Clayton, isn't it, eh?" went on the Major. Meredith nodded. "And that's the face of the chap that served me with petrol. Good enough—what? If you want a second opinion, I'll ring for my wife."

"It might be as well," remarked the Inspector. "Not that I doubt your identification. But it was a dark night, remember, and one can't be too careful in a case of this sort."

The Major, therefore, pressed the bell and sent the maid to fetch Mrs. Rickshaw. After introductions had been effected, Mrs. Rickshaw, a somewhat wispy, faded lady of about fifty, corroborated her husband's evidence in a tremulous voice, which drew forth a triumphant "I told you so!" from the bed.

Satisfied that he had gained all he could from the Rickshaws, Meredith drove back to the station in a thoughtful frame of mind. It was extraordinarily curious how the Nonock Petroleum Company kept cropping up. First there was Higgins's customer, the manager of the Penrith depot. Then his encounter with the fast-driven lorry on the road just outside Braithwaite. And now on Saturday night a Nonock lorry had been drawn up beside the Derwent petrol pumps. He had already determined that inquiries would have to be made about the men on the lorry, and he decided to drop in at the Penrith depot on the following day.

In the meantime, what exactly had he learnt from his interview with Major Rickshaw? Precisely—nothing! It was annoying that the Major hadn't stopped at the garage, say, at eight-thirty.

He already knew that Clayton was alive and kicking at seven-thirty-five. He had Freddie Hogg's word for that. What he really wanted, was to narrow down the time in which it was possible for the murder to have been committed. If only somebody turned up who had called at a later hour at the garage!

The next day, Inspector Meredith, in plain clothes, boarded the Penrith bus. The day was clear and sunny, though a cold wind was blowing up from the Borrowdale valley at the end of the lake. The vast hump of Saddleback rose gilded in the frosty air, laced with the white threads of distant waterfalls. Little patches of snow still clung to the weather-sides of the higher peaks, but already in the valleys there stirred the first subtle promise of approaching spring. The wine-like air filled Meredith with energy and optimism. Somehow he had a premonition that before the end of the day he would be able to look back on a considerable amount of progress. Why this feeling was so insistent he could not say. He rather doubted if he was going to gain much from the lorrymen. They must have left shortly after Major Rickshaw, because when Freddie Hogg cycled past some ten minutes later the lorry was no longer there. Still, as a matter of routine, the men would have to be questioned.

Nearing the depot, Meredith stopped the bus and alighted. He did not want anybody to see him entering the place and he knew that one or two Keswick people on the bus had already recognized him. The less the locals knew about his peregrinations the better were his chances of solving the case.

After a brisk walk he came to the entrance of the depot. The entire place was surrounded by a tall corrugated-iron fence, above which projected the roofs of the garages and stores. About a hundred yards behind, and slightly above the rear of the depot, ran the Cockermouth–Whitehaven branch-line of the L.M.S. Meredith noted a tank-car which had been shunted off on to the

Nonock siding and a couple of stout poles from which dangled two flexible pipes, obviously used to connect with the union on the tank-car. Open meadows rose in a gradual slope from the siding, and the depot itself, standing quite on its own, looked unutterably bleak despite the clear March sunshine.

Just inside the gateway, which was ajar, Meredith noticed a little brick-built office raised on a platform of cement. At first glance the place seemed entirely deserted, and it was not until he drew level with the office that he noticed a man watching him from a window. Mounting the steps which led up to the office door, the Inspector rapped sharply and the face disappeared, to reappear a few seconds later in the open doorway.

It was then that Meredith had one of the biggest thrills in his life!

It was all he could do to suppress a sharp cry of astonishment, for the face which peered uncertainly into his was as clearly impressed on his memory as the title on the cover of a book. Not that he had ever met the man before. He hadn't. But there was no gainsaying those thin, clean-shaven features, the weak eyes enormously magnified by the thick lenses of a pair of horn-rimmed spectacles. Even if Meredith had doubted the evidence of his eyes, the moment the man opened his mouth he knew that he had not been deceived in his belief. That slight stutter offered conclusive proof. The man who confronted him was the man whom Mrs. Swinley had, on two occasions, seen at the garage cottage!

"Well," demanded the man, with a rather truculent air, "what can I do for you?"

"Can I speak to the manager of the depot?" asked Meredith with emphasized politeness. "It's a personal matter."

"You're speaking to him," replied the man shortly. "My name's Rose. What's the trouble?"

Again Meredith suffered a sudden surprise. So this was the man with whom Mark Higgins had made that appointment on Sunday morning! It looked as if Mr. William Rose had a pretty close connection with the partners of the Derwent.

"I won't keep you a moment. May I come in?"

Meredith grew more affable every minute.

"All right," said the manager, kicking an office stool in his direction. "Sit down, won't you?"

"Thanks," said Meredith. "First let me introduce myself, Mr. Rose. My name's Johnson and I've just rented a place for the winter at Braithwaite. Well, two days ago I was driving round a sharp bend in the middle of Portinscale when I was nearly run down by one of your lorries. I shouted to the driver to stop but I'm sorry to say, Mr. Rose, he ignored my summons and drove on. If I hadn't had my wits about me I don't mind telling you that I shouldn't be here now talking to you."

"Well?" demanded Rose acidly. "What do you want me to do about it?"

"My first idea," went on the Inspector in an unruffled voice, "was to take up the matter with the police. But on thinking things over I decided to come over here and see you first. After all, I don't want your man to lose his job or have his licence suspended. My idea was that you might give the fellow a straight talking-to and leave the matter at that."

"I see." Mr. Rose seemed to contemplate the facts for a moment, then: "You're quite certain it was one of our lorries, I suppose?" he asked.

"Of course."

"What time did this happen?"

The Inspector smiled to himself. It was rather a novelty being cross-examined for a change; besides, the fertility of his invention amused him highly.

"Let's see—about seven-thirty in the evening."

A look of sneering triumph came over the manager's sunken features.

"Then I've got you! Our lorries aren't on the road after six o'clock. They're scheduled to garage here at six when I check in their returns. You've made a mistake, Mr. ... Mr. ..."

"Johnson," smiled the Inspector pleasantly. "But I assure you that. ..."

"Impossible," snapped the manager. "If you doubt my word, you can darn well stay here till six o'clock and see 'em come in. They're all out to-day. Six lorries. So you can stand in that gateway and count 'em. That's fair enough, eh?"

"Well, really. ..." Meredith's confusion was admirably genuine. "I don't quite know what to say, Mr. Rose. It looks as if I must have been mistaken. I apologize, of course. Can't imagine how I could have made an error like that. Your lorries *are* green aren't they? Green with yellow lettering?"

"That's settled it! You *have* made a mistake. Blue and red—that's us !"

Meredith's apologies grew profuse. He couldn't imagine how he could have been so stupid. Now he came to think of it, the Nonock lorries had blue tanks with red lettering, hadn't they? He'd noticed them about quite a lot in the district.

"I expect you've got a pretty flourishing connection in these parts? Interesting work, eh?"

"So-so," said the manager in surly tones.

"Oh, well," observed Meredith spaciously, "we all think other people's work more interesting than our own. Now I'm a commercial traveller—at least, I was until I had a nervous breakdown. Haberdashery—that was my line. Ever been on the road, Mr. Rose?"

The manager eyed his interlocutor suspiciously, and nodded.

"Off and on," was his non-committal reply.

"But now that you've got a regular round for your lorries I suppose it means you're tied to the office?"

"That's about it."

Meredith rose suddenly, with an apologetic air, and held out his hand.

"But I mustn't take up all your time, Mr. Rose. I'm sorry I've troubled you. I still can't see how I made that mistake. Well—good morning."

"Good morning," answered Mr. Rose in level tones as he escorted the Inspector down the steps.

Aware that the manager had followed him cautiously to the gates and was now watching his departure, Meredith sauntered casually along the road in the direction of Penrith. There was no bus due for another forty-five minutes, so he decided to walk into the town and improve the shining hour at the Beacon. Once round the bend of the road, screened by a high stone wall, Meredith swung into a brisk stride, a form of exercise which always acted as a stimulant to his brain.

He was delighted with the result of his visit to the depot. He now felt sure that there was some definite connection between the manager and the partners of the Derwent. That it was a purely business interest Meredith dismissed. Rose had as good as told him that his work lay solely in the little brick office. The Nonock company had already worked up an excellent connection with the garages in the surrounding areas, as witness the number of places which sported their blue and scarlet pumps. He had already noticed a pump of this description at the Derwent. So it hardly seemed probable that Rose's nocturnal visits to the cottage could be connected with a desire to further the trade of the petrol company. What, then, was the basis of the intimacy between the two factions? Was the Chief right in his theory? Were these men united in the running of some nefarious concern under cover of their respective trades?

Meredith could not suppress a chuckle when he recalled the shock he had received when Rose had confronted him in the office door. Thank heaven his powers of invention hadn't failed him at the crucial moment! As Mr. Johnson, the retired commercial traveller, he had at least gained a glimmer of useful information, which would most certainly have been denied him if Rose had guessed his real identity. Complications had accrued, of course. He would now have to interrogate the lorry-men away from the depot. It would never do for Rose to see him cross-examining the men. That would immediately put him on his guard.

And why had the lorry been seen at the Derwent at seven-twenty when he had the manager's assurance that all the Nonock transport was in the depot by six o'clock? The significance of this discrepancy struck Meredith at once. Did it mean that the lorry-men were vitally concerned with Clayton's death—in brief, *were they the murderers*? It was a possibility, but a possibility discounted by Freddie Hogg's evidence. The lorry was no longer there when he passed at seven-thirty and Clayton was definitely alive. The men might have parked the lorry up a side-turning and returned on foot to the garage. That was another possibility. If only he could have established the time at which the lorry reached the depot on Saturday night! On the other hand, why not follow up the supposition that the lorry had parked and make an exhaustive examination of the probable side-turnings up which it could have been concealed? Meredith decided that this, coupled with a cross-examination of the lorry-men, must be his next move.

Charlie's amiable countenance expanded into a vast grin when Meredith walked into the hotel entrance of the Beacon.

"Hullo, Inspector. Taking a day off?"

"You've said it!" replied Meredith with a wry grimace. "No such luck, Mr. Dawson. Can I have a word with you in the office?"

"Right-o. This way. Mind the mat!" He went to a side-table and poured out a couple of whiskies and sodas. "No need to ask," he observed with a sly chuckle as he handed Meredith the tumbler. "Here's luck, Inspector!"

Meredith grinned as he raised his glass.

"I need it," he answered tritely. "You saw the result of the inquest on Clayton, I suppose?" The manager nodded. "Well, between ourselves, I've got a hunch that I'm on to something. Nothing certain. But I believe you've got some information that I can do with, Mr. Dawson."

"Right-o. Go ahead, Inspector."

"What exactly do you know about the Nonock Petrol Company? That's my star question."

Dawson considered the query for a moment, pulling at the lobe of his right ear, a habit of his when thinking.

"Well, I don't know much," he acknowledged, at length. "Ormsby-Wright is the owner of the concern. It's a newish business. Been running about ten years. The company's well organized and paying their shareholders an annual dividend of seven and a half per cent. As far as I know, there are only two depots—one here and one just outside Carlisle. I can't tell you anything about the Carlisle place, but I've picked up a good bit of information about the local depot."

The Inspector leant forward eagerly.

"Good—that's just what I'm after. To begin with, how many people are employed there?"

"Let's see—there's Rose, the manager. I've mentioned him before, you remember. Then there's six lorry-drivers and their mates. That's another twelve. And a yard-man. That's the lot, I think."

"There are always two men to a lorry, then?"

"Always—yes. I'm sure of my facts in this case, Inspector, because most of the lorry-men patronize my public bar of an evening."

"What time do they knock off?"

"Six. They start off at nine in the morning, see? Each lorry has a definite itinerary to cover. If they can do their round in less than the scheduled time then they garage their lorries before six. Actually their itineraries are so worked out that it takes them a full working day to cover the mileage. Fast driving, as you can guess, is not encouraged. They're heavy machines, at the best of times, and the wear and tear is pretty bad, without the chaps speeding."

"Quite. Does the same lorry always cover the same itinerary?"

"That's the idea. There are six lorries, see, and six different districts to be covered. For example, one chap does the Kendal district, another runs between here and Carlisle, a third takes in Keswick, Cockermouth and the coast towns. Get me?"

Meredith nodded.

"You've given me some useful information, Mr. Dawson."

"Always ready to oblige the police," grinned Mr. Dawson. "Anything more, Inspector?"

"Yes. Do you know the men who work the Keswick–Cockermouth route?"

"Course I do. Bettle's the driver—big, bull-necked chap with a fist like a leg o' mutton. Carnera, I call him on the Q.T. Slow-thinking sort of chap he is. Never says much. Just the opposite to his mate, Prince. He's a lively little box o' tricks. Wonderful with cards! Sleight of hand and so forth. A darn good mimic, too. I tell you, Inspector, things always look up in the bar when young Prince sticks his head round the door. Talk? He never *stops* talking. Keeps us all in fits."

"You say that Higgins is often over here. Ever seen Higgins talking to these men?"

"Well, only in a general sort of way. Higgins never seems particularly pally with 'em. I reckon they're a cut below his style.

Mark Higgins rather fancies himself as a bit of a dandy. Least-ways, that's my opinion."

"What about Rose?"

"Oh, he knows *him* all right. Whenever Mark Higgins is over from Keswick it's ten to one that he and Rose will have fifty up in the billiards saloon. Both keen players. Good, too. Why I've seen young Mark make——"

Meredith tactfully allowed Dawson the satisfaction of deliv-ering a eulogy on Higgins's skill with a billiard cue before glanc-ing up at the clock with the information that his bus was due to start in three minutes.

Feeling more than pleased with his morning's investiga-tions, he returned home, ate a hearty lunch, and shortly after two o'clock tramped off across the sodden fields to Portinscale. He had already decided on four possible by-lanes in which the lorry could have been concealed. Two of these, on the right-hand side of the road, petered out in farm-yards by the head of Bassenthwaite, whilst the two on the left eventually converged on the main, lakeside road to Grange and Seatoller. Meredith, for obvious reasons, chose to examine the right-hand roads first. The men would have naturally selected a road on which traffic was negligible. Passing the first of the side-turnings, he came to the second, which was a little over a quarter of a mile from the garage. Unobserved, he turned into the narrow, grass-bordered lane and, working up each side, made a close examination of the ground.

Although the lane itself was stony and unyielding, the turf at the sides was still soft from the recent rain. If, then, the lorry had drawn in at all when stopping, it was almost certain that the tyre-marks would be visible. On the other hand, if the driver had his wits about him, this was just the sort of clue he would avoid leaving. So when, at the end of half an hour, Meredith found his way barred by a high gate, he was disappointed but still disinclined to abandon his theory. It was true that there were several vague outlines which suggested the recent passage of traffic up the lane, but the heavy rainfall disallowed any possibility of distinguishing one blurred track from another.

He felt, however, that it was imperative for him to make a number of inquiries at the farm-house, in the hope that one of the inmates had noticed the stationary lorry. But although he questioned some half-dozen people about the place, nobody could give him any information. The owner of the farm, a Mr. Thomas Thornton, felt sure that if anybody had seen the lorry there on Saturday night the news would have soon got around. Anything unusual would certainly be made much of, for the simple reason that unusual happenings so seldom occurred in the district. Meredith felt inclined to agree with this line of reasoning and, after thanking Mr. Thornton for his help and courtesy, he made his way back to the lane.

Whatever faults may be attributed to the British police force by the American or continental critics, a lack of thoroughness is not one of them. And in accordance with his early training, Meredith patiently re-examined every foot of the lane and its grass-grown skirtings. And this time his thoroughness was rewarded! He found something. Not exactly what he was looking for, but something unexpected enough to rivet his attention.

Scattered over an area of about a yard square, almost invisible in the grass, were hundreds of tiny pieces of glass. There was nothing in the shape of a bottle-neck or base to indicate their origin. The individual bits were so tiny, in fact, that Meredith concluded the original object must have been deliberately broken up. Probably with one of the several loose stones lying nearby. With immense patience he at length collected a good handful of the jagged pieces and poured them carefully into an envelope. A cursory inspection of his find had brought one fact to light. A distinct curve was noticeable in the larger pieces, suggesting that the original object might have been a bottle or a globe. But the extreme thinness of the glass puzzled Meredith intensely. Offhand, he could think of no commonplace article which would have been manufactured from such fragile stuff. The idea of an electric-light globe flashed through his mind. But surely the filament was welded into a thick tongue of glass, projecting from the metal holder? A watchglass, too, was out of the question. One wouldn't collect a large handful of remains from a shattered watch-glass. Meredith therefore decided to call in Dr. Burney to perform, what he mentally registered as, a *post-mortem*!

The rest of his afternoon's work proved disappointing. Although he spent the best part of two back-aching hours examining the other three turnings he found absolutely nothing in the shape of a clue. If the lorry had parked for a quarter of an hour up any of the four lanes it was obvious that unusual care had been taken to cover up all traces of the fact. That the broken glass had any bearing on the crime, Meredith doubted. Try as he would, he could forge no link which would connect his discovery with Clayton's death. At a quarter-past five, therefore, he flagged the local bus and returned to Keswick. Before going to his desk he called in on Dr. Burney and asked his opinion about the glass. The doctor, after a meticulous examination, was non-committal.

"It's the sort of glass that is manufactured for laboratory use—beakers, test-tubes, retorts and so on. But I'm not going to say that the original object belonged under that category. Foreign glass, for example, used for ordinary domestic articles is notoriously thin."

THE LAKE DISTRICT MURDER

"I suppose you wouldn't hazard an opinion as to what the vessel contained?"

Burney laughed sarcastically.

"What? After it's been lying out there in the rain—probably for days. Rather not. A laboratory test would be waste of time. Sorry!"

Meredith returned disgruntled to the police station. Although outwardly he had expected no result, subconsciously he had rather hoped that the broken glass *would* supply some startling data. Oh, well—this detection business was full of annoying *cul-de-sacs*. One took a likely road and after a tiring tramp it ended abruptly in a blank wall. Frustration, confound it, was part of his job!

The Sergeant was off duty and Railton *pro tem* in charge of the office.

"That clock right, Constable?" asked Meredith, jerking his thumb at the wall.

"Ten minutes past five—yes, that's right, sir."

"Well, I want you to go on point duty until six o'clock. Understand?" Railton looked puzzled.

"Point-duty? Where, sir?"

"At the bottom of the street on Greta Bridge. I'm expecting a Nonock petrol lorry to come through Keswick within the next few minutes. If it does, stop it, and bring the occupants up here. I want to talk to 'em."

Railton, secretly disgusted at having to abandon the comfortable heat of the office, put on his helmet and departed.

CHAPTER VIII

PRINCE AND BETTLE EXPLAIN

In ten minutes the constable rapped on the door of the inner office.

"The gentlemen are outside, sir."

"Show 'em in," said Meredith briskly. "And I shall probably want you to take down a statement."

For all his outward calm, Meredith was experiencing a lively undercurrent of excitement. Although as a practical-minded man he was inclined to scoff at intuition, he could not help feeling that the approaching interview would prove of paramount importance to his investigations. If these men failed to tell him anything then the future of the case stretched out before him with all the uncompromising bleakness of a moorland road.

The moment the bull-necked Mr. Bettle came through the door Meredith appreciated the aptness of Charlie Dawson's nickname. Brute strength was the keynote of his physical appearance; accruing from a massive torso, a somewhat smallish head and a broad and prominent jowl. Mentally he looked, if not actually deficient, considerably under average quota, whilst the slow roving of his eyes spoke of a nature that was suspicious rather than credulous. Beside this cumbersome giant his companion offered a strange and ludicrous contrast. Well under average height, dapper and nimble of movement, Prince was a Cockney to his finger-tips; embodying in his small, dynamic person all the ready wit and intelligence of the type. In view of the dissimilarity between the two men, Meredith decided, at once, that it would be politic to question them apart.

After they had revealed their names, the Inspector stated his reason for wanting to see them. And although he was watching them closely he was unable to detect the flicker of an eyelid at his first mention of the murder. Bettle looked straight at him with a sort of bewildered stupidity, whilst Prince seemed over-whelmed with an impatient desire to speak. Both men acknowl-edged that they had seen the report of the inquest in the local paper, also the police demand for information, but as they had only stopped for a short time at the garage, and as Clayton was alive and in a normal frame of mind when they left, they had decided that there was no point in their coming forward.

The Inspector hastened to correct this mistaken viewpoint.

"In a case of this sort any information, however slight, may be of importance. You were the last people to see Clayton alive, so I'm afraid you'll have to tell me all you can. Any objection?"

"Not as far as I'm concerned," replied Prince promptly.

"Same 'ere," grunted Bettle.

"Very well. Suppose I take your statements separately? It will make things easier." Meredith opened the door and called the constable. "The Sergeant back yet?"

"Just come in, sir."

"Good. Then suppose you sit in the other office for a minute, Mr. Bettle, whilst Mr. Prince and I have a word together in here. All right, Railton. I shall want you. Now, then, Mr. Prince—let's have the details of your visit to the garage on Saturday night."

Prince seemed more than ready to oblige. He delivered his evidence with such swift volubility that it was all the constable could do to take down the main points of his statement.

"Well, it's like this," began Prince. "Me and my mate work the Keswick–Cockermouth district for the Nonock. We don't have no half-day off on a Saturday. That's a rule of the firm. Thursday's our day, see? Well the last garage on our round is the Derwent. We'd had an order through on Friday to deliver two 'undred gal-lons without fail next day. So we pulls up and, after a word or two with Clayton in the office, connects with the tank and delivers as per schedule. I suppose we were the best part of 'arf an hour on the job, what with one thing and another. Clayton's a talkative chap—leastways, I suppose I should say he *was* a talkative chap—and we had a bit of an argument about 'oo was going to win the F.A. Cup this season. At any rate, about 'arf-past seven, after Clayton had signed the delivery slip, taken a dip of the tank and O.K.'d the load, we left for the depot. He was right as rain *then*, though a bit absent minded, if you take me. I've heard he's a moody chap, Inspector, but whether that's true or not I can't rightly say."

"You didn't notice anybody hanging about the place when you left?"

"No, sir."

"Are you certain about the time you started for the depot?"

"Pretty near positive. You see, I 'appened to look at my watch, because we were already overdue at the depot."

"Overdue?" said the Inspector sharply. "Why was that?"

"Engine trouble. Spot of water in the carburettor feed, as it turned out. Took us the best part of an hour to set the thing right."

"Where did this happen?"

"D'you know Jenkin 'Ill, about 'arf-way between Hursthole Point and Braithwaite Station? We called on time at the Lothwaite and then ran into this patch of trouble. Consequence was we didn't arrive at the Derwent until near on seven o'clock."

"I see. And after you left the Derwent you returned straight to the Penrith depot? No stops, I take it?"

"None. A clear run. Mr. Rose—that's the manager—was waiting back for us and checked us in."

Meredith rose from his desk and held out his hand for Railton's hurriedly written statement.

"Thanks, Mr. Prince. Perhaps you'd just read this through and attach your signature."

As soon as this had been done, Railton ushered in Bettle, whilst Prince vanished into the outer office.

Bettle was far less glib in the delivery of his evidence. Whenever Meredith slipped in a terse question, the driver pondered deeply, rubbed the back of his head with his cap, and answered with a deliberation that was distinctly irritating. Every one of his slow utterances seemed to have a heavy chain attached to it, and it was all the Inspector could do to drag the necessary information out of Bettle's dull cranium. But the sum total of his evidence coincided in every detail with that of his mate. They had been overdue because of carburettor trouble. They had stayed for a time at the Derwent arguing with Clayton about the chances of the various football teams, and left for the depot at seven-thirty. Bettle remembered Prince taking out his watch and looking at it. His mate, in fact, had mentioned the time and suggested that they ought to get a move on. They had had a straight run home and Mr. Rose had checked them into the depot.

When Bettle had laboriously read through his deposition and attached an ill-written signature, Meredith explained that there was nothing more he wished to see them about, and the men hurried out into the street and climbed into their lorry.

In a second Meredith was back at his desk. Opening a drawer, he took out a Bartholomew's mile-to-the-inch map of the district and began to scale the exact distance between the Derwent and the Nonock depot. His final reckoning was exactly nineteen and a half miles. Assuming that the tank was more or less empty, Meredith concluded that the lorry could have covered the distance in an hour or a little over. At the most, it could not have taken longer than an hour and twenty minutes. Suppose, therefore, he compromised and said an hour and ten minutes—that would mean Rose had checked in the lorry at eight-forty. One of his next moves was to get a glimpse of the manager's books without Rose's knowledge. How the devil he was to manage that Meredith could not imagine. He would have to think out a scheme.

And beyond this matter of times, what exactly had he gained from the interview? Little enough! The promise of his intuition had not been fulfilled. The men had put foward a perfectly feasible explanation for their belated arrival at the Derwent. It was raining. What more natural than a spot of water in the petrol feed-pipe? He ought to check up on their statement and find out if anybody had noticed the lorry parked on the roadside between Hursthole Point and Braithwaite Station. Their last call had been at the Lothwaite. He could easily check up there with the proprietor the time of the lorry's departure. He could, in fact, kill two birds with one stone. He had already decided to have a look over the lakeside garage in consequence of the Superintendent's story about the Hursthole Point tragedy. Was it, he wondered, in any way suggestive that the lorry formed a link between the two fateful garages? Possible but not probable, was Meredith's inward comment.

He then turned his attention to the other half of the lorry's journey. Surely he could find somebody who had noticed it either on the open road or passing through Keswick? They might not know the exact time they had seen it, but a rough idea would be enough to gauge the truth of the men's story.

Suddenly the Inspector whistled. Why the devil hadn't he thought of it before? He knew somebody who could give him the desired information! Hadn't Freddie Hogg been cycling home from Keswick at a time when the lorry should have been on its way to the depot? Freddie had passed Clayton at the garage at about seven-thirty-five. The lorry had left the garage at seven-thirty. So Freddie must have met the lorry on the road somewhere just outside Portinscale.

Burning with impatience, Meredith searched through the telephone directory. Yes—there it was—Hare and Hounds, Braithwaite. Briskly he dialled exchange and in a few seconds he was through to the public house.

Freddie Hogg himself answered the phone.

"Look here, Mr. Hogg," said Meredith after he had revealed himself, "I've got a question of vital importance to ask you. Think well before you answer. I want you to cast your mind back to Saturday night again. Yes—it's to do with the Clayton affair. Now, did you on your way back from Keswick pass a Nonock lorry anywhere on the road between Portinscale and the Derwent?"

Freddie seemed to be thinking for a minute, then: "No, Inspector. I'm quite sure I didn't. There was so little traffic on the road, that if I had, I'm certain I should have remembered the fact."

"Then what about between Portinscale and Keswick?"

"No. I never passed a Nonock lorry at all. Positive!"

"You went straight from Keswick to Braithwaite—main road all the way?"

"Yes. Where else could I have gone? There's only the one road, isn't there?"

"That's true." The significance of this fact struck Meredith at once. Hogg was right. There *was* only one road. "At what time did you leave the picture-house?"

"About five past seven."

"Thanks," concluded Meredith tersely. "That's all I wanted to know."

For the first time since the case had opened, excitement was Meredith's predominating emotion. At last he had gained some really substantial information. He could only interpret Freddie Hogg's evidence in one way—the lorry *had* left the garage at seven-thirty but before the cyclist could have met it the lorry had turned off the main road and parked, probably without lights, up a by-road. There seemed to be only one plausible explanation for this. Major Rickshaw had called at the garage when the lorry was parked beside the petrol pumps. Bettle and Prince would therefore realize that there was no hope of concealing the fact that they had called on Clayton. What then is their move? They drive off and when the road is clear, park up a side-turning. Prince then returns on foot to the main road and waits there until he sees somebody pass in the direction of Braithwaite. In this case—Freddie Hogg. He realizes that there is every chance of Hogg seeing Clayton, which is exactly what he wants, since the lorry is no longer there. The coast being clear, he then returns, on some pretext or other, to the garage. He probably explains that the carburettor is giving trouble again and asks Clayton to lend a hand. Before they leave the garage, however, Prince gets Clayton to take a drink out of his whisky-flask. Whilst waiting for the trional to take effect, he engages Clayton in conversation and the moment he is unconscious, drags him to the garage, sits him in the car, arranges the hose and mackintosh, starts up the engine and rushes off to rejoin Bettle on the lorry. By driving the lorry all-out they manage to make the depot in plausible time and thus establish an alibi.

So far so good. "Now," thought Meredith with a wry smile, "for the snags." He was too old a hand at the game to expect everything to go his own way without difficulties. Almost immediately several objections to his new-found theory reared their undesirable heads.

First he dealt with the time factor. The road was clear for Prince at seven-thirty-five—say, five minutes for him to walk from the first of the side-turnings (the one in which he had found the

glass) to the garage. Say another five minutes offering an explanation for his return and getting Clayton to have a swig from his
whisky-flask. Twenty minutes, at least, according to Dr. Burney,
for the trional to take effect. At least another ten minutes to get
the unconscious man into the car, fit up the apparatus and start
the engine. Then another five minutes to get back to the lorry. In
all—forty-five minutes. That was to say, the lorry would set off
for the depot at eight-twenty, arriving there somewhere about
nine-thirty. But both Prince and Bettle had assured him that they
started at seven-thirty and had a clear run to Penrith; and they
must have known that it would be a simple matter to check up on
this statement. So it rather looked as if his nice little theory was
already knocked on the head.

That Clayton had been given the drugged whisky before the
lorry left the Derwent, Meredith refused to believe. It would be
too risky. Clayton might easily have collapsed before Prince was
able to return to the garage, in which case the chances were that
anybody passing by might notice that something was amiss.

Again, would the lorry-men have gone to the trouble of parking up a side-turning and returning to murder Clayton, when
the vital point in their alibi was that Clayton should be seen by
a chance passer-by? They couldn't wait up the lane for ever. On
the other hand, it was Saturday night. Traffic, though not very
heavy, would be fairly frequent along the Cockermouth road at
that time of the evening. Meredith reckoned that on an average one vehicle or pedestrian would pass the garage about every
ten minutes. He was inclined to think, therefore, that this was
a fairly safe gamble for the men to take despite the fortuitous
element in their scheme. His final conclusion on this point was
that it offered no real objection to his theory.

The time factor was the real trouble. Even if the apparatus
had been previously fitted up in some way—Meredith let out

a sudden exclamation! What about Higgins? He could have done it. He knew where the hose was kept, and the dimensions of the exhaust-pipe. What was to prevent Higgins from secreting the pipe and the mackintosh in some prearranged spot, locking the garage and hiding the key with the other objects and then clearing off to Penrith? There was probably only one key to the lean-to, so even if Clayton had wanted to get at his car he would have been unable to do so. Or better still, Higgins could have fitted up the whole deadly apparatus and just hidden the key. That would take at least eight minutes off Prince's time. But was that enough? Surely it would still leave too much time unaccounted for?

Try as he would, Meredith could not persuade himself into a confident frame of mind over his first reconstruction of the crime. Everywhere there were loose ends lying about. If Prince, in company with Bettle, *had* murdered Clayton—*what was the motive?* That was the biggest query of the lot. Then there was the matter of the £2,000, the Lothwaite tragedy, the bits of broken glass, Rose's nocturnal visits to the garage cottage and the undeniable fact that the Nonock lorry *must* have returned direct from the Derwent to the Penrith depot.

"As healthy a brood of problems as one could ask for," thought Meredith as he trudged home dispirited to his long-awaited meal.

CHAPTER IX

INVESTIGATIONS AT THE LOTHWAITE

AFTER a somewhat restless night, in which the various problems surrounding Clayton's death hovered on the fringe of his consciousness, Meredith returned in an irritable mood to his office. The case, instead of clarifying with the progress of his investigations, grew more complex at every turn. There were now so many different clues to be followed up that the Inspector was at a loss as to where it would best profit him to begin the day's work. He finally decided to take a look at the Lothwaite, interview the proprietor, and corroborate the lorry-men's story about the breakdown on Jenkin Hill.

One thing was essential. He must without further delay forward a full description of Higgins, Rose, Prince and Bettle to Scotland Yard. From their speech he had gauged them to be southerners and, from his knowledge of dialects, Londoners. If any of the men had been convicted of a crime in the metropolitan area then Scotland Yard would be able to give him an idea as to their particular "line". But how was he to obtain the necessary photographs of the four men? A verbal description was all right as far as it went, but it wouldn't establish the identity of the men with any degree of certainty.

In the case of Higgins there would be no difficulty. The *Cumberland News* had already published an excellent portrait of the man in conjunction with their mid-weekly report of the tragedy. But what about the Nonock trio?

Meredith cast his mind back to the depot and its near environs. The picture was quite clear in his mind. On one side of the Penrith road the high, corrugated-iron fence and the tall gates; on the other, directly opposite the entrance, a thick clump of holly bushes. What was to prevent him from posting a man with a camera in the bushes, with instructions to "snap" Mr. Rose as he left the depot at lunch time? He felt quite certain that the manager would return to 32 Patterdale Road for his mid-day meal. Bettle and Prince presented a more difficult problem. They did not return to the depot until after dark, which meant that the only chance of taking their photograph was in the early morning before they started work. The men lived in the town and it was pretty certain that they would either walk or bicycle out to the depot, arriving there a little before nine.

Having decided on this line of action Meredith swung up Main Street to Vernon's the photographers. The proprietor himself came forward in answer to the shop door bell. When he saw the Inspector he grinned.

"Hullo, Meredith! Your young scallywag been up to something? In for a paternal lecture, is he?"

"Not this time, thank heaven. But I'd like a word with Tony if he's about."

"He's in the dark-room. I'll fetch him," said Vernon.

In a short time Tony himself came into the shop obviously at a loss to explain his father's unexpected visit. Particularly as they had parted at the breakfast table only half an hour before.

"Hullo, Dad? What's the idea? Nothing wrong at home is there?"

"Rather not, Tony. Listen here a minute."

In a few brief sentences Meredith explained what he wanted, whilst Tony's blue eyes grew bright with interest and excitement. This was an adventure after his own heart. A relief from the rather boring routine of the shop at which he was apprenticed.

"Well, Tony? Do you think you can do the job?"

"It's as good as done," Tony assured his father with all the bragging optimism of seventeen. "If you can fix it with the boss, Dad, I'll look out my camera and get on to the job straight away."

Vernon raised no objections when the Inspector had explained the importance of getting hold of the photographs. And after warning both Vernon and Tony to keep the affair secret, he strode off briskly to the police garage and took out the combination. Shortly after ten he swung right off the Braithwaite road and headed for Bassenthwaite lake. About a hundred yards beyond the turning which led to Braithwaite station, he drew up at the roadside and consulted his Bartholomew's map. He reckoned Jenkin Hill to be a little over a mile ahead, at which point the railway line was shown as being some three hundred yards away from the road. This fact was of vital importance to Meredith, as he knew there was a Cockermouth train due in at Braithwaite station at 6.25 on Saturday evening. So the chances were that the train had passed within a reasonably close distance of the parked lorry. True, it would be dark, but the lorry would be showing lights, and any stationary vehicle at that particular point at that particular time would offer a strong hint as to whether Bettle and Prince had been telling the truth or not. Arriving at Jenkin Hill a quick review of the locality showed that it was not only possible for the lorry to have been seen from the passing train, but probable. The road at that point, for over a quarter of a mile, was raised on a slight embankment and the intervening meadows were as flat as a pancake and destitute of vegetation.

"So much for that," thought Meredith, his depression lifting a little. "Now for the Lothwaite!"

Opening the throttle, the Inspector was soon level with the head of the lake. Here the railway line swung in, running close to the right of the road, whilst on the left the fell-sides rose in a spruce-covered slope to a gradually declining ridge. Soon the glorious expanse of Bassenthwaite opened out, shining with the transient beauty of the early spring light; its far shore backed by the sombre immensity of the Skiddaw range. But Meredith had little time to appreciate the subtle loveliness of the landscape, for rounding a corner he came suddenly on a scene which sent him braking and skidding into the side of the road.

Not two hundred yards ahead was the garage and drawn up beside the petrol pumps was a blue and scarlet Nonock lorry! Three men stood talking in the garage entrance, luckily facing in the opposite direction, but even at that distance Meredith had no difficulty in recognizing the bull-necked Mr. Bettle and his loquacious companion, Prince.

The Inspector acted quickly. Running his bike behind a row of tar barrels, which stood on the edge of a little draw-in beside the road, he climbed the low wall at the foot of the fell-side and plunged into the spruce wood. Dodging this way and that among the thick and brambly undergrowth, he worked his way to a position somewhat behind and above the small group of buildings which constituted the Lothwaite. From a quick survey of the lie of the land, he realized with a thrill of excitement that it would be possible for him to get within ten yards of the group without any danger of revealing himself. The garage had been erected in a natural hollow, rather like a small, disused quarry, so that anybody approaching through the trees could look down almost on to the roofs of the building.

At first Meredith was unable to distinguish a single word of the conversation proceeding below, but by dint of further cautious manœuvring he finally succeeded in catching a few isolated sentences. In a flash he had drawn out note-book and pencil and begun to set down the drift of the men's talk.

First there was Prince.

"Thought we might have something to take in … working overtime … Mark's naturally out of the running … the Derwent … settled down."

Then the proprietor—a short, stocky man, Meredith noted, with bowed legs and long arms like a baboon.

"… all very well … the boss can't expect … up the output … impossible. … "

Then he heard Bettle's rough voice break in with:

"That's not our fault, Wick. Orders is orders. O.W. gets a bee in 'is bleeding bonnet … not our look-out!"

Then Prince entered in again, but this time in so low a voice that Meredith was unable to catch a word. At the conclusion of his remarks Bettle let out a raucous laugh and the three men moved toward the lorry. Prince uncoupled the union, which joined the lorry's delivery-pipe to the countersunk pipe attached to the underground petrol tank, and replaced the iron lid of the manhole. He then curled up the flexible tube and laid it in a wooden box parallel to the base of the blue and scarlet lettered container, whilst Bettle climbed up into the driving-seat. After Prince had given the starting-handle a couple of twists the powerful engine broke into a roar, and in a few seconds the lorry had lumbered out of sight.

Wasting no time, Meredith plunged back through the wood, mounted his bike and drove up to the garage. The man whom he had just seen in conversation with Prince and Bettle came forward to attend to his customer's needs.

"Yes, sir?"

"I'll take a gallon of Nonock," said Meredith. "I hear it's good stuff and I've never tried the brand before."

"It *is* good stuff," agreed the man. "The best."

"Sell a lot of it, I daresay?" asked Meredith innocently, as the man stuck the nozzle of the pipe into the petrol tank and returned to work the handle of the pump.

"Fair bit."

"You must do," continued the Inspector, watching the man closely. "Two deliveries in about six days looks like a roaring trade to me!"

"What do you mean?" asked the man sharply.

"This," replied Meredith. "Last Saturday night a Nonock lorry called here and made a delivery at your pump. This morning, a few minutes back, they made another delivery. Hence my remark—a roaring trade."

"That's just where you're wrong. The lorry called here last Saturday night, but it didn't make any delivery. I wanted four hundred gallons and they'd only got a couple of hundred surplus left in their tank. So I got 'em to call on their way out this morning with the full load. It was the earliest delivery they could make. Anyway," added the man with the sudden realization that he'd been drawn unwittingly into giving an explanation where it was not actually due. "Anyway, with all due respects, sir, I don't quite see what it's got to do with you."

"Possibly not," replied Meredith. "Here, take a look at those and then perhaps you'll understand."

The Inspector drew his credentials out of his trench-coat pocket and showed them to the proprietor. The man looked puzzled.

"Police, eh? Sorry, sir! I didn't realize—you not being in uniform."

"Quite. Well, I'm Inspector Meredith if you want to know. Let's see—your name is?"

"Wick—Gurney Wick."

"You're the proprietor of this place?" Wick nodded. "Nobody work with you?"

"Yes—I've got a lad who comes in from Cockermouth every day in the summer. But in the winter I run the place myself to keep down the overhead. I was in partnership here two years ago, but I daresay you remember that rotten affair at Hursthole Point?"

"You mean Peterson's suicide?" Wick nodded and made a mournful grimace.

"Never understood it myself, though I daresay the loneliness got on his nerves. It's pretty dull here in winter."

Meredith smiled to himself. Wasn't this a replica of Higgins's suggestion as to the reason for Clayton's supposed suicide?

"Where do you live?" he asked.

"There," answered Wick, pointing to a dilapidated wooden shack attached to the side wall of the brick garage. "Do for myself and everything, as a matter of fact. I've no time for a woman about the place. More trouble than they're worth."

Wick expectorated with a mingled air of disdain and disgust and pulled out a packet of Woodbines. He had now completed the charging of the petrol tank and was leaning back against one of the pumps, watching the Inspector with ill-concealed impatience.

"Now look here, Wick," said Meredith briskly. "I want to know something. What time did the Nonock lorry leave your garage last Saturday night?"

Wick slowly lit his cigarette, considering the point.

"About a quarter to six or a bit earlier, perhaps."

"Wasn't that rather late for them? I mean, they usually pass here on their homeward run earlier than that, don't they?"

"It varies," answered Wick shortly. "Can't be too cut-and-dried on their job. What I mean is this—if they've got to deliver in comparative small quantities it takes 'em longer to do their round. Then again it depends on where they've got to place their load. Some of their garages lie a bit off the beaten track, you know."

"I quite see that. So you wouldn't consider them particularly overdue here on Saturday?"

Wick shook his head. "Though I did hear that they made the depot pretty late on account of engine trouble. I was talking about it only this morning because it made 'em late at the Derwent—and I've no need to tell you what happened *there* on Saturday night, have I, Inspector?"

"Exactly. And you can see why I am anxious to trace the exact movements of the lorry."

Wick broke out into a sudden roar of laughter.

"You don't mean to tell me, Inspector, that you suspect Bill Bettle and young Prince had a hand in the job? Good Lord— that's ripe—that is!"

"It's my job to suspect everybody and nobody," replied Meredith tersely. "You'd better think that over, Mr. Wick. Now, how much was the petrol?"

The Inspector paid what was due and after a quick yet comprehensive glance round the place, he straddled his bike, turned in the road and made for Braithwaite Station.

There, as luck would have it, he found he had only ten minutes to wait before a train was due in from Penrith. The sole official at the station was able to supply him with all the information he needed. The Penrith–Cockermouth route was a shuttle-service, divided into two shifts, and after consulting a timetable, the station-master-cum-porter assured Meredith that the driver and fireman of the approaching train would have run the 6.25 from Cockermouth into Braithwaite on Saturday.

Dead on time the train steamed into the station and drew up with a jerk. In a matter of seconds Meredith had clambered on to the fire-step and stuck his head into the overheated, oil-reeking cabin. The driver, a Keswick man, recognized the Inspector at once.

"Good Heavens, Mr. Meredith, what on earth are you doing here? Not bad news, is it?"

Meredith quickly set the man's mind at rest and explained the reason for his appearance. After a moment's consultation, both the driver and the fireman came to the conclusion that they had seen the lights of a stationary vehicle on the Cockermouth road, but neither of them could say exactly where it had been parked. They thought it was about a mile up the line.

"Well, we can easily make certain as to that," cut in Meredith. "How far was the road from the line when you saw the vehicle?"

The driver scratched his chin with the tip of a grimy forefinger.

"Now you've got me, Mr. Meredith. Let's say from about here to that haystack over there. Not nearer, eh, Ted?"

The fireman agreed.

"Good enough," replied Meredith. "About three hundred yards. Thanks, gentlemen." Then with a broad wink: "You'll have to step on it if you want to keep up with schedule. Still, blame the police if there's trouble. Good day."

On his way back to Keswick Meredith's attention was equally divided between keeping a watch on the road and trying to elucidate certainties from the various new facts which he had gleaned.

He now felt quite sure that the Chief was right. Behind Clayton's murder lurked the shadowy suggestion of a well-organized, criminal activity. What it was he could not say, for the simple reason that there were so many illegal practices to choose from. That the Derwent and Lothwaite garages were in some way under the thumb of the Nonock Petroleum Company seemed more than probable. Hadn't Wick spoken to Bettle and Prince about "the boss"? Hadn't the whole of that overheard conversation suggested that the men were united in carrying on some form of illicit business? "Orders is orders" had been Bettle's trite remark. That hinted at what the "twopenny bloods" would call a "master-mind"—a master-mind behind the working of the organization. Was the master-mind Rose? Meredith thought not. The depot manager had not impressed him as a particularly subtle or intellectual man. Then what about this O.W. that Bettle had so picturesquely referred to? Who was O.W.? Was he the brain behind——?

In a sudden rush of inspiration Meredith narrowly escaped collision with an oncoming farm-cart. What a fool he'd been not to take up the point at once! O.W. *could* only be one person! Ormsby-Wright—the owner of the petroleum company! What better alibi could a man have than a position of authority, responsibility and trust, when secretly engaged in the running of some nefarious organization? Who would suspect the respectable head of a well-known business concern of being a criminal? The more Meredith thought about it the more certain he grew that he'd hit the nail on the head.

But if this were so, the police were up against a bigger thing than they had first suspected. A man of Ormsby-Wright's calibre wouldn't dabble in petty criminality. If Meredith knew anything about crime he would set about things in a big way. He would demand big profits. And to make those big profits the turn-over of his illegal concern would have to be considerable. Whether this would prove a stumbling-block to the solution of the mystery the Inspector could not rightly say. But he was inclined to think, perhaps optimistically, that the more people there were in a "racket" the greater were the police's chances of running that "racket" to earth.

He knew one thing all right. If he could bring off the job single-handed it would be a feather, not only in his own cap, but in that of the County Constabulary.

CHAPTER X

DISCOVERIES AT THE DEPOT

MEREDITH lingered over his lunch, waiting for Tony to return from Penrith. He suffered a mild lecture from his wife for sending the boy on what she called "one of your silly underhand police tricks". Mrs. Meredith bore no love toward the Force. In her opinion it made enough demands on her husband's time, without it having to interfere with Tony's proper lunch-hour. Hadn't she done all in her power to kill the boy's absorbing interest in police affairs? She really thought Meredith might have shown a little more consideration for her feelings.

Tony's entry put an end to a well-worn argument. He was excited and triumphant.

"Got three beauties, Dad!" he announced before he was half-way through the door. "The chap came outside the gate and stood chatting to another chap. Gave me just the chance I wanted!"

"Good lad, Tony. You weren't seen?"

"Oh, don't you worry," cut in Mrs. Meredith witheringly. "He's not been a Boy Scout for nothing."

And with this Parthian shot she swept into the kitchen.

Tony laughed.

"There's something in what mother says, you know. Boy Scout training does help in this sort of job."

"You couldn't hear what they were talking about, I suppose?"

"Couldn't I! I never missed a word, Dad."

"Then you were luckier than I was," thought Meredith. Aloud, he added: "Well?"

"It was about that Rose chap not being at the depot this afternoon. He'd got business in Penrith and the other chap was not to expect him back until five o'clock. Then our chap gave the other chap a few orders about things he wanted done in the yard and then cleared off."

"And this other chap," grinned Meredith. "What did you take him for?"

"Sort of odd-job chap, I should say."

"Now what about these photos, Tony—when can you let me have the prints?"

"Well, I ought to get the second lot before nine tomorrow morning, hadn't I? So if I rush through the developing and printing I ought to have the whole lot ready for you by four o'clock."

"Splendid! I shall be able to get them off to the Yard by the evening post. You've done well, Tony."

"Thanks," said Tony. "By the way, that new three-speed Raleigh in Simpson's——"

Meredith laughed and reached out for his cap.

"It won't hurt you to go on thinking about it," he said. "Thinking never hurt anybody."

And with this non-committal remark he set out for the station.

Hardly had he arrived at his office when the Superintendent stuck his head round the door and asked if he could come in. Meredith placed him a chair.

"Anything new, Inspector?"

Meredith outlined his morning's work.

"So we can take it," observed the Superintendent when Meredith had concluded, "that Bettle and Prince were telling the truth about that breakdown?"

"Well, they were seen on the road at the time stated. So I think we can safely say that they did stop for about an hour on Jenkin Hill. But whether they did have carburettor trouble is another matter."

"But what other reason would they have had for stopping?"

"This," answered Meredith. "The Keswick F.C. were playing Cockermouth on the away ground last Saturday. A good few people would be over watching the match. That would mean a tidy bit of traffic past the Derwent until well after six o'clock. Bettle and Prince must have known this. Assuming that they did murder Clayton it would be essential for them to offer a plausible reason for arriving at the Derwent as late as seven o'clock, wouldn't it? Hence the carburettor trouble."

"There might be something in that," acknowledged the Superintendent. "At any rate, with all those people coming back along the Cockermouth road you ought to be able to check up on the engine-driver's statement."

"Re the parked lorry? Yes—I'd thought of that."

"Then there's another thing which has occurred to me," went on the Superintendent. "That's the chief reason why I've come over. I was looking through that copy of Mrs. Swinley's deposition, which you sent over. Didn't it strike you, Inspector, that the conversation she overheard between Higgins and Clayton was pretty significant?"

Meredith looked puzzled. "Just a minute, sir." He searched through a file on his desk and produced a small sheaf of papers. "Here we are—this is the bit you mean, isn't it?" He pointed to a paragraph of his own neatly written report.

"That's it. You notice that Clayton says, 'It's all very well for you, but I've got to get out of this concern'?"

"Exactly. A reference, I take it, to the garage partnership."

"But is it?" demanded the Superintendent quickly. "That's just where I'm inclined to disagree. Notice Higgins's reply. He says something about it being the worse for Clayton if he does back out. According to Mrs. Swinley it sounded as if Higgins was threatening his partner. But why such a strong attitude if it was the mere dissolution of the partnership in the garage?"

"You mean?"

"That Higgins wasn't referring to the partnership at all! He was referring to something of far more vital importance to his well-being."

"The illegal business running under cover of the garage!" exclaimed Meredith. "The Chief's supposition? I see it now!"

"And you see how it suggests a motive for the crime? The motive already put forward by the Chief. Clayton was clearing off to Canada with the girl to make a fresh start. Once over there, what was to prevent him from turning King's evidence? His silence was essential. It could be guaranteed in only one way. So they murdered him in time to prevent his get-away."

"And this illegal business, sir?"

"You've got me there. I'm inclined to think that the Nonock company has got something to do with it."

"You mean in conjunction with the garage."

"Garages," corrected the Superintendent. "Don't forget the Lothwaite. My theory is that the lorry forms the link between, what we might call, H.Q. and company headquarters. Your report of what you overheard this morning helps to strengthen my theory. If O.W. stands for Ormsby-Wright, what more natural than Wick and the lorry-men speaking about him as 'the boss'? A common boss at the head of the illegal concern."

The Superintendent settled himself more comfortably in his chair and thrust out his feet toward the glowing coal-fire.

"It seems to me, Meredith," he went on after a pause, "that we're up against two problems. Clayton's murder and the nature of this illegal concern. From the data already to hand I think we can assume that the two problems are pretty closely connected. Solve one and I think we shall solve the other. But the question is—on which of the two problems shall we concentrate first? I agree that we have collected more information about the murder. That was natural because the idea of the illegal concern didn't enter our heads when we started our investigations. Again the murder is a fact. We haven't got to ask ourselves, 'Was Clayton murdered?' We know now that he was. The second problem, on the other hand, is still in the realms of pure theory.

When we come to look closer into it, we may find that it doesn't exist. So on the face of it, it looks as if we ought to settle with the murder problem first. The question remains, can this be done without bothering our heads further about the solution of problem number two?"

"Well, sir," said Meredith cautiously, "we've got to assume problem number two if the motive you put forward for the murder holds good. It seems to me that we ought to tackle both problems at the same time."

"I don't agree with you there, Inspector," said the Superintendent bluntly. "And I'll tell you why. Once let any of the gang suspect that we're investigating something more than the murder, and we'll have them on their guard. At the moment all they'll be concerned with is covering up the facts of Clayton's death. Always assuming, of course, that Bettle and Prince are the murderers. The probability is that they're still running the illegal business without a thought that we suspect anything."

Meredith agreed.

"You know, sir—the same thing occurred to me when I was sitting over lunch to-day. You remember what I overheard this morning?" Meredith pulled the notebook out of his pocket and handed it to his superior. "Take a look at that first sentence again, sir. What do you make of it?"

"*Thought we might have something to take in,*" read the Superintendent slowly. "*Working overtime ... Mark's naturally out of the running ... the Derwent settled down.*" He looked up inquiringly. "That the bit you meant?"

"That's it. Remember it's Prince speaking to Wick. Now I tried filling in the gaps and the result I got went something like this—'*We thought we might have something to take in since you've been working overtime. Mark's naturally out of the running until affairs over at the Derwent have settled down.*' Does that let the light in at all, sir?"

"By Jove, it does!" exclaimed the Superintendent, suddenly sitting upright in his chair. "It means that since Clayton's death Higgins has had to lie doggo. He can't carry on with the illicit job until police interest in the garage has calmed down a bit. In consequence, Wick, at the Lothwaite, has had to work overtime. And further it looks as if the lorry acts as a sort of collecting van for the 'racket.' You agree, Meredith?"

"In detail, sir," said Meredith warmly. "Now take the next bit." He held out his hand for the proffered notebook. "*... all very well ... boss can't expect ... up the output ... impossible*," read the Inspector. "Which I read something like this—'*That's all very well, but the boss can't expect me to keep up the output. It's impossible!*' Which suggests that Wick was finding himself hard put to it, to do the Derwent work as well as his own."

"But what? What?" demanded the Superintendent with a comical note of despair. "What work?"

Meredith shook his head.

"That *is* problem number two," he pointed out. "Find out what they're up to and I reckon we should be able to get 'em inside the net. Do you know anything about this Mr. Ormsby-Wright, sir?"

"Little enough, I'm afraid. He's got a big house up on the Carlisle road near Penrith Beacon. 'Brackenside', I think it's called. But beyond the fact that he's a member of the local Conservative Club, a churchgoer and a sound business man, I know nothing. I've heard he's worth a bit, of course. It's common property that he's got a finger in a good many industrial pies. But although the Nonock's his chief concern, he takes no active interest now in the running of the company. More or less leaves it to his two branch managers, I understand."

"He's not married, sir?"

"No."

"What do you suggest as my next move, sir?" asked Meredith with his customary tact.

"Follow up the murder," replied the Superintendent as he got up from his chair and buckled on his cape. "If your investigations take you into localities where you might pick up information about the 'racket', then keep your eye skinned. But, for heaven's sake, don't let them get wind of our suspicions, Meredith. Play the murder for all you're worth but not a hint about the second problem. Understand?"

Meredith understood only too well, and when the Superintendent had departed for Carlisle, he swore softly under his breath at the cussedness of the double-barrelled case. It was all very well for the Superintendent to talk glibly about solving the murder first, but suppose it proved impossible to do so without further investigation of the other crime? These sort of official limitations were annoying. At any rate he had discovered a means of keeping an eye on the Lothwaite, which would not result in any of the suspects being put on their guard. Tony's information, too, had provided him with a heaven-sent opportunity to find out a bit more about the Nonock depot and its personnel. With Rose away for the afternoon he could question the yard-man and perhaps get a glimpse of the manager's books. He glanced at his watch. Ten minutes to three. If he drove over straight away he would have plenty of time to interview the man before the manager returned at five.

Before he departed, however, he left instructions with the Sergeant to find out who had driven over to the football match at Cockermouth on Saturday afternoon.

"Get all the information you can about a parked petrol lorry at a point near Jenkin Hill. Find out if they appeared to be in trouble—bonnet up or anything like that. There must have been plenty of people on the road at the time."

"Very good, sir."

Meredith was soon speeding over the all-too-familiar Keswick–Penrith road through a dull and muggy afternoon. The higher mountain peaks were swathed in blankets of white mist. Although it was March there was an almost autumnal feeling in the air. Meredith half expected to see patches of decayed heather and the sere and golden bracken on the fell-sides. The melting drifts of snow still clinging to the windward sides of the higher gullies, the bare, black trees and the general desolation of the wintry landscape seemed strangely out of place.

As an imaginative man, fond of the open air, Meredith had grown to love the sweep and the grandeur of the valleys and the hills. Even the realistic and often sordid nature of his job had failed to take the keen edge off a naturally poetic appreciation of his surroundings. Often he would tramp for miles over the fells with no other companions than his pipe and his thoughts. He was thinking then, as he sped between the age-old, grey, stone walls—not of the patch of watery sunlight on the distant slope of Clough Head, nor the blue shadow caught in the trough of a far-off valley, but as to why a certain Nonock lorry had parked up a side-turning on the night of Clayton's murder.

Try as he would he could not see how Prince or Bettle could have found time to do their dastardly work and arrive back at the depot before nine o'clock. If only he could lay his finger on the weak spot of his reconstruction of the crime! Was it, he wondered suddenly, that Bettle had returned alone to the depot? Had he left Prince to do the job and return to Penrith by train or bus? If so, what was the point of Bettle waiting up the side-turning? It would have been far better for him to have dropped Prince a little way up the road from the Derwent and driven directly back to Penrith.

Still turning these problems over in his mind, Meredith drew up in front of the corrugated-iron gates and dismounted. As on his previous visit he found the gates ajar. Ignoring the apparently closed office, he crossed the yard to the big garage in which a light was burning. Inside he found a man in blue overalls, engaged in swilling down the cement floor with a length of hose.

Meredith's first impression was of a quiet, respectable individual, who would probably prove to be a conscientious and efficient employee. In age he looked to be fifty or a little over.

At the Inspector's unheralded appearance the man looked up quickly.

"Hullo, sir! And what may you be wanting?"

"Manager about?"

"No, sir. He won't be back till five. Anything I can do?"

"Yes," replied Meredith brusquely. "I'm Inspector Meredith—county police. You can probably help me. Won't keep you a minute."

The man laid the bubbling hose on the floor, and, walking over to the tap, turned off the water.

"Now, sir?" he said, turning to the Inspector.

"What's your position here?" asked Meredith.

"Yard-man. Odd-job man if you like—it more or less amounts to that. If there's anything extra to be done they drops on me to do it."

"Name?"

"Dancy—Robert Dancy."

"What time did you leave here last Saturday night?"

"Darn late," answered the man promptly. "I should have got away by seven, but No. 4 had trouble on the road and didn't get in until near on nine."

"No. 4?"

"That's the Keswick–Cockermouth lorry, sir."

"I see. Was the lorry checked in?"

"Yes, sir. By Mr. Rose. He's the manager."

"Could I see the book?"

The man hesitated, obviously reluctant to interfere with something that was strictly outside his province.

"Well?" demanded Meredith. "Yes or no?" Then realizing the man was still undecided he determined to try a bluff. "You realize that I could get a search warrant anyway, don't you? But I don't want to waste time on that. There's no need for your boss to know that you've let me have a look at the book, if it's that what's troubling you."

"All right," agreed Dancy. "Since you put it like that, Inspector."

The yard-man pulled a bunch of keys out of his pocket and Meredith followed him over to the little, brick-built office. Unlocking the door Dancy preceded the Inspector to a knee-hole desk near the window and picked up a black-bound book.

"Here you are, sir. This is what you're after."

Meredith took the book and soon found the page in which he was interested. He noted that each page was ruled into several columns, headed respectively—Date. Lorry No. Time Outgoing. Load. Deliveries At. Time Incoming. On Saturday, March 23rd, Lorry No. 4 had apparently left the depot at 9.10 with a load of 1,000 gallons. Deliveries were to be made at five various garages *en route*, including the Derwent. There was, however, no mention of the Lothwaite. The lorry had arrived back at the depot at 8.35. Five minutes earlier, in fact, than his own estimate for a direct run, allowing that the lorry had left the Derwent at 7.30. So unless Rose had cooked his books Prince and Bettle *had* told the truth.

"I see that No. 4 got in at 8.35 on Saturday," observed Meredith to the yard-man. "Does that strike you about right?"

"Within a minute or so, I reckon. Since I was kept hanging about I looked at the yard clock pretty frequently, and that check-in just about fits in with my idea of the time, sir."

"Who regulates the yard clock?"

"I do."

"Tell me, Mr. Dancy—when a lorry goes out with a load does it only deliver to order? Or do the men carry enough surplus to deliver an order on request?"

"Well, sir, for the most part they only deliver to orders received in advance. The garage writes in to Mr. Rose, stating the number of gallons required, and the load is usually made up so as to cover these advance orders. On the other hand when there's only half a load, we usually shove in another three or four gallons in case it may be wanted. On a round of that sort it's usual for our chaps to visit all our customers on their route."

"I see. What about Saturday's load on No. 4?"

"I can tell you about that all right, sir, because I helped to run it in. It was made up exact to advance orders. No surplus, see? Thousand gallons, I think it was."

Meredith's interest quickened. Something was wrong there! Wick had spoken that morning about wanting four hundred gallons on Saturday for delivery at the Lothwaite. But according to him there was only a surplus of 200 gallons in the tank and so he had asked for the full load to be delivered that morning. But how could there have been a surplus of 200 gallons if Saturday's load was made up exact to orders? When the lorry reached the Lothwaite there should have been just enough petrol left in the tank for the advance order at the Derwent.

Another point flashed through Meredith's mind. He hastily turned the pages of the black-bound book. Yes—there was to-day's entry. He went through the list of garages under the heading of "Deliveries At". The Lothwaite was not there! But it should have been there! Wick had given an order on Saturday night for 400 gallons. Why hadn't the order been entered in the book? Hadn't he himself seen the lorry making the delivery that morning?

"Is there an order book, Mr. Dancy?"

"There," said Dancy, pointing to a foolscap-size ledger lying in a wire tray. "All the advance orders are posted up in that book by Mr. Rose."

The Inspector examined the more recent entries with the closest attention. Saturday's order from the Derwent was there all right, but there was no record of Wick's order for the 400-gallon delivery to be made that morning.

"Tell me this, Mr. Dancy—if one of your lorry-men gets a verbal order *en route*, does he have to report it to Mr. Rose?"

"Of course. Otherwise the office wouldn't be able to keep a proper check on the outgoing loads. *Every* advance order received, sir, is shown in that ledger."

"Thanks. Now do you think I could just take a look round the premises?"

Dancy, although obviously puzzled by the Inspector's interest in the depot, readily assented. The two men set off on a brief tour of the place, the yard-man explaining things as they went along. But Meredith found nothing out of the ordinary to interest him. The place was well kept, roomy and so constructed as to minimize any risk of fire or explosion.

"Tell me, Mr. Dancy—what's the procedure from the moment a petrol consignment arrives at the port of entry until it reaches here?"

"It's like this, sir," explained the yard-man. "We've got our own store down at the dock-side. The petrol's discharged from an oil-tanker alongside the storage tanks in our own wharf-depot, see? As it's run in from the ship the Excise people check up on the amount and levy the necessary duty. When we find ourselves getting low here we let 'em know down at the dock-side store. We then get an advice note to say that a tank-car has been des-patched to us containing so-and-so gallons of petrol. When the tank-car arrives here, the railway people shunt it off on to our own siding round the back of this place. From there, by means of that pump I showed you just now, we empty the tank-car into our own storage tanks. There's an underground pipe from the siding which runs into the tanks via the pump."

"I see. Very interesting," commented Meredith. "Can you tell me the capacity load of one of your lorries?"

"Thousand gallons, sir. Same in each case. All our bulk-wagons—that's the trade name for the lorries—are built to the same pattern. They're three-compartment jobs. Two compartments holding four hundred gallons each and the remaining one two hundred gallons."

Satisfied that he now had a fairly extensive idea as to the *modus operandi* of the petrol company, Meredith accompanied Dancy back to the garage, where he thanked the yard-man for his attention and cautioned him to keep quiet about the visit.

"I'm afraid I've kept you from your job," he concluded, with his usual politeness.

"Oh, that's all right, sir," Dancy assured him. "With this new, high-pressure nozzle I can wash down the yards in half the time. Ever seen the gadget? Neat, isn't it?"

The Inspector, after a quick examination of the patent, agreed that it was—very neat. He noticed, too, that the length of hose to which the nozzle was attached was also brand new. It started a sudden train of thought coursing through his mind.

"New hose as well, I see. No chance of my getting hold of the old length for my garden, is there?"

The yard-man chuckled.

'Well, if you like to patch up the holes in it, you can have it for the asking, Inspector. I chucked it over the fence on to the dump about a fortnight back. Daresay it's the worse for wear now!"

"I only wanted a short length," explained Meredith glibly. "Perhaps I could cut off a sound piece and take it with me. You must use at least a forty foot hose to cover the yard from one tap, eh?"

"Thirty feet," corrected Dancy. Still, if you only want a dozen feet or so I daresay you'll find what you want."

"The dump's round the back, is it?"

"That's it, sir. I'll come round if you—?"

"No—don't worry, Mr. Dancy. I'll rummage round on my own." Just as he was about to walk off, Meredith asked with studied casualness: "By the way, was Mr. Rose in his office until No. 4 lorry returned?"

"Yes, sir—he never left the yard until after nine on Saturday night. He was at his desk making up the books. I could see him through that window."

"Thanks."

Leaving the yard-man to make up for lost time, Meredith passed out through the gates, hastily climbed the low wall by the roadside and followed the curve of the corrugated-iron fence to the back of the depot. The dump consisted of all sorts of odd bits of junk—old tyres, dented petrol tins, a couple of rusting mudguards, rotting sacks and empty oil-drums. It did not take the Inspector long to find what he was looking for. Shoving aside some of the rubbish, he pulled out a dirty length of rubber hosing. At first glance his interest quickened. Although the hose was now covered with a thick coating of oil and grime, it was obvious that its original colour had been white. Was his long shot in the dark going to find a billet?

It was the work of seconds to lay out the hose flat on the ground and draw a flexible steel rule from his pocket. With growing excitement he measured up the length—then, with an exclamation of delight, he pulled out his pocket-knife and cut off about six inches from the end of the hose. Rubbing the clean end against the ground, he thrust the remainder back into the dump and pocketed his specimen.

This done, tremendously elated, he returned to the motorbike, climbed into the saddle and headed full speed for the Derwent.

CHAPTER XI

PROBLEM NUMBER TWO

WASTING no time in Keswick, Meredith drove straight through the town and made for the Derwent. He could hardly suffer a moment to elapse before following up the hose-pipe clue to a definite conclusion. So much depended on a positive result of the test he was about to make. If the test were successful, then there would be no doubt that he had, at last, forged the first definite link between the murder and the murderer.

Reaching the Derwent, he hastily dismounted and took stock of the place. The sliding-doors to the main building were closed and locked, and a large, crudely-written notice announced: "These premises will be closed until Monday next." Meredith smiled. So his luck was holding! With Higgins out of the way it would make his investigations far simpler. He wondered if he might not be in the cottage, but there again he found the windows shut and the doors bolted.

"So much for that," he thought. "Now for the shed!"

The wood-shed door was merely on the latch and it did not take Meredith long to unhook the piece of hose-pipe off the nail and measure up. The instant he had done so he realized, with a thrill of excitement, that his theory had been metamorphosed by that simple operation into a fact! Here was the tangible proof he had been looking for! Here, at last, was a blazed trail leading from the Derwent to the Nonock depot at Penrith!

There was no gainsaying the certainty of his test. The length of hose in the wood-shed was just over six feet. The piece which had been cut from it and used over the exhaust of Clayton's car, was, as he knew from previous measurement, just under eight feet. The length of the piece in the dump was sixteen feet, almost to an inch, and Dancy had assured him that the original hose was thirty feet long. But that was not all! Comparing the bit which he had cut off from the piece on the dump, with the piece in the wood-shed, he saw at once that they were identical. The colour, the thickness of the rubber, the diameter of the pipe itself corresponded exactly. There was no doubt left in Meredith's mind now, that the hose used to convey the fumes from the exhaust to the mackintosh over Clayton's head, had been cut from the discarded length on the dump!

But one thing still remained to puzzle him. From his previous examination he had noticed that there was one, clean-cut end to each piece of hose. This meant that if the length used by the murderer in setting up his lethal apparatus were joined to the length in the wood-shed, a complete hose would result. But how could this be if the two lengths at the garage had originally been cut off from the thirty-foot hose on the dump? If this *had* been done, then one or the other lengths at the garage should show *two* severed ends.

For a moment Meredith's elation was usurped by the profoundest despair. Was this after all just another wild goose chase? Another one of those damnable blind-alley investigations? It certainly looked like it.

Then suddenly he asked himself: "But is it? *Is* it?" Wasn't it possible that the murderer had so arranged things as to make it *look* as if the two lengths formed a complete hose? With this in mind he made a careful examination of the length he held in his hand. Acute disappointment was his first reaction. Although one end was startlingly clean, the other was definitely soiled. Almost instinctively he rubbed the soiled end with the palm of his hand. To his amazement a black patch immediately appeared on his skin, and the whiteness of the rubber began to show through. He sniffed at the black patch. The odour was distinctive. At first he could not place it, but the next moment he broke out into a delighted chuckle, which resolved into a deep sigh of relief.

Boot blacking! So that was it! The test had not failed. It was certain now that the man who had murdered Clayton was an employee at the Nonock depot—otherwise, how had he known that the discarded hose was in the dump? It looked as if Messrs. Bettle and Prince were booked for an uncomfortable half-hour when next he questioned them!

But had he accumulated enough evidence against the men to warrant a further cross-examination? The time factor still demanded an explanation. Rose might have made a false entry in the last column of the black-bound book, but what about Dancy's corroboration? Unless he was part and parcel of the conspiracy he would not have troubled to lie about the matter. And somehow Meredith felt that Dancy was not mixed up with the mysterious doings of Rose, Higgins, Wick and the lorry-men. For one thing, he had not refused to let him inspect the manager's books, although strictly he would have been within his rights if he had done so. He could easily have forced Meredith to procrastinate his search by pretending that the manager had gone off with the sole key to the office. That would have given Rose time to decide on a line of action and allow him to cover up all discrepancies between the lorry's deliveries and his own entries in the ledger. Again, hadn't Dancy been quite open about the length of worn-out hose? If he was in league with the murderer or murderers, to draw Meredith's attention to the hose would have been little short of lunacy. Combining these facts with his own judgement of the man's character, the Inspector came to the conclusion that Dancy had been speaking the truth. The lorry *had* arrived back at the depot at 8.35. In other words, Bettle and Prince seemed to have an unassailable alibi.

Meredith was loath to omit that little word "seemed" from his conclusion. He knew how unreliable these unassailable alibis could turn out to be. But unless he could shake that alibi, wasn't he forced to relegate both Prince and Bettle, as potential murderers, to the background?

Now, as Meredith saw it, the only other persons who would be likely to know of the existence of the discarded hose on the dump were Rose, the remaining ten lorry-men and possibly Higgins. And although a certain amount of suspicion had accumulated about the manager of the depot and the proprietor of the Derwent, it was impossible for either of them to have actually committed the murder. They may have been in league with the murderer, but they couldn't possibly have been anywhere near the Derwent at the estimated time of Clayton's death. Between the hours of 7.30 and 9.30, the vital hours in the case, Higgins had been at the Beacon, and Rose was in his office at the depot. Dawson had vouchsafed for Higgins, and Dancy, whose evidence Meredith had every reason to trust, had sworn that the manager had been working solidly at his books until the arrival of No. 4 lorry at 8.35. Even on a high-powered motor-cycle, Rose could not possibly have got over to the Derwent, administered the drugged whisky, waited twenty minutes for it to take effect, placed the body in the car, started up the engine and got clear of the premises before Luke Perryman's arrival at the garage, shortly before 9.30.

That left the other ten lorry-men, and, as much as the Inspector felt inclined to dismiss them, he realized dismally that the movements of every one of them on Saturday night would have to be followed up. He decided to get the Penrith police on to the job early the following morning.

Such were the thoughts which occupied Meredith's mind as he drove slowly back to the police station. Coupled with his ruminations about the murder, were further thoughts pivoting on the nature of problem number two, the illegal business which was obviously being run by Rose in conjunction with the two garages. He knew now that Wick had lied to him that morning at the Lothwaite. Why, he could not say—at least, not at the moment, and he determined to shelve the second puzzle until such times as he could give it his undivided attention.

On his return, the Sergeant had good news for him. Not only had he run to earth two people who had noticed the stationary lorry on Jenkin Hill, but a third had offered a voluntary statement that, although they had not been over to the football match, they had seen a Nonock lorry pass through Threlkeld just before eight on Saturday night.

Meredith, although more interested in the second half of the lorry's journey than the first, dealt with the statements in their proper order.

"And your first two witnesses thought the lorry was in trouble of some sort?"

"Yes, sir," replied the Sergeant. "Hobson—that's the local reporter for the *Cumberland News*—actually stopped his car and asked what was up. The driver told him it was carburettor trouble, but they thought they'd nearly got matters right. The bonnet was up and the driver's mate was shining a torch on to the engine."

"Good enough," was Meredith's brief comment. "Now what about this Threlkeld information. Reliable?"

"Perfectly, sir. I got it from Frank Burns, who farms that big stretch of land under Gategill. I happened to see him up the town this afternoon, and knowing he was a football fan, thought I'd have a word with him. Seems lucky that I did, sir."

"Very. Go on, Sergeant."

"Well, sir, just before eight, Burns was standing outside the Legion Hall, talking to the Vicar. There was a whist drive on—Women's Institute or something like that. They were standing a bit out in the road it appears. Suddenly one of them

Nonock tankers comes hell for leather round the corner and nearly runs them down."

"Speeding, eh?" was Meredith's sharp comment. "How did Burns know it was just on eight?"

"The Vicar had just looked at his watch, sir. He was due to start the ball rolling at the whist drive at eight o'clock, and he'd just told Burns that it was time he was going when the lorry dashes round the corner."

Before the Sergeant had finished speaking, Meredith had spread out his Bartholomew's map on the desk.

"Let's see—from here to Threlkeld?"

"Best part of four and a half miles, sir."

"That's about six and a half from the Derwent. Which means that if the lorry left the Derwent at 7.35 and passed through Threlkeld, say at 7.55, it must have covered the distance in about twenty minutes. How does that strike you, Sergeant?"

"About right, sir."

Meredith nodded.

"And Burns's information just about fits in with the lorry's arrival at the depot at 8.35." He folded up the map and put it away in a drawer of the desk. "It looks as if we've now got that confounded lorry's movements taped out to a second. But even now, I'm hanged if I can see why it went up that side-turning!"

Alone at his desk, Meredith pondered that question again. It now appeared to be the one suspicious fact associated with the lorry's homeward run from the Derwent. And apart from that one inexplicable fact it seemed certain that neither Bettle nor Prince could be incriminated.

Realizing that he could get no further with that problem for the moment, Meredith switched his mind over to the second puzzle. Why had Wick spoken about those 200 surplus gallons when they weren't in the tank? Why hadn't his order for the

400 gallons been entered in the order book at the office? *And why had the pipe been connected with the tank of the petrol pump that morning?* Wick's order had not been recorded, so on whose authority had that delivery been made?

Leaning back in his chair, with narrowed eyes, the Inspector smoked and pondered, cursed under his breath, and returned to his smoking and pondering.

Then suddenly he sprang up, knocked out his pipe, and began to pace quickly up and down the room.

Why the devil hadn't the idea occurred to him before? But that was always the case—when an explanation was simple, one overlooked it just because it *was* simple. It was like searching a wood for a pair of dropped spectacles, when all the time they were pushed up on to one's forehead.

The Nonock Company dealt in petrol. So did the garages. Then wasn't it obvious that if the two factions were combined in the nefarious job of making illicit profits, that those profits would most likely accrue from the sale of petrol? What could be simpler? Rose sent out an unordered surplus with the lorry and this surplus was discharged into the tanks of the dishonest garages. The load was not paid for and the profits from the sale of the petrol to the public were divided between the manager and the garage proprietors. In that case it was Ormsby-Wright who was the plucked pigeon. How Rose managed to balance the amount in store with the sale returns of the amount which had gone out of store, Meredith could not imagine. But if he was clever enough to cook his books in one direction he was probably clever enough to cook them in another.

The petrol, so Meredith had learnt from his talk with Dancy, was despatched by rail from the dock-side depot. On arrival at the local siding it was transferred to the storage tanks by means of an underground pipe. There would be two checks on the amount consigned by rail. One kept by the manager at the wharf-side, the other recorded by Rose when the consignment was run out of the tank-car into storage. How then, was Rose to fake his books so as to make an illicit profit, when the amount in storage was known to the dock-side manager? Meredith, after a prolonged bout of hard thinking, had to acknowledge himself beaten on this point. Unless Rose was in league with the dock-side manager, it was beyond his powers to say how the fraud was worked. The only plausible explanation which did finally occur to him was that Rose omitted to enter up the full amount consigned to him by the dock-side depot, whilst his colleague at the wharf made a similar error in his record of the load consigned. After all, both the managers were in a position of trust and unless Ormsby-Wright grew suspicious of fraud, he naturally wouldn't trouble to compare his manager's figures with those relative to the shipments received at the port. And if an identical omission was made throughout in the company's books, the accounts could not be challenged by the auditors. There was an element of risk, of course—but in view of the owner's personal disinterest in the company, by no means a fatal one!

Tired out after his strenuous day, the Inspector went home to his high tea, in a mood vacillating between extreme optimism and the blackest despair. He was perfectly ready to acknowledge that he had made progress during the last twelve hours, but he was beginning to think that the more he found out in this peculiarly perplexing case, the more complex and baffling the case became. It was something to have forged that unbreakable link between the Derwent and the depot, but until fresh links could be fitted into his broken chain of evidence, the hose-pipe clue was valueless. It was now Friday. Nearly a week had gone by—a crowded, tiring week of investigation, cross-examination and theorizing, and yet he really had very little to show for it.

He had narrowed down the search for the murderer. That was something. But the second mystery, for all his ideas about fraudulent profits being made from the sale of Nonock petrol, was still a long way from a definite, *proof-positive* solution. It was all very well to expound suppositions, but the cleverest supposition in the world was quite worthless in the eyes of the law, unless backed by proof. To reconstruct a crime was fairly simple but to prove the truth of that reconstruction was a task that called for tremendous patience, acute observation and the devil's own amount of hard work!

CHAPTER XII

FRAUD?

By the time Meredith was astir the following morning, the enthusiastic Tony had already left for Penrith on the 7 o'clock bus. It was a clear, cold day and there was no reason why he should not succeed in getting some really excellent photos. Over breakfast Meredith busied himself with planning out his day's work.

Shortly after nine he was in touch with Sergeant Matthews at Penrith. After giving him a rough idea of his progress in the Clayton case, he came to the business in hand.

"So you see what I'm after, Sergeant? I must find out if those ten men were in or about Penrith on Saturday night. My suggestion is this. Send up a man to quietly waylay Dancy, the yardman, on his way home to lunch. You can't mistake him. There'll only be him and Rose at the depot at mid-day. Rose is a short-ish chap, with horn-rimmed glasses and weak eyes. So all your man will have to do is to avoid the manager and cotton on to the other chap. Whatever happens, don't let Rose see your man interviewing Dancy. Get that? With any luck, Dancy will be able to give the addresses of the ten men. If he can't do so on the spot, get him to find out without Rose's knowledge, from the pay-book in the office. Once you've got those addresses it should be fairly simple to find out something about the men's movements. I daresay Charlie Dawson at the Beacon may be able to help you. A lot of the Nonock fellows drop into his bar of an evening. At any rate, Sergeant, keep at it until you get results. It's absolutely essential that I should find out, and the sooner the better. Speak to the Superintendent about it, of course, when he comes in. But make him realize that it's very important. Understand?"

"Perfectly, sir."

"Get hold of Dancy's address, too, will you? I may want to question him myself later on and I don't want to do it at the depot. Give me a ring here."

"Right, sir. Is that all?"

"No, wait a minute! There's another thing. I want you to get in touch with all the Penrith banks and find out if Mark Higgins or Gurney Wick ... no, Wick! W. I. C. K. Got it? Good. Find out if either of them run a banking account over there. Phone that through with Dancy's address, if you will. That's all. Good morning, Sergeant."

Meredith's next call was through to the Cockermouth police, where he made a similar request in regard to the banking accounts. This done he got a local directory and compiled a list of the Keswick banks. These he dealt with himself, but neither Burton, the Barclays manager, nor Goreleston at the Westminster, nor any of the other branch managers numbered Higgins or Wick among their customers.

About ten-fifteen, Tony walked into his father's office and made his report.

"I've got 'em all right," he announced with justifiable pride. "I recognized the chaps from the descriptions you gave me, Dad, but to make quite sure I took a photo of every blessed chap that arrived. I'll develop and print them off at once and then you can pick out the two you want."

"That's smart work, Tony. What about Rose—did you see him again?"

"Yes—but it was lucky I got a snap of him yesterday. He came out by bus and was round the other side of it before I could count two."

Meredith grinned.

"I slipped up on that, Tony! It was lucky none of the lorry-men happened to arrive the same way. We'd have been properly in the soup if they had! How many chaps, as you persist in calling them, turned up at the depot?"

"Thirteen, I counted. Not including the Rose chap."

"Good lad—that's the lot. Now hop off and hurry through those prints."

The moment Tony had departed, Meredith got through to Carlisle.

"Inspector Meredith—Keswick station speaking. The Superintendent in?"

"Yes, sir. I'll put you through," answered the distant voice.

In a few seconds Meredith was in touch with his superior.

"Well, Inspector, what's the trouble now?" demanded Thompson in bantering tones. "Not another *post mortem*, I hope?"

"Not yet, sir," replied Meredith with a short laugh. "But if this Derwent case gets any more complicated I shouldn't be surprised if Dr. Burney has to perform on me!"

"I've just been through your report, which came in early this morning. You've done some neat work over that hose-pipe. Congratulations, Meredith!"

"That's all very well, sir," objected Meredith, "but it doesn't get us anywhere. As far as I can see it at the moment—my investigations of the murder have come to a dead end. Unless anybody else comes forward with new information, I don't see what I've got left to work on."

"I see. So what do you want me to do?"

"I want your permission, sir, to concentrate on problem number two. I'm beginning to think that until we learn something more about this illegal business, we shan't get any forrader with the murder case. What's your opinion, sir?"

"Well, frankly, at this instant, I haven't got one! But suppose you come over here and have lunch with me. Then we can talk things over and decide on our next line of action. Let's say twelve-thirty at the Royal Star—that's the biggish hotel in Botchergate. Know it?"

Meredith acknowledged that he did, thanked the Superintendent for the invitation and rang off.

When an hour and a half later Meredith reached the imposing façade of the Royal Star, he found Thompson, in plain-clothes, waiting for him in the reception-hall. They went through, at once, to the dining-room, and after an excellent lunch found a quiet corner in the deserted lounge and began their conference. At the end of twenty minutes Meredith had detailed all the facts of his discoveries in Rose's books, drawn the Superintendent's attention to the unauthorized delivery at the Lothwaite and elucidated his theory about the fraud which Rose, in conjunction with the two garages, was practising on the Nonock Petroleum Company.

"So you see, sir, I couldn't help feeling that our next move should be to follow up this discrepancy in the amount of petrol going out of store and the amounts recorded in the advance order book and, presumably, the sale-returns."

The Superintendent pondered the question for some minutes in silence. He was still loath to abandon the murder investigation and direct the energies of the police to the solving of the second problem. On the other hand, he was inclined to agree with Meredith that little progress could be made, at the moment, with the inquiries centring on Clayton's death.

At length he looked up and asked: "What do you propose to do now, Inspector? I mean, if we decide to shelve the murder problem and concentrate on the other? Have you thought of a new line of inquiry?" Meredith nodded.

"It will need your co-operation over here, sir. But I think we shall get results. Perhaps I'd better explain my idea so that you can then judge for yourself."

"Do," said the Superintendent eagerly. "I'll just light my pipe and let you do the talking. Now then—fire ahead."

"Well," began Meredith, "the first thing we've got to do is to get hold of a copy of all the advance orders which have to be dealt with by Lorry No. 4 on any particular day. I suggest Wednesday. I'll explain my reason for this choice in a minute, sir. For this copy we'll have to rely on Dancy, and from what I know about the man, he'll have no difficulty in getting into the office and taking a look at Rose's books. For the sake of argument, let us suppose that the total number of gallons accruing from Wednesday's advance orders is eight hundred. Now we shall know the number of gallons which is to be delivered at each garage and the names of the garages which have sent in requests for a specified delivery. From Dancy we can find out if the load on No. 4 is made up exact to advance orders or whether a surplus is run in over and above the eight hundred gallons. If it is, Dancy can further tell us the exact amount of this surplus.

"Now, this is where I shall want your help, sir. We must, before Tuesday next, find out the name of every garage on No. 4's round—that is to say, every place which sports a Nonock pump. I doubt if Dancy would be able to lay his hands on a comprehensive list of these places, but at any rate he will be able to give us a fairly good idea of the district covered by No. 4. I've already learnt from Dawson, at the Beacon, that Bettle and Prince deal with Keswick, Cockermouth, Whitehaven, Workington and Maryport. So it should be simple to make up a list of the Nonock customers in those particular towns. Then if one or two men could be put on to the job of unearthing the village and roadside places, we should then have a pretty accurate list of Nonock customers on No. 4's round. You follow me so far, sir?"

"Perfectly."

"Our next move," went on Meredith, "would be to post a man to watch every one of these garages. My idea was that I should cruise round on the motor-cycle and take a note of all those places which could be watched without arousing suspicion. Those that can't be dealt with in this way—say, the more open and isolated garages—will be marked by me and tackled differently. At some suitable point on the roadside a motor-cyclist could be concealed, with instructions to follow up the lorry and find out if it stopped at the specified garage. Each of these would then have to make a note as to whether No. 4 coupled up with the Nonock pump and discharged a delivery. In this way we could draw up a list of every garage dealt with by No. 4—that is to say, every garage *at which a delivery was made*. With our previous knowledge of the make-up and concents of the lorry's load, coupled with a reference to our copy of the day's advance orders, we could then find out if any unauthorized delivery was made, and if so, at what garages. I'm inclined to think that if there is anything in my theory, we shall find that these illegal deliveries are only made at the isolated places. That's more or less my scheme, sir. What do you think of it?"

The Superintendent smiled.

"Extremely neat, Meredith. It will call for a lot of careful organization, but I think it can be done all right. Luckily, the Chief himself was the first to suggest the existence of this illegal concern. He'll probably be as keen as you are on putting the scheme into practice."

"There's another thing," went on Meredith. "We ought to check up on two or three days—not just on Wednesday's round. There's always the chance that the deliveries on that particular day may be in order."

"Quite. I see that. Suppose we follow up Thursday, Friday and Saturday as well. Will that meet the case?"

"Not Thursday, sir," corrected Meredith. "Don't forget that's the men's half-day. But I think that if we include the Monday and Tuesday of the following week we shall find out as much as it is possible to find out. You see now why I suggest Wednesday for a start? It will take us at least three days to get the scheme organized and collect the necessary information. You agree, sir?"

The Superintendent nodded.

"And I suggest we go round now and have a word with the Chief. He happens to be in his office."

At the termination of this interview Meredith was elated. Colonel Hardwick was enthusiastic, and after complimenting Meredith on the progress he had made, the trio had settled down to a detailed discussion of ways and means. It was finally arranged that Carlisle should supply the list of garages and provide the necessary watchers and motor-cyclists. Meredith was to get hold of the advance-order copies for Wednesday, Friday, Saturday, Monday and Tuesday, and also to procure from Dancy a statement of the loads taken out of store on these particular days. The Inspector was also to cover the route and take note of suitable hiding-places from which the garages could be watched and earmark those places which would have to be dealt with by the cyclists.

After they had taken leave of the Chief, Thompson accompanied the Inspector to the garage where he had left his motor-bike.

"By the way, Meredith, I don't want to damp your ardour, but two points occurred to me just now when you were talking to the Chief. You remember the conversation you overheard yesterday morning at the Lothwaite?"

"Word by word, sir," said Meredith promptly.

"Well, in the face of your theory, how do you account for the following points? Firstly, why did Prince, in speaking to Wick, say, 'We thought we might have something to take in since you've been working overtime'? Doesn't that strike you as rather curious? If the lorry was making a fraudulent delivery, why should Prince talk about 'taking in'? Surely that should have been Wick's expression. Again, what about that reference to 'overtime'—where exactly does that fit into your theory?"

For the moment Meredith was nonplussed. In the excitement of working out and perfecting his plans, he had entirely overlooked this point.

"I suppose Prince couldn't have been joking," was his final suggestion. "The 'taking in' expression might have referred to the money due on the last fraudulent delivery. And the 'overtime' rather suggests that Prince was pulling Wick's leg because he had sold more petrol than was usually the case. With Higgins out of the running at the Derwent, this increase in Wick's sales would be understandable. He would be getting a good deal of the Derwent's custom over at the Lothwaite."

"That's a possible explanation," conceded Thompson. "Particularly as Prince made a remark about Higgins being out of the race. Again—what about Wick's reference to 'output'? You remember he said something about it being impossible to keep up the output? How do you account for that?"

"Simply, sir. Wick meant that it was impossible for him to sell enough petrol at the Lothwaite to equal the average amount usually sold by the Lothwaite *plus* the Derwent."

"Again I agree that it's a plausible explanation. But now for my second point. If Rose is the head of a concern defrauding Ormsby-Wright, why does Bettle say something about orders being orders and that if O.W. gets a qualified bee in his bonnet it's no concern of his? Can you explain that away Inspector?"

This time Meredith shook his head and had to acknowledge himself beaten. Try as he would, he could not fit Bettle's racy observation into the theory which he had formed. According to that theory, Ormsby-Wright was the pigeon and Rose the plucker. Why, then, should Bettle suggest that Ormsby-Wright was the man from whom he received his orders?

"Mind you," went on the Superintendent, noticing Meredith's comical look of disappointment, "I'm not suggesting that you're wrong in your theory. I was merely trying to see if we could fit these awkward bits into the puzzle. In any case, we've every-thing to gain and nothing to lose by following up your proposed scheme. The only thing we've got to guard against is rousing the gang's suspicion. Once do that, and they'll shut up shop before we can say 'knife'. Well, keep in touch with me, Inspector, and I'll let you know all about our progress at this end."

His ardour somewhat cooled by the Superintendent's perfectly justifiable criticism of his theory, Meredith drove back over the bleak, undulating road to Penrith on his way to Keswick. He kept on turning over Thompson's last point in his mind. Why had Bettle mentioned Ormsby-Wright as his boss, instead of Rose? It was inconceivable that Ormsby-Wright was running the petrol racket. He had nothing to gain by cheating *himself*! There was the possibility, of course, that the major-ity of the capital invested in the company was not his own. In which case, to increase his own share of the profits, he might be in league with his manager over the cooking of the books. But somehow Meredith felt that the method was too clumsy, and that the resultant profits would be too small for a man of Ormsby-Wright's calibre.

To a man who thinks in thousands, a hundred pounds one way or the other would make little difference, and as far as Meredith could gauge the profits resulting from the fraudulent sale of the petrol could not amount to more than a few hundreds in a year. It would depend, of course, on how many garages were collaborating in the dishonest scheme. But even if there were a dozen or more, and even if hundreds of gallons were secretly discharged into their tanks per week, the Inspector was still disinclined to believe that the game would be worth the candle for an already wealthy man.

But the question remained. Why had Bettle mentioned Ormsby-Wright? Meredith cast his mind back to the conversation he had overheard. He ran that particular sentence of Bettle's through his mind, over and over again, as one might run a short length of film through a projector. Then suddenly—an idea struck him!

Had Bettle mentioned Ormsby-Wright? He had certainly referred to somebody as O.W., but these initials might not apply to the owner of the Nonock Company. Was it possible he had not heard aright? Mightn't Bettle have said something about 'old W.'? Meredith recalled the difficulty he had had in catching the gist of sentences, let alone any isolated word. In that case, might not "old W." refer to "old William"? And wasn't William the manager's Christian name? He remembered the occasion in the Beacon when Charlie Dawson had first given him Rose's name and address. Surely he had hit on the real explanation of the puzzle! Rose *was* the boss! Not Ormsby-Wright! And if Rose was the boss of the gang, then it was pretty well certain that his theory about the fraud was correct.

It was in an elated frame of mind that Meredith called in at the Penrith station and inquired for Sergeant Matthews. The Sergeant, however, had little to report. He had gathered in replies from all the Penrith bank managers but none of them knew anything about a Mr. Mark Higgins or a Mr. Gurney Wick. Dancy had been waylaid in the lunch hour and had provided six of the ten addresses necessary to the tracing of the lorry-men's movements. He had promised to supply the remaining four that evening, after a look at the wage-sheets. He thought he would have no difficulty in getting into the office, as the manager was due up at the railway goods yard that afternoon, to check in the new petrol consignment that had come in during the morning. His own address was—24 Eamont Villas, Careleton Street. The Sergeant assured Meredith that his men were already making inquiries about the men at the six addresses which, so far, had come to hand. He promised to let the Inspector know the result of these inquiries at the earliest possible moment.

At Keswick Meredith found another message waiting for him, on his desk.

> *Cockermouth reports unable to trace banking accounts of Mark Higgins or Gurney Wick in this town. All listed banks applied to for necessary information.*

"So much for that," thought Meredith. "It looks as if Wick and Higgins are a bit more cautious than their one-time partners!"

But for all the negative result of his inquiry, he could not help feeling that somewhere the men had hidden away a couple of nest-eggs similar to those which had been discovered in the case of Peterson and Clayton.

A thought struck him. Was it possible that Higgins was living up to his income? That would do away with the necessity of banking any surplus cash. Dawson had spoken of him as being a bit of a dandy and it was obvious that he spent pretty freely over at the Beacon, let alone the local pub at Braithwaite. Goreleston, the manager of the Westminster, had stated that once a month Clayton drew out £16, which was divided between the partners. That meant Higgins's share in the garage profits was £2 a week. Ten shillings went to Mrs. Swinley for her services, which left Higgins with thirty-five shillings. Out of this he had to pay his food, clothing, personal expenses, and share the general running expenses of the cottage. On top of this he ran a high-powered motor-bike and made frequent journeys to Penrith, often staying over the week-end at the Beacon. The singularity of these facts so impressed Meredith that he decided to put through a call there and then to Charlie Dawson.

The manager's cheerful voice boomed at him over the wire.

"Hullo, Mr. Meredith. What's the trouble to-day? You can't persuade me that you've rung up to inquire after my health."

Meredith laughed.

"Right, as usual. I haven't. It's about Mark Higgins again. Have you any idea how much he spends over at your place? I don't mean the actual amount, but does he appear to be pretty free with his money?"

"Free's not the word!" chuckled Dawson, thickly. "He fairly throws the stuff about. I've known him stand every chap in the bar a couple of rounds or more when he's a bit on. To say nothing of taking a bottle of whisky up to his room when he's staying in the hotel. The best room, mind you. Nothing's too good for friend Higgins. He's that sort, Inspector. He likes to cut a dash."

"Just as I imagined," said Meredith. "I suppose he'd run through a good bit of money in a week-end?"

"Two or three quid, easy, what with one thing and another. To say nothing of what he loses on dead certs and napped doubles and the like!"

"Horse-racing!" exclaimed the Inspector.

"Oh, don't sound so shocked, sir!" was Charlie's laughing reply. "Registered bookie! All above board, I assure you."

"All right, Mr. Dawson. I wasn't casting any reflection on the good behaviour of your house. Well, I think you've told me exactly what I wanted to know. Thanks very much. Good-bye."

Meredith registered an oath, there and then, that if Mark Higgins wasn't obtaining money from illegal sources he'd eat his hat! No man could carry on as he was carrying on unless he had money to burn. And it was certain that this money did not owe its origin to the garage business. Higgins might have a private income, but if so, why didn't he run a banking account? That, in the circumstances, would have been the normal and sensible thing to do. On the other hand, if his money did accrue from illegal sources, Meredith realized that Higgins was gifted with enough cunning to avoid any official record being kept of his finances.

He had just reached this point in his argument when Tony burst into the office with a sheaf of damp prints in his hand.

"Take a look at these," was his triumphant command, as he spread out the photos on the desk. Meredith examined them in silence and finally selected the three portraits which were to be sent to the Yard.

"Good work, Tony. There should be no difficulty in identification if any of these men have passed through the hands of the Metropolitan Police. They're beautifully clear. Now, if you'll wait here while I finish drafting this letter to Scotland Yard, we can get the photos away by the night mail."

"Righto," said Tony, dropping into a chair by the fireplace. "And then, if you're coming home to tea, dad, we could take a look in at Simpson's on the way back. That new three-speed——"

"Quiet!" exclaimed Meredith sternly, without looking up from his work. But, in secret, he was smiling for all he was worth! The single-mindedness of this younger generation! Phew!

CHAPTER XIII

MEREDITH SETS HIS SCHEME IN MOTION

On Sunday Meredith took a well-earned rest and spent a lazy day before a roaring fire with the newspapers and the wireless. But Monday saw him early at the station in anticipation of a hard day's work. Now that the Chief had sanctioned his plan for keeping watch on the garages he was eager to work out and perfect every detail before the organization was put in motion. His two principal jobs were to interview Dancy and persuade him to get copies of the advance-orders for the specified days and to make a round of the Nonock garages in order to find out where his men could be concealed.

In the meantime, a long report had come in from Penrith. To date, undeniable alibis had been established in the case of seven of the lorry-men, and Sergeant Matthews hoped that the movements of the other three would be accounted for in the near future. As Meredith had anticipated, no less than five of the men had spent the evening in the Beacon public-bar. Another had been at the cinema with his wife—a fact which had been verified by the commissionaire, who knew the man intimately. The seventh had spent the evening in one of the Working Men's Clubs; his presence being vouchsafed for by the secretary of the concern and several reliable habitués.

The result of these inquiries was much as Meredith had expected. Right from the start he had seen no reason why any one of these ten men should be connected with Clayton's murder. Not one of them had been seen near the Derwent on the night of the crime. Whereas Bettle and Prince had called at the garage shortly before Luke Perryman had discovered the body. Their lorry had acted in a suspicious way after leaving the Derwent. That it had parked up a side-turning was now certain, though in cross-examination both Bettle and Prince stated that they had made the homeward run direct. This meant that the men had been lying, and what other reason could they have for lying than that they wished to conceal something from the police? Everything, in fact, pointed to Bettle and Prince as being the murderers. But until Meredith could prove his suspicions he was bound to explore every other avenue of possibility—which, as he clearly saw it, meant an establishment of the other lorry-men's innocence.

Another point puzzled him. Were these other Nonock employees part and parcel of the manager's illegal traffic? Did it mean that the fraudulent sale of petrol took place not only on No. 4's round, but on the company's other five routes as well? To verify this would necessitate a county-wide police investigation, the cost of which would be enormous. But, in Meredith's opinion, it would be time enough to enlarge the scope of the police inquiries when No. 4's activities had been duly noted and recorded.

A call through to the Penrith station was sufficient to ascertain the time Dancy arrived home for his lunch, and punctually at twelve-thirty the Inspector turned into the end of Careleton Street on his way to 24 Eamont Villas. He had no difficulty in locating this uncompromising block of cottages. Every door and window in the unbroken, yellow-brick façade was identical with those to either side, and only the numbers on the doors distinguished one cottage from another. Strolling casually down the length of the street, Meredith became intensely interested in the windows of a pawnbroker's shop. For nearly ten minutes he seemed to be engaged in sizing up the multifarious objects displayed behind the plate-glass. Then suddenly he turned from the window and returned smartly up Careleton Street, where he almost ran into the arms of Mr. Dancy.

The yard-man recognized the Inspector at once.

"Surprised to see you in these parts, sir," he observed. "You weren't looking for me, by any chance, were you?"

Meredith nodded.

"I understood you live at 24 Eamont Villas, and as I want a quiet word with you, I thought I'd catch you on your way home to lunch. Is there any place we can talk?"

"As a matter of fact, sir, my old woman's away for the day. She's visiting a relative over at Shap. So if you care to come inside we'd be all alone. Perhaps we could have our talk over my dinner, like?"

Meredith thought this an excellent proposal, and a few minutes later he was seated opposite Dancy in the clean little kitchen-parlour of No. 24. A cold meal had been laid ready on the table, and at the Inspector's instructions to "Go ahead," Dancy settled down to appease a healthy appetite.

"Now, Mr. Dancy," began the Inspector with deliberate solemnity, "I'm going to take you into my confidence. There's absolutely no reason why you should fall in with my request, but I'm sure you'll agree with me that fair-dealing comes first in my business. Now, the police have good reason to believe that certain irregularities are being practised on the public by some of the employees of your firm. I can't tell you more than that—but I want you to understand that it's a serious matter. The good name of the Nonock Company depends on our being able to lay our hands on the culprits. And that's where we need your help. We need certain inside information which you alone can procure for us. The question is, Mr. Dancy, will you supply us with that information?"

The yard-man laid down his knife and fork and champed his food, for a moment, in meditative silence.

Then: "Depends on what you're going to ask me to do," he said cautiously. "It might be more'n my job was worth if I was caught giving away the firm's private business to outsiders. Even if they did happen to be the police."

"Well," said Meredith expansively, "I really don't think you need trouble on that account. There's nothing particularly private about the facts I'm anxious to get hold of. It's just that I'd like a copy of your advance-orders for the Wednesday, Friday and Saturday of this week, and the Monday and Tuesday of next. You realize, of course, that I could get this information by making inquiries at every garage that takes in Nonock petrol and finding out from them if they have placed an advance-order with your firm. So you won't really be telling me anything that I couldn't find out for myself. Only that would take time. And, unfortunately, I haven't got time to waste. So I'm looking to you instead. Well, what about it, Mr. Dancy?"

"All right," said Dancy, nodding his head slowly. "I suppose it can't cause no harm, since you put it like that. Now, perhaps you'd explain exactly what you want me to do, eh?"

Meredith explained in detail, whilst Dancy listened with undivided interest to his instructions. He was to obtain complete copies of every advance-order to be sent out from the depot by No. 4 lorry on the scheduled days. So as to include even the most belated orders, he was not to make up these copies until the evening prior to the date to which these orders referred. To make quite sure that there should be no mistake in this direction, Meredith elicited the information from the yard-man that no order was ever dealt with on the day of its arrival. This was a strict rule of the firm. Reasonable notice had to be given when a delivery was wanted, so that the loads could be made up accordingly and dealt with in rotation. The manager, in fact, did not attend to the morning post until after the lorries had left on their rounds. But, as Dancy pointed out, if a request for immediate delivery was received overnight, it might be dealt with on the following day if there was the requisite room left in the delivery-tank.

Once he had obtained the necessary copy, Dancy was to hand it over to a man in plain-clothes, who would be waiting for him at the north-end of Careleton Street.

The next point was to discuss with the yard-man how best he could effect an entrance into the manager's office without arousing suspicion. According to Dancy, the manager usually left the premises shortly after 6.30, sometimes earlier, depending on the time of the last lorry's arrival. It was his, Dancy's, job to see that everything was locked up securely for the night, and to see that all lights were turned out. For business reasons, the yard-man had a duplicate key of the office and, although Rose usually locked the office himself before leaving, it would be perfectly simple for Dancy to re-enter the building once the coast was clear. Should the manager, by any chance, return unexpectedly, Dancy felt sure that he could offer a reasonable excuse for his presence in the office. He promised Meredith to think up something in case this excuse was needed.

"Now, there's just one other thing, Mr. Dancy," went on Meredith. "It's absolutely essential that I should know to a gallon the amount of petrol loaded on to No. 4 on the mornings I've already specified. Not only the amount run in to cover the advance-orders, but the surplus amount run in to make up a reasonably full load. You remember that you told me on Friday that when the advance-orders were small it was usual to fill out the load, in the hope of making a 'spot' sale *en route*?"

"That's quite right. I did. It's not always done. In fact, during the winter, when there's no tourist traffic on the roads, the lorries more often than not *don't* carry a surplus."

"I see. What would happen if an advance-order was cancelled at the last moment—say, by phone?"

"We should probably put in a surplus in that case. But it doesn't happen that way more than once in the blue moon."

"Still, to be quite sure, Mr. Dancy, even when the advance-orders total up to a capacity load, you'd better drop us a note saying, 'No surplus'. Then we shall know there has been no last-minute cancellation of an order. Well now—do you think you can let us know about all this?"

Dancy nodded.

"Easy, sir. It's part of my job to help with the filling of the tanks, and I'll take good care to keep a check on the number of gallons run into No. 4. The question is, how soon will you want the return?"

"Suppose we say noon of the same day. I'll have the same man that takes in the advance-order copies waiting for you outside the George in Devonshire Street. You can give him the figures on your way home to lunch."

"That's the idea, sir!" agreed Dancy with enthusiasm. Now that he was in possession of the details that were required of him, all trace of his previous reluctance had vanished. It was obvious to the Inspector that he now had in Dancy a fervent ally, who would not be likely to let him down. The man was evidently flattered to be working in such close co-operation with the police. Meredith, therefore, left Eamont Villas more than satisfied with the result of this rather delicate interview.

After a late lunch at his house in Greystoke Road, Meredith returned to the police station, where he was informed by the Sergeant on duty that Carlisle had been calling him on the phone. Anxious to ascertain what progress had been made in the listing of the Nonock customers, Meredith got through at once to the Superintendent. Thompson was elated at the smart-ness displayed by the men he had put on to the job.

"I think we've got the complete list already," he informed the Inspector. "My men have been working hard on the job over the week-end and the last report came in about half an hour ago. We've traced forty-two customers—most of them in the towns. Thirty-six of these are garages, and the remaining six licensed premises sporting a Nonock pump for the convenience of their customers. You know the type of place, Inspector. Not exactly hotels, but sort of glorified pubs with a limited number of bedrooms. Three of these places are in Whitehaven, two in Workington and one in Maryport."

"And the garages, sir? What's the proportion of town and country places?"

"Twenty-nine of the thirty-six garages are in towns. Two in Keswick, four in Cockermouth, eight in Workington, twelve in Whitehaven and three in Maryport. The seven country places include, of course, the Derwent and the Lothwaite. Of the remaining five, only two are really isolated."

"Which suggests," put in Meredith, "that we ought to keep particular watch on these two places. Could you hold on a minute while I get my map, sir, and then perhaps you could let me know exactly where they're situated."

The Superintendent waited until Meredith declared himself ready.

"You've got a Bartholomew's mile-to-the-inch, I suppose?"

"Yes, sir."

"Well, follow the Cockermouth road from the Lothwaite until it crosses the railway line and makes a sudden bend westward. Got that?"

"Yes, sir."

"Right! Now, about two miles from this right-angled turn you'll find a place called Stanley Hall. Got that? Good. Well, the first of the two isolated places lies about midway between the bend and

Stanley Hall. According to the constable who investigated that district there is no cover of any sort within a hundred yards of the building. Just pasturage bounded with stone walls. So you'll probably have to get a motor-cyclist on to that particular place."

"Right, sir, I've made a note of that. And the other place?"

"Between Cockermouth and Workington. You see the railway station marked at Broughton Cross. Well, continue along the road from the station for about half a mile, and you just about reach the point where the garage stands."

"Yes, I've got that, sir. Not far from Nepgill Colliery?"

"About a mile I should say. Open country again, as you can see from your map, but this time we've got a bit of luck on our side. Opposite the garage, on the other side of the road, there's a derelict barn. The constable who covered this stretch of country says that it would be easy to conceal a man in the barn. There's not much of the roofing left, but the walls are still standing, and on the garage side there's a small ventilation hole."

"Sounds promising, sir," was Meredith's comment. "Could I have a list of the garages and hotels sent over soon?"

"You can have the list now over the phone. Is there a constable in the office?"

"No, sir—but Sergeant Brown's on duty."

"Well, get the Sergeant to come to the phone. I've got a constable here ready to read over the list. Then you can start locating the various places on your maps this afternoon."

"Right, sir."

Meredith changed places with the Sergeant and as he was buckling on his cape in the outer office he heard the drone of the man's voice checking over the names and addresses of the Nonock customers.

His next visit was to Ferriby's garage at the top of Main Street. The proprietor himself—a tall, bony, round-shouldered individual—was leaning against the bonnet of a lorry talking to a mechanic. On seeing the Inspector, he threw away the stump of his cigarette and came forward to greet him.

"Evening, Mr. Meredith. Want me?"

"A moment, if you will. Can we go into the office?"

Ferriby nodded and the moment he had closed the door of the higgledy-piggledy little room, Meredith plunged into the reason for his visit.

"I want some information, Mr. Ferriby. Some technical information."

"Anything I can do," answered Ferriby obligingly.

"You used to work with the Greenline Petroleum Company, I believe?"

"That's right. About seven years ago."

"Then you can probably tell me this—how long would it take to discharge a hundred gallons of petrol from a lorry into a garage-tank?"

"You mean from the bulk-wagon into the pump? I think I can tell you that. We used to reckon on seven to eight minutes to run off a couple of hundred gallons. Say, three and a half minutes per hundred gallons. Mind you, it depends on the diameter of your feed-pipe."

"Naturally," said Meredith. "What's the usual size of the pipe?"

"Three-inch diameter."

"Is a three-inch pipe used on the bulk-wagons of all the petrol concerns?"

"Well, I don't know about all. But it's used on the Greenline, Redcar, North British and Nonock—to mention a few."

"Thanks very much, Mr. Ferriby," said Meredith as he made ready to go. "You've told me exactly what I wanted to know."

"Nothing more?"

"No, I don't think—wait a minute, though! There is. Why did you reckon out the time it took to run off two hundred gallons instead of a hundred? Any particular reason?"

"Matter of instinct, I suppose," answered Ferriby, lighting another cigarette. "You can't send in an advance order to most of the petrol firms for less than two hundred gallons when it's to be delivered from the bulk-wagon. After that it ascends in hundreds—three hundred, four hundred, and so on."

"Does that apply, say, to the Nonock people?"

"Well, I don't sport one of their pumps, but I happen to know that their ruling in the matter is the same as my old firm, the Greenline."

"Thanks."

On his return down Main Street to the police station, Meredith felt that he had gained some very useful knowledge. Utilizing Ferriby's information, it was only necessary to instruct his watchers at the various garages to make a note of the time it took to discharge the petrol in order to gain a fairly accurate idea of the petrol delivered. In this case, if any unauthorized deliveries were made, he would know almost to a gallon the quantity of petrol discharged at the dishonest garages. And by a simple calculation he could then find out what profits Rose and his confrères were raking in from the fraud.

Two sheets of paper awaited him on his desk. The first was a report from the Penrith station, which had come in ten minutes before. The movements of the remaining three Nonock lorry-men had been accounted for. Two had left for Carlisle by the 6.45 bus and were known to have spent the week-end with friends. The other man, not feeling well, had returned to his lodgings and gone straight to bed. Although Meredith had anticipated this result, he could not help feeling that it had considerably strengthened the case against Bettle and Prince. By a process of elimination the other suspects had now been cleared and, to his way of thinking, it was no longer a case of "Who murdered Clayton?" but a case of "How and why was Clayton murdered?" Find an answer to those two questions and surely he would then be in a position to make an arrest?

The second document on his desk was a copper-plate copy of the Superintendent's list of the Nonock customers. The Inspector, spreading out the two Bartholomew's maps which covered the complete district, began the arduous task of locating the places and marking them on the maps with a tiny circle.

An hour and a half later, this task completed, he yawned widely, stretched his legs, and returned home to his customary high tea. It would mean another long and strenuous day on the morrow. A round of the garages and detailed arrangements for the placing and concealment of his watchers, a final conference over at Carlisle and a talk to Penrith about the runner who was to collect that all-important information from Dancy.

CHAPTER XIV

THE QUART IN THE PINT POT!

As luck would have it, the following day was warm and sunny. Great masses of fleecy clouds floated idly through the deepest of blue skies, and the wrinkled faces of the higher fells stood out sharply in the tiniest detail. It was the first day of April and there was every promise of seasonable weather—bright periods alternating with typical April showers. The touch of spring in the air infused Meredith with more than his customary keenness and energy, and it was in something approaching a holiday mood that he and Railton, both in plain-clothes, set out on a tour of the Nonock garages.

They had already discussed their intended line of action. The towns were to be dealt with on foot, as the Inspector considered that this method of survey would attract less attention. Before leaving his office he had, therefore, rung through to the police-stations at Cockermouth, Whitehaven, Workington and Maryport and arranged for them to have a plain-clothes constable ready to act as local guide. The six country places were to be investigated by the simple expedient of calling at each of the garages and ordering a half-gallon of petrol. While this was being run into the tank of the combination, Meredith and the constable were to take in all the details of the near locality. If the tank of the motor-cycle became too full, then they were either to take in oil instead of petrol, or to run out some of the surplus spirit when a safe opportunity presented itself.

The Keswick garages were to be dealt with by the local Sergeant, and Meredith had already decided to keep an eye on the Lothwaite himself. Passing the Derwent on their way out that morning, he noticed that Higgins had evidently returned, for the garage doors were open and smoke was coming from the cottage chimneys. When they were well by the place, Meredith called out to Railton above the noise of the engine:

"I shall leave you to cover the Derwent to-morrow. You'll have to use the motor-cycle, of course, and find some excuse for stopping if you notice the lorry drawn up in front of the pumps."

Shortly after, as they sped by the Lothwaite, Meredith caught a glimpse of Wick, tinkering with an engine in the interior of the garage. Their first stop, however, was at the isolated garage between the railway arch and Stanley Hall. It was, in fact, named after the big house in the vicinity—the Stanley Hall Filling Station. Railton placed the order for petrol, whilst Meredith made a quick survey of the surrounds. He saw, at once, that the Superintendent was right. The place would have to be dealt with by a motor-cyclist. Except for the two low stone walls bordering the road, the locality was destitute of cover.

The Inspector also made a careful note of the man who came forward to serve them. But beyond the fact that he was small, wizened and white-haired there was nothing remarkable in his appearance.

At Cockermouth the guide was waiting and at the end of half an hour the four garages had been accounted for and detailed arrangements made for the posting of the watchers. They then drove on to the other isolated garage near Nepgill Colliery, where Meredith had soon endorsed the constable's report which had gone into Carlisle. If, in the early hours before it was light, a man was introduced into the derelict barn, the garage across the road could be easily observed through the ventilation hole. The proprietor, in this case, proved to be a broad-shouldered individual, more like a farm-labourer than a mechanic. But his manner was free and pleasant and he seemed quite ready to stop and have a talk. Meredith noted that the name of the garage was the "Filsam".

Thereafter they followed an unvarying routine. At the three remaining country places, all of which proved to be in villages, Railton drew up and ordered petrol or oil, whilst Meredith took note of suitable observation posts. The three big coast towns they covered on foot, sponsored by a local police guide, and by three o'clock the whole forty-two places had been accounted for.

Quite a number of the town garages, including two of the six licensed premises, were so situated that they could be kept under perfect observation by uniformed constables on point-duty. The remainder were, for the most part, in such populous districts of the towns that a casual lounger at a street corner would cause no comment.

Satisfied, at length, that he had drawn up a comprehensive report on the forty-two places and their environs, Meredith directed Railton to drive back as fast as possible to Keswick.

Shortly after four-thirty he was in touch with the Superintendent at Carlisle.

"My suggestion is this, sir," went on Meredith, after he had made a concise report of his day's work. "Except in those few cases where there is a fool-proof hiding-place, the men must hang about in the vicinity of their scheduled garage. Then when the lorry puts in an appearance they can stroll along until they are opposite the petrol-pumps. In most cases they will have a shop-window to look into or, failing that, they can stop and read a newspaper. But I think we can leave that more or less to the men's own ingenuity. You agree, sir?"

"Perfectly. Since you were last on the phone I've arranged with Workington, Whitehaven, Maryport and Cockermouth stations to put their own men on to the garages in those particular localities. To avoid the risk of the constables being recognized, they are taking them from their usual districts and putting them on to watching those places where there's little chance of their being known. We're dealing with the country places from here. I suggest that you send over your written report at once. I'll then run through it and issue the necessary orders to the various stations and include a copy of your report. We ought to have every man in position early to-morrow morning. They will then be able to get the lie of the land an hour or so before the lorry turns up. By the way, Meredith, the man that we intend to post in that barn should be in position before daylight."

"That's just what I thought, sir."

"Any other point occurred to you?"

"Yes—one more, sir. I want each man to make a careful note of the time that elapses between the opening and the shutting of the valve on the lorry's feed-pipe."

"I don't quite see—" began the Superintendent.

"Let me explain, sir," offered Meredith; and in a few words he detailed his plans for arriving at a rough estimate of the profits accruing from the fraud.

The Superintendent then arranged to be over at Keswick by six o'clock the following evening. He further arranged that all reports, as soon as they were available, were to be phoned direct to the Keswick police station. After making sure that the Inspector had provided for the collecting of Dancy's information, the Superintendent rang off.

An hour later Meredith had filled out his hastily scribbled notes on the day's investigations into a clear and concise report. This done, he jumped into the waiting side-car and ordered Railton to drive him to the Penrith police station. The constable was then to rush the Inspector's report over to Carlisle and return to pick up Meredith on his homeward run.

As soon as he had explained what he wanted, Sergeant Matthews detailed a plain-clothes constable to accompany

Meredith to Careleton Street. It was then six-thirty and Meredith reckoned that Dancy would have had time enough to reach Eamont Villas. Leaving the constable on the corner opposite the pawnbrokers, the Inspector rapped on the door of No. 24. Dancy opened to him in person.

"I've got the man who is to collect your information just up the street, Mr. Dancy," he said quickly. "I'd like you to slip out quietly in five minutes' time and join us there. Just stroll up casually. I don't want your neighbours to get curious."

"Right," was Dancy's quiet answer. "In five minutes, sir."

"You've got the first copy of advance-orders?"

"Yes."

"Then bring it along with you."

With this Meredith ambled off up the street and joined the constable, who was looking in the pawnbroker's window. Five minutes later Dancy strolled along and the three men set off slowly together down a deserted side street. As they came within the lighted radius of a street-lamp, Meredith said softly:

"As we pass this lamp I want you to take a good look at the constable here. Understand, Mr. Dancy?"

Dancy nodded. When they had passed out of the light into the shadows again, Meredith added: "Now that copy." He felt a folded piece of paper being thrust into his hand. Good. "No difficulty?"

"None," answered Dancy.

"Don't forget about the surplus—if any—to-morrow."

"Right, sir."

"The George, Devonshire Street, at twelve-thirty."

"Right," said Dancy again.

"Well," announced the Inspector in a louder voice, "This is where we turn off. Good night, Mr. Dancy."

"Good night," replied Dancy heartily.

Back in Sergeant Matthews's office, Meredith examined the paper which he had received from the yard-man. It told him all that he wanted to know. Five garages were listed, with their addresses, and opposite each name was written the number of gallons on order. The total load was one thousand gallons, split up into five deliveries of two hundred gallons each.

The Inspector was acutely disappointed. From his previous conversation with Dancy at the depot he knew that the capacity load of No. 4 was exactly one thousand gallons. And since there was now no room left in the tank for a fraudulent delivery, it followed that No. 4's outing on the following day must be genuine.

Much as Meredith hoped otherwise, this in fact turned out to be the case. Shortly after six on Wednesday evening, when the final report had come into the Keswick station, Meredith and the Superintendent looked at each other and made a wry grimace.

"No luck!" observed the Superintendent dolefully. "Five advance orders and five deliveries. Looks as if the day's work has gone west, Meredith. According to these reports, the lorry made no stop at any other garage or hotel."

"Much as I anticipated, sir," replied Meredith, equally depressed. "Particularly when Dancy handed over his mid-day note with 'No surplus' on it. If we *are* barking up the right tree, then it's one of the gang's off-days."

"At any rate," the Superintendent assured him, "we'll carry through with the full programme. We may get a result to-morrow."

"Friday, sir," corrected Meredith. "Half-day to-morrow."

"I was forgetting. Well, let's fix Friday at six for our next meeting here, shall we?"

"Right, sir."

On Thursday evening, after an annoyingly blank day, Penrith phoned through the contents of Dancy's message, which had been slipped into the waiting constable's hand by the pawn-broker's shop earlier that evening.

When Meredith had jotted down the details and rung off, he sat for a long time staring dejectedly in front of him. Was No. 4 to go out every day with a capacity load? Were the advance orders always to total up to the full one thousand gallons? At the thought of this *contretemps* he cursed under his breath, angrily stuffed the tobacco into his pipe and began to pace up and down the room.

Did it mean that, after all his elaborate schemes, his theory was going to be violently knocked on the head? Had he led half the county police on a wild-goose chase? It would, in spite of the Superintendent's ready collaboration, go hard with him at headquarters if these county-wide investigations were unproductive of result. Still, there were the facts staring him in the face. Four garages—three with two hundred gallons on order—one with four hundred—total load one thousand gallons—capacity of tank one thousand gallons. Where was the loophole for fraud in a perfectly orderly statement of that sort? The deliveries *must* be genuine. Already he could see Dancy handing over that confounded negative report to the constable outside the George—"No surplus". So his great scheme had failed! Did it mean that the Chief's theory of an illegal concern had also gone overboard? Meredith prayed heaven that this wasn't the case—otherwise, where was he to look for the motive of the murder?

On the other hand, what about the report which had come in from Scotland Yard that morning? Two of the men suspected to be members of the gang had most certainly been through the hands of the Metropolitan Police. It was down there in black and

white—William Bryant Rose, convicted of embezzlement—
three years' imprisonment. Joseph Bettle, alias Sam Shaw—two
charges of petty larceny—one conviction—three months' hard
labour. Those facts in themselves surely lent colour to the Chief's
theory? If Rose had cooked his books once, why not again?
Though Meredith was at a loss to see why Ormsby-Wright had
engaged the man without inquiries into his past record. Be that
as it may, Rose was once more in a position of trust and Meredith
felt, that faced with a strong enough temptation, the man might
easily pander again to the criminal streak in his make-up.

Bettle's offences, though of a milder nature, threw an equally
unfavourable light upon the man's character. If it had been part of
Rose's job to engage the lorry-drivers, wasn't Bettle just the type of
man he would look for if he had a fraudulent scheme at the back
of his mind? The men had served their sentences some eight years
before and, according to Dancy, both the manager and the driver
of No. 4 had been in the firm's employ for a matter of seven years.

Wasn't it significant that both Rose and Bettle had come
North about the same time, in each case shortly after they
had served a prison sentence? It looked as if London and
the Home Counties had grown a little too warm to hold
them. Hence this new start in Cumberland. Had they been
acquainted before coming North? Was it possible that Rose
had already planned the fraud before leaving London, but
after he had received notification of his engagement to the
Nonock Petroleum Company?

The Inspector gibed at himself inwardly. All very well to dabble in suppositions of this sort, but all the facts, at the moment,
combined to prove that no fraud *was* being practised on the firm.
Utterly disheartened, Meredith returned home to his wireless-set
and attempted to drown his depression in a programme of light
music. The further he went with the case, the more abstruse the
problems became!

A little after one o'clock on Friday Penrith delivered the expected information from Dancy. "No surplus." At five o'clock the earlier reports began to dribble in. At six the Superintendent walked into the office with an anxious, inquiring look on his features, and without preliminary demanded to know the latest news.

"There isn't any," said Meredith shortly. "We're wasting our time, sir. That's my feeling, anyway."

He handed over Dancy's messages.

"Four garages to-day," observed the Superintendent, after he had read through the brief reports. "And another full load! How many reports still to come in, Meredith?"

"Only two, sir. The Stanley Hall and the Filsam. They're the two isolated places."

"And the Lothwaite?"

"I watched that myself, sir. Railton dealt with the Derwent. Both O.K. I stayed in hiding until the lorry had passed on its homeward run."

"Then surely those two reports should be in by now?"

"I expect them at any minute, sir. The trouble is there's no phone in the vicinity of either of the garages."

"In the meantime, let's take a look at what we know to date. Now, let's see—advance-orders for two hundred gallons have been placed by the Ennerdale and the Queens Street in Whitehaven—Whittaker's Garage in Maryport—and a four hundred gallon order by Drake's in Cockermouth. All accounted for, I suppose?"

"Yes, sir. I've set aside the four reports." The two men crouched forward over the paper-littered desk. "You notice that in each case a note has been taken as to the length of time taken by each discharge. By comparing——"

The phone bell rang jarringly at Meredith's elbow.

"Excuse me, sir." He took up the receiver. "Yes—Inspector Meredith—Keswick speaking. Covering the Filsam. Yes—I see. You're sure about that? Right! Thanks." Meredith hung up and turned to the Superintendent. "That was Constable Wilson, sir, covering the Filsam. Nothing to report. No. 4 passed both on its outward and inward run."

"Damn!" was the Superintendent's sole comment.

"That leaves the Stanley Hall place. And," went on Meredith as the phone bell broke forth anew, "it sounds as if we're booked for a final disappointment straight away."

With a languid gesture he unhooked the receiver again and held it to his ear. After revealing himself to the distant voice, he resigned himself with a disinterested air to the reception of a further negative report.

Then suddenly his whole attitude changed. In a moment he was alert, tense, listening absorbed. Thompson, noting his expression, took a quick step forward,

"Yes. Yes. I've got that! On the homeward run? I see. Did you time the delivery. Good! Right—I've made a note of that. Anything suspicious to report? Nothing out of the way in the men's behaviour? I see. No, that's all. Put in a written report, of course. 'Night, Constable."

"Well?" demanded the Superintendent the instant Meredith had hung up.

"Something at last, sir!" exclaimed Meredith with a note of triumph. "The news would have come through earlier if Constable Brennen's bike hadn't petered out. He's only just got into Cockermouth. He reports that No. 4 stopped at the Stanley Hall Filling Station at five-fifteen this evening!"

"Splendid, Meredith! Splendid!"

"He waited about a hundred yards up the road, pretending to tinker with the engine of his bike, until the feed-pipe had been coupled up with the garage tank. His idea was that once they were coupled up, even if he did put in a sudden appearance, it would be too late for them to cover up the fact that a delivery was being made. The moment Prince opened the valve, Brennen noted the time. He then began to walk slowly toward the garage, pushing his bike. Twice on the way he stopped to fiddle again with his engine. Reaching the pumps, he got into conversation with the proprietor and mentioned that he had got some sort of engine trouble. His arrival, so he reports, caused no sort of consternation. Bettle was still seated at the wheel of the lorry and Prince was at the rear of the tank with his hand on the control-valve. The proprietor said he'd attend to Brennen when he was finished with the lorry-men.

"They stood talking for two or three minutes before Prince turned off the valve. Brennen managed to lift his cuff, unob-served, and get a glance at his wristwatch. Prince then accom-panied the proprietor to the office, where Brennen saw them signing some form of receipt. When Prince returned, about five minutes later, to the lorry, he uncoupled the feed-pipe, stowed it away, and screwed on the safety cap over the valve union. Then he climbed up beside Bettle and the lorry drove off."

"Good man, Brennen," said the Superintendent. "That was a smart piece of observation. Now then, Inspector, let's see exactly where we are. Firstly, how long did it take to make the Stanley Hall delivery?"

"According to Brennen, just on seven and a half minutes, sir."

"Which means?"

"Two hundred gallons—or near enough that it doesn't matter."

"Good. So it looks as if one of the four advance orders was delivered short. I suggest Drake's order at Cockermouth—you remember, Meredith, that that was the four hundred gallon request?"

"But that couldn't be done without the knowledge of the garage people, sir," objected Meredith.

"Quite! I'm not suggesting it was. I'm suggesting that one of those advance-orders was faked. Drake really ordered two hundred gallons and the other two hundred was planted at the Stanley Hall place."

"But that's impossible, sir!" exclaimed Meredith. "For one thing, Dancy took that copy from Rose's books in the office. If four hundred gallons was entered up against Drake's name, then Drake would have to be charged for the full amount. Otherwise Rose wouldn't be able to balance his accounts. Secondly, sir— take a look at this little table I've drawn up. It's compiled from those four reports I showed you on the genuine deliveries."

The Superintendent took up the sheet of paper and examined it carefully. It ran as follows:

Garage	Address	Advance Order	Time taken to Deliver
Ennerdale	11 High St., Whitehaven	200 galls.	7 ½ mins. appr.
Queens St.	63 Queens St. „	200 galls.	7 mins. 20 sec.
Whittaker's	Marine Place, Maryport	200 galls.	7 mins. 35 sec.
Drake's	The Memorial, Cockermouth	400 galls.	15 mins. appr.

"Good heavens, Inspector!" ejaculated the Superintendent when he had fully absorbed this astonishing document. "What the devil does it mean?"

"I only wish I knew, sir! But there's no doubt that the full four hundred was delivered at Drake's, is there? These times are just what we should expect. The Cockermouth order *should* have taken just twice as long to deliver as the other three orders."

"That's obvious. Then how on earth——?"

"Exactly, sir. How on earth, since the capacity load has been accounted for, could No. 4 deliver a further 200 gallons at the Stanley Hall garage?"

For a moment there was a silence, broken only by the tinkling of falling coals in the grate. Then——

"What about a false tank, Meredith? Or perhaps Dancy was wrong about the lorry's capacity being only 1,000 galls."

"Impossible, sir. These things are checked up by the Weights and Measures official. A dip is made of every new lorry that goes out on to the road. Dancy wouldn't lie in the matter. He'd know as well as we do that it would be a perfectly simple matter to check up on the tank's registered capacity. As for a false tank, sir. Well, that's out of question. You couldn't conceal a couple of hundred gallons surplus petrol on a lorry without altering the whole construction of the chassis. It's too big an amount."

"But good heavens, Meredith, have you any other sugges-tion? It's obvious now that some sort of fraud is going on. You've offered objections to all my theories. It's time you put up one of your own."

"As far as I can see," went on Meredith after a long silence, "there *is* only one other way in which the business could be managed."

"And that?"

"The tanks of the genuine garages have been tampered with. In consequence of this a short delivery is made at each place, leaving a surplus in the bulkwagon."

"But how could the garage tanks be tampered with?"

"Well, sir, I don't quite——"

"Exactly!" snapped the Superintendent. "Neither do I! Now I'm going to make a suggestion. As this is a technical matter I think we should call in an expert. Mr. Weymouth, the Weights and Measures official over at Penrith, happens to be a friend of mine. It's now seven o'clock. Suppose we motor over there straight away and have a word with him."

CHAPTER XV

THE INSPECTOR OF WEIGHTS AND MEASURES

In consequence of the Superintendent's decision, shortly after eight, a police car pulled up outside a largish house in Milton Avenue, Penrith. In answer to Thompson's inquiry, the maid informed him that her master was in, and a minute or so later the three men were seated before a cheerful fire in Mr. Weymouth's sitting-room. The official, though elderly, was a keen, quick-witted individual, with twinkling blue eyes and a decisive, almost blunt manner of speaking.

While Thompson outlined the reasons for his visit, Mr. Weymouth refrained from uttering a word. At the conclusion of the Superintendent's story he let out a sharp whistle, however, and began to ply him with questions.

"You say the bulk-wagon went out with advanceorders totalling 1,000 gallons, and that after these deliveries had been made a further delivery of 200 gallons was run into the Stanley Hall pump?"

"That's correct."

"But the thing's manifestly impossible, Thompson! The capacity load of those Nonock tanks is exactly 1,000 gallons. I checked them myself before they went out on the road."

"How long ago was that?"

"About seven years. When Ormsby-Wright's new manager took over, an entirely new convoy of lorries was put on to the road. Three-compartment affairs. Up to date."

"And you haven't checked them since?"

Weymouth shook his head.

"No need. Once a dip has been taken of a new tank it's never taken again. After all, you couldn't squeeze in more than the registered capacity load without altering the shape of the tank, could you?"

Thompson and Meredith agreed in unison.

"When was this Stanley Hall delivery discharged—on the outward or homeward run?"

"Homeward," said Meredith promptly.

Weymouth glanced across at him sharply.

"You're sure? But, good heavens, they passed that garage on their outward run, didn't they?"

The Inspector nodded.

"Well, it beats me," exclaimed Weymouth. "It's odd, to say the least of it. Here is a 200-gallon delivery to be made and instead of lightening the load on the outward run, they carry the stuff with them all round the coast towns. Now why the devil did they do that?"

"Perhaps Meredith has got an explanation," said the Superintendent, with a sly chuckle. "He's knocked all my pet theories on the head. Now it's our turn, Weymouth!"

"Well, Mr. Weymouth," said Meredith diffidently, "my suggestion was this. If they could deliver short on their genuine orders, they would then have something left over for their dishonest delivery at the Stanley Hall. That, at any rate, would account for their failure to deliver there on the *outward* run."

"Umph," grunted Weymouth. "Something in that. But how the deuce *could* they deliver short?"

"That's just what we've come to you for, Weymouth—to find out!" put in Thompson. "Tell us—how do these garage people keep a check on a lorry's delivery?"

"Simple!" said Weymouth, settling himself deeper into his arm-chair. "I don't know if you're familiar with the construction of a petrol pump? No? Very well—I'll explain. First of all there's the storage tank under the pump, and as that's the part which concerns us, I won't bother with the mechanism of the pump itself. When a new tank is installed, it's my job to supervise the business. I have to see that the tank is, what you might call, well-founded. That is to say cemented into the pit and a good lining of sand laid between the cement and the surrounding earth. A fire precaution, of course. I then take a dip of the tank, check up the pump itself and see that the whole business is properly sealed in. After that I make periodic visits to see that the indicator on the pump is registering the true amount. That's to protect the public. There are two inlets to the storage tank. Both in the form of countersunk pipes. On one of these there is a union to which the lorry's delivery pipe is coupled. This countersunk pipe is also fitted with a padlocked cap, of which the employees of the petrol company hold the key. The second inlet is, in the strict sense of the word, not an inlet at all. It's merely there so that the garage people can take a dip after a delivery has been discharged. You understand, gentlemen?"

Thompson and Meredith both nodded.

"You keep on talking about taking a dip, Weymouth. How is this done exactly?"

"By means of a calibrated brass rod. This rod is fixed to a cap, which seals up the second of the countersunk pipes. This cap, like the other, is usually locked and the key kept by the garage people. When a delivery has been made, the cap is unlocked and the brass rod pulled up from the tank. By the simple method of breathing on the rod, they get an indication of the petrol level. The dry part mists over and the dividing line between the misted and clear surfaces is then checked off on the numbered calibrations. That's the complete process in a nutshell."

"And very interesting, too," commented Thompson. "The question remains, could a tank be so tampered with that a short delivery would pass unnoticed?"

"Well, it *could* be done," acknowledged Weymouth with a faint smile. "But the chances of the fraud not being detected are slight. For example, if small stones or quantities of lead shot were poured down the intake pipe, the petrol level would be automatically lifted. Where the original capacity of the tank was say, 500 gallons, it might be diminished by this trick to 400 gallons. The petrol company would therefore have to deliver a hundred gallons less to bring the tank up to capacity. But even so, I don't see how the fraud could go undetected for long. As soon as the garage people began comparing their pump sales with their delivery costs, they'd be bound to notice the discrepancy. Quite frankly—I don't think there's a single way in which a garage could be successfully cheated by a petrol company."

At the conclusion of Weymouth's speech the police officers looked at each other despairingly. Then how, in the name of heaven, was the fraud being managed? If the bulk-wagon was in order on leaving the depot and the garage tanks had not been tampered with, how could 1,000 gallons of petrol be metamorphosed into 1,200 gallons? It was surely inconceivable that the lorry had stopped at some unknown spot and taken in that extra two hundred? What would be the point of it, anyway? The extra petrol would have to be paid for, so where would the profit come in?

Meredith had not felt so utterly depressed since the case had started. Try as he would, he could see no way out of the labyrinth. And on the top of the first puzzle Weymouth had set another. Why had the bulk-wagon made the Stanley Hall delivery on its homeward run?

Suddenly Meredith sat up! The homeward run! What about No. 4 on the night of the crime? That order which had to be delivered at the Derwent?

"Good heavens, sir!" he said, turning to Thompson. "I believe I've hit on something!"

"Out with it then!"

"Why did No. 4 leave the Derwent delivery till last on the Saturday night when Clayton was murdered? Doesn't it strike you as significant, sir?"

"You mean that they deliberately made a late delivery so as to arrive at the garage after dark?"

"Precisely, sir."

"But you're not suggesting that the reason why they delivered late to-night at the Stanley Hall was because they intended to murder the proprietor?"

Meredith laughed.

"Hardly that, sir. The two cases aren't the same. Remember the Derwent delivery was a genuine advance order. I've seen the record of it in Rose's books. To-night's was——"

"Well, what was it? You can't answer that question, Meredith, so it's no good trying. But I agree with you about the other point. It's certainly an incriminating bit of evidence against Bettle and Prince."

Weymouth looked bewildered.

"I'm afraid I don't quite——"

"Sorry, Weymouth," laughed the Superintendent. "Just shop. I forgot you weren't in the know. Now we really must be getting on, my dear chap. We've taken up enough of your valuable time. Any other point, Inspector?"

"Just one, sir. Would it be possible for Mr. Weymouth to take a dip of No. 4 and certify that thousand gallon capacity?"

"Officially, you mean?"

"Not exactly. An official inspection would put the men on their guard. Particularly as it's not usual to take a second dip after the tank has been certified correct. My idea was to get Dancy's help. We could then slip into the yard after dark and have a look at the lorry. On the Q.T."

"You give me a ring," said Weymouth promptly. "I'll be there, Inspector."

"Good," concluded Thompson. "Now it's time we were off. Come on, Inspector!"

As the Superintendent was returning direct to Carlisle, Meredith had arranged to catch the 9.40 train back to Keswick. Thompson, therefore, directed the constable at the wheel to drive at a slow pace to the station. There were still some twenty minutes to go before the train was due, and he felt the time could be profitably spent in a discussion.

"What are you going to do now, Meredith?" was the Superintendent's first remark, when they had dropped into the back seat of the car. "It's your case, remember."

"No need to rub it in, sir," replied Meredith with a rueful laugh. "I don't quite see what we *can* do. We might get a line on the dockyard manager and try to prove the fraud from that end. But I'm doubtful if we'd get results. I still think Rose is the brain of the gang. Of course," he added, brightening a little, "we've got these garages under observation for another three days. There's a chance something *may* turn up. But the outlook's none too bright at the moment."

"I'm not so sure," countered the Superintendent in measured tones. "We know now that something irregular is going on and we didn't know that for *certain* this morning. That spells progress, anyway. Then there's that bit of incriminating evidence about No. 4's late delivery on the night of the crime. Further, we've discovered a number of ways in which the fraud is *not* being carried on. Negative, I admit. But helpful."

"Then there's another point which struck me," went on the Superintendent, after a moment's silence. "Don't you think,

Inspector, that we might find out as much by watching one garage as by keeping the whole lot under observation? I don't mean abandon our wholesale test at once. We'll carry through with that according to plan. But take the Lothwaite, for example. We're pretty certain now that it's mixed up with the racket. When you questioned Wick that Friday morning, it was obvious that he was lying to you. Then there was that very suggestive conversation you overheard. Combine these facts with the suspicious circumstances surrounding Peterson's suicide, and I think we've got good cause to keep the place under observation. What I suggest is this. Watch the place, according to plan, until the Tuesday test is over. After that keep the place under *constant* observation. Day and night. It might even pay us to shadow Wick if he leaves the garage. He must get away sometimes to shop and so on."

"You mean work it in shifts, sir?"

"That's it. You might split up the work between yourself, say, and a couple of constables. Try it for a few days, at any rate, then if you get no result we can discuss the matter again."

"Very good," said Meredith as the car slowed to a standstill. "This looks like the station now, sir. Meeting at the same time to-morrow night, I take it?"

The Superintendent nodded and after "good nights" had been exchanged, Meredith saluted and hurried off to catch his train, which had just drawn into the station. An hour and half later, tired out, chilled to the marrow and dispirited, he reached Greystoke Road. There, after a long-deferred meal and a short domestic, fireside chat with his wife, he switched off the wireless, locked the front door and wended his way to bed.

On reaching his office the next morning he found Dancy's overnight report lying ready for him on his desk. The make-up of the lorry's load was virtually the same as that of the day before.

Advance orders again totalled 1,000 gallons. Three orders were for 200 gallons and one for 400. Two of the garages were in Workington, one in Maryport and one in a coastal village near Whitehaven.

Constable Brennen had also sent in his written report of the Stanley Hall incident. But although Meredith perused it with extreme thoroughness, he gained no more than he had done over the phone the previous evening.

In a dissatisfied mood he set off, therefore, to take up his position in the larch wood overlooking the Lothwaite. Hiding his motor-cycle behind the opportune tar-barrels, he was soon installed at his post, where he settled down for a long and dreary wait. Several cars and tradesmen's vans passed along the road. A goods train chuffed laboriously up the valley. Later a motor-cyclist drew up at the Lothwaite pumps and Meredith saw Wick come out of the garage office and attend to his customer's wants. Then followed a blank half-hour. For the time being all traffic on the road and rail seemed suspended. A thin rain began to fall, sweeping in misty pillars up the grey and silvered surface of the lake. Meredith, cursing under his breath, drew his muffler tighter round his neck and buttoned the collar of his trench-coat. How he loathed this waiting job! And some people imagined that the detection of crime was an exciting and glamorous pastime! Little they knew about it! Glamorous? Brrr!

Then suddenly he was jerked back to the realities of his job. From up the road he heard, unmistakably, the approach of a heavy lorry. Wick, too, seemed to have caught the sound, for he shot out of the garage and took a hasty look up the road. Then, to Meredith's amazement, he made tracks for the door of the adjoining cottage and disappeared within. A minute later the Nonock lorry drew up at the pumps.

Prince climbed down from the cab, whilst Bettle switched off the engine. After a quick look up and down the road, Prince then began to couple up the feed-pipe. He removed the manhole lid which protected the countersunk pipe, unlocked the padlock and took off the metal cap. Returning to the lorry, he opened the long wooden box, which ran parallel to the base of the tank, and drew out the feed-pipe. With a second key he then unlocked a metal box, which overhung the lorry's rear light and coupled the feed pipe, by means of a union, to the middle of the three valve pipes projecting from the tank. This done, he completed the job by connecting the other end of the feed-pipe to the garage tank.

Wick then reappeared in the doorway of the cottage and called out something, which, owing to the adverse direction of the wind, Meredith was unable to hear. Prince's reply was a wave of the hand and an observation which sounded like "O.K." He then crossed to the rear of the tank and opened the valve. Meredith looked at his watch. 10.44. He made a note of it.

Then for some minutes nothing happened. Prince lit a cigarette ("A dangerous policy," thought Meredith), and lounged back against the door of the cab. Although he couldn't see him, Meredith imagined that Bettle was still seated at the wheel. Wick, for some unearthly reason, had retired again into the cottage!

After a short period the proprietor emerged once more and made a quick signal with his hand. Prince must have been waiting for this signal, for he went forward, at once, and shut off the petrol valve. Again Meredith glanced at his watch. 10.53½. So far, so good, he thought. What now?

But if he was expecting any sensational action on the part of the men, he was destined to be deceived. Prince strolled over to the garage and disappeared with Wick, presumably into the office. Five minutes later they reappeared. Prince with a blue-covered book in his hand; Wick with a single sheet of paper.

The lorry-man then uncoupled the pipe, stowed it away, locked the metal box at the rear of the tank, replaced the cap and padlock on the intake pipe and dropped the manhole lid into place. The three men then held a desultory conversation (none of which Meredith could catch) at the conclusion of which Prince swung over the starting-handle and climbed up into the cab beside Bettle. Then with a grinding of gears the bulk-wagon slowly gathered way and lumbered out of sight round the corner. Wick returned, at once, to his office.

Knowing that No. 4 was booked for a round of the coastal towns, Meredith decided that he need keep no further watch on the Lothwaite until 4.30 that afternoon. He, therefore, exe-cuted a cautious retirement through the larch wood, mounted his motor-cycle out of sight round the corner, and made for Keswick.

On the journey he occupied himself with an analysis of the facts which had now come to light. He was highly delighted with the results of his observation, though as yet quite unable to set value on what he had learnt. First, he dealt with the time factor.

Prince had opened the valve at 10.44 and closed it at 10.53½. The delivery had therefore taken exactly 9½ minutes to discharge. Meredith was puzzled. Calculating on a basis of 100 gallons flow in 3½ minutes, it meant that No. 4 had discharged something in the region of 270 gallons into the Lothwaite tank. But why the odd amount? Ferriby had assured him that most petrol firms, including the Nonock, delivered a minimum of 200 gallons from the tank and that thereafter the amounts ascended in hundreds. But here was a delivery which obviously did not comply with the rule. What was the explanation? There could be only one. The delivery was outside rules and regulations—in brief, a *fraudulent* delivery.

Wick's strange behaviour was his next consideration. Why had the man disappeared into the cottage at the sound of the lorry's approach? And why had he reappeared some minutes later and signalled Prince to turn off the petrol valve? Did it mean that there was a second tank inside the cottage, connected by means of a secret pipe to the genuine intake pipe under the pump? That, at any rate, would offer a reason for Wick's singular behaviour. There was probably some form of gauge fitted to this illegal tank and as Wick wanted to avoid an overflow, it was necessary for him to disappear and take a reading of the level. When capacity was nearly reached he naturally came to the door and signalled Prince to stop the flow. That would account, too, for the odd gallonage discharged. But if this *was* so—what was the idea? Why a second tank? Why should Wick throw himself open to risk of discovery when he had a perfectly genuine storage place under the registered Nonock pump. Weymouth was concerned solely with the pump itself. Once the tank had been certified correct and sealed, it was not examined further by the Inspector of Weights and Measures.

Still wrestling with this problem, Meredith drew up outside the Keswick police station. Railton was in the outer office.

"Well, constable, anything to report?"

"Nothing, sir. She went right by the Derwent. No sign or anything."

At one o'clock Dancy's report came through from Penrith. It was the usual disheartening message—"No surplus". It gave proof, however, that no advance order had been cancelled overnight. The lorry was, therefore, out on the road again with a capacity load.

"Then how, in the name of thunder," was the Inspector's inward demand, "could she have delivered an extra 270 gallons at the *start* of her run?"

This point had struck him forcibly. The Stanley Hall delivery had been made *after* the advance orders had been dealt with—the Lothwaite's *before*! Did it mean that the general report that evening would announce a non-delivery at one of the four garages on Dancy's list?

But the problem was not to be solved as simply as that. When, shortly after seven, Meredith took in the final report over the phone, he realized that all the advance-orders had been accounted for. And more than that—the scheduled amount to be delivered at each place coincided exactly with the observer's notes as to the time taken for each discharge.

"Confound it, Meredith!" exclaimed the Superintendent. "The more we go into this, the more impossible it seems. Here is a 1,000-gallon bulk-wagon, delivering on consecutive days, amounts of 1,200 and 1,270. I don't see how the devil it can be done! We know they don't deliver short. Weymouth has more or less knocked that theory on the head. As far as we know they don't collect extra petrol *en route*. I know we haven't absolute proof of this—but, even so Meredith, what would be the point? I don't see how they could make a profit that way, do you? Finally we have come to the conclusion that it would be impossible to conceal a large amount of petrol in a secret tank on the lorry. What are we left with? Nothing. The whole thing's a mystery from start to finish. You agree?"

"I must," said Meredith tersely.

"Any suggestions?"

"What about an examination of the bulk-wagon?"

"To-night?"

"Why not? If you could ring Mr. Weymouth, I'd get Sergeant Matthews on to Dancy. We could then meet at the depot and run our eye over No. 4. I shan't feel really satisfied until we've done this."

"Very well, Meredith. A forlorn hope, I feel, but better than inaction."

Twenty minutes later the necessary arrangements had been made and within the hour Thompson and Meredith were shaking hands with Mr. Weymouth, on the deserted road outside the Nonock depot. Weymouth had picked up Dancy at the Penrith police station. Instructing the police chauffeur to run the car up a side-turning, some hundred yards down the road, Thompson got Dancy to unlock the entrance gates. In conspiratorial silence the little group filed in, whilst Dancy closed and locked the doors behind them.

"The lorries are over here in the garages," said Dancy. "I've got the keys all right."

"Good," answered the Superintendent in low tones. "Lead the way. We'll follow."

Dancy repeated his actions of the moment before, and as soon as the garage doors were closed and locked behind them, Meredith flicked on a powerful pocket-torch and shone it over the line of blue and scarlet bulk-wagons.

"Here we are, gentlemen," he said. "This is No. 4—see, there's the number on the hood of the cab."

"Now what exactly do you want me to do," asked Weymouth, obviously thrilled by the adventurous outing. "Take a dip, I suppose?"

Meredith nodded.

"That will satisfy us, at any rate, as to the genuine capacity of the tank, Mr. Weymouth."

"That's all very fine!" countered Weymouth. "But we're up against a nasty snag. The tank will be empty. I can't take a dip of an empty tank, can I? There'd be no level."

"Anything to suggest, Dancy?" was the Superintendent's brusque demand.

"'Fraid not, sir," replied Dancy with a slow shake of his head.

"I suppose we couldn't run in a full load and then run it back into the storage tanks?"

"Impossible, sir. We couldn't get at the discharge valves. They're in this locked box at the back of the lorry here. Bettle holds the key."

"No duplicates?"

"No, sir."

"Confound it!" exclaimed the Superintendent with irritation. "We must do something!"

"I think I can see a way out," put in Weymouth, who had been making an external examination of the tank. "I can measure up the circumference, length and diameter of the tank and get a fairly close estimate of the cubic contents. If we remove one of the compartment lids I can also get the thickness of the plates and make due allowance. See how I mean? By deducting the thickness I shall get an inside measurement."

"Excellent!" was the Superintendent's observation. "Let's get to work."

While Weymouth and Thompson were running over the bolt with a 60" flexible steel rule, Meredith made an exhaustive examination of the lorry itself. Dancy had produced a lantern, so Meredith was able to wriggle under the chassis and search out every nook and cranny with his torch. But, if he hoped to unearth some cleverly contrived secret tank, he was doomed to disappointment. The stout wooden base, into which the tank fitted, was innocent of any appendage. The engine, too, appeared to be bedded into its framework in a perfectly normal manner. Meredith made a further examination of the other five lorries, but in no case did he find any discrepancy between their design and that of No. 4. Satisfied, at length, that everything was in order, he joined Thompson and Weymouth who were now crouching over the repair bench.

Weymouth had already covered a page of the Superintendent's note-book with a mass of tiny figures. His pencil flickered here and there with lightening rapidity, adding, dividing, subtracting, and in a few minutes he straightened up with the declaration that he had arrived at a total.

"And that, sir?" asked Meredith eagerly.

"The expected total!" was Weymouth's flattening reply. "1,000 gallons. I don't say my figures work out exact to that amount—but near enough that it doesn't matter. That tank's in order. Can't deny it! If it hadn't been I guess I should have seen it at a glance. But since you gentlemen wanted proof ... well, there it is!"

And he thrust the note-book into Thompson's hand.

"What about you Meredith?" asked the Superintendent.

"Nothing, sir. As far as I can see there's nothing abnormal about the lorry at any point."

Weymouth's blue eyes twinkled.

"And a 200-gallon tank is hardly a thing you would overlook, is it, Inspector?"

Meredith responded to his broad grin and broke into a laugh.

"I know—that's the whole point. Here we are, arriving at the most exact calculations, when a glance should tell us if anything was wrong. It's beyond me, Mr. Weymouth. I can't see——"

"You don't think," broke in Mr. Weymouth suddenly, "that your precious gang is dealing with something quite different from petrol?"

"But what, Mr. Weymouth? What?"

"Well, that's your business to find out. There are plenty of possibilities, surely? Counterfeit notes, perhaps."

"Then how would you explain away these extra petrol deliveries?" was Thompson's immediate query.

"Perhaps they're a blind. Bettle and Prince may need a plausible excuse for stopping at certain garages, so they couple up and *pretend* to make a delivery."

Meredith whistled. "Pretend!" This point hadn't struck him before. He turned with a questioning look to the Superintendent. "What do you think, sir?"

The Superintendent rubbed his chin reflectively.

"It's an idea, Weymouth. Though at the moment we haven't the smallest scrap of evidence which points to counterfeiting. The opposite, in fact. Everything points to a petrol fraud. Still it's a theory, and in my opinion, a good one. You agree, Meredith?"

"I do and I don't, sir," answered Meredith cautiously. "If Rose is counterfeiting the notes and passing them out through the garages, he might use the lorries as a go-between. On the other hand it's a trifle elaborate and clumsy, isn't it? I mean as a method of transport. I can't help feeling that a motorcyclist would meet the case better. Again it would be easy to trace the counterfeit notes to the garages, the moment we got to know they were in circulation. So with all due respects, Mr. Weymouth, I'm rather doubtful about your theory."

"I wonder," concluded the Superintendent after a short silence, "if there is any way of making sure that No. 4 *does* actually run out the petrol when it couples up with certain of the pumps. It might prove extremely interesting to find out!"

CHAPTER XVI

THE BEE'S HEAD BREWERY

OVER the week-end Meredith thought more than once of Mr. Weymouth's theory. Although he recognized the possibility of a pretended delivery, he was still sceptical about the idea of counterfeit notes. He was doubtful, too, as to whether there was any means of making sure that petrol actually flowed through the feed-pipe when No. 4 connected up with certain of the garages. For all that early on Monday morning he got in touch with the constables covering the Stanley Hall and the Filsam and instructed them to get as near as possible to the lorry if any extra delivery should be made. He had an idea that it might be possible to hear the petrol passing through the pipe. The Filsam was to be covered by a motor-cycle instead of from the derelict barn, so that the constable would have a natural excuse for appearing on the scene when the bulk-wagon was coupled up.

But for all these elaborate preparations Meredith was doomed to further disappointment. On Monday's round No. 4 completely ignored the Stanley Hall and the Filsam. In fact an entirely new line of investigation was opened up.

Dancy had taken a copy of Monday's advance orders whilst Weymouth was working out the cubic capacity of the tank. He had thrust the paper into Meredith's hand just as he was leaving the depot on Saturday night. For the first time since Meredith's scheme had been put into action, the lorry was not travelling with a capacity load. Advance orders totalled 800 gallons—four orders for 200 gallons each. This left room for a surplus 200 in the tank.

After an abortive watch on the Lothwaite, Meredith returned to Keswick, where at one o'clock the usual phone call was put through from Penrith. Dancy's message ran as follows—"*Surplus of* 200 *run in to make up capacity load.*"

Meredith therefore anticipated that No. 4 would call at a number of garages in the hope of discharging this extra petrol.

But a surprise awaited him. When all reports had come in he found that the lorry had only called at five garages. No more. Four of these were the places accounted for by the advance-orders. The fifth was "The Admiral Hotel" in Whitehaven. The constable posted to watch the place had noted down the time taken to deliver. It was exactly seven minutes. In other words exactly 200 gallons had been discharged at the pump.

"Which means", put in the Superintendent, "that to-day's deliveries are all above board, Meredith. The full 1,000 gallons has been accounted for."

Meredith nodded.

"All above board, sir, except for one rather curious fact. Instead of going round to a number of customers, the lorry makes straight tracks for 'The Admiral Hotel'. What I want to know is, how did Bettle and Prince *know* that the hotel were in need of this 200?"

"Perhaps they rang through to the depot early this morning before the lorry left, suggesting that if there was a surplus 200 they'd like to have it."

"Well we can easily make sure about that, sir. Dancy should know something about it. Suppose I get through to Penrith and ask them to get the information straightaway?"

Twenty minutes later Penrith replied.

"Report from Dancy, Inspector. He says no phone message came through this morning before No. 4 left the depot. Further neither Bettle nor Prince mentioned 'The Admiral Hotel'. In his opinion they had no idea as to where that extra 200 was to be placed when they set out on their round."

"Good. That's just what I was after." Meredith rang off and swung round on the Superintendent. "So that's that, sir! It seems pretty obvious to me that No. 4 made straight tracks to 'The Admiral' because the whole business was prearranged."

"Suggesting, of course, that this hotel is 'in' with the gang?"

"Exactly. Which rather kills our idea about the isolated garages. I happen to know 'The Admiral', and it's in one of the most thickly populated districts of Whitehaven."

"You know, Meredith," said Thompson, in measured tones, breaking a long silence, "I'm beginning to think that we've been barking up the wrong tree. All along we've adhered to the supposition that Rose and his little crowd are out to diddle Ormsby-Wright. Let's return again to that conversation you overheard at the Lothwaite. Because the expression 'O.W.' didn't fit in with your theory, you twisted it round to mean 'Old William'. In other words, a reference to Rose himself. But suppose your original interpretation was correct? Suppose 'O.W.' does actually refer to Ormsby-Wright? Where are we then? Surely it means that the gang is trafficking in something quite different from petrol. Weymouth suggested counterfeit notes. But over that I'm inclined to agree with you. The only reasonable way to get rid of false notes is to unload them over a large area. The question we're up against is this—if the gang is not concerned with petrol or counterfeit notes, what is their racket?"

"And I'd like to have a ready answer to that question, sir," put in Meredith with a faint smile. "It's the crux of the whole business."

"Well," said the Superintendent quietly. "I think I *have* got an answer to the question. It was to-day's fifth delivery which first gave me the idea. 'The Admiral Hotel'. Why an hotel? Does it suggest anything to you, Inspector?"

"I don't quite see—" began Meredith with a frown.

"Well, let's put it like this. The major profits of a place like 'The Admiral' come from the sale of intoxicating liquors. The hotel is really a side-line. A minute ago, while you were phoning, I looked up 'The Admiral' in the A.A. book. It's a 2-star concern with a dozen bedrooms. On the other hand, if memory serves me right, it's got very large public and saloon bars. Now consider its position. It's in a coastal town. There's a good bit of shipping passing up and down just off the coast at that point. A lot of it, as a matter of fact, puts in at the Scotch ports on the Solway Firth. Now, Meredith, can you see any immediate connection between shipping and intoxicating liquors? Does it suggest any form of illegal traffic to you?"

Meredith let out an exclamation of delight.

"Smuggling, sir! Rum-running!"

"Precisely," was Thompson's dry observation. "Though I suggest brandy rather than rum. There's a high duty on the stuff coupled with a pretty ready sale. Well, I looked at it like this. Suppose 'The Admiral' is mixed up with a crew of smugglers. The job would be worked something like this, I imagine. The stuff's put ashore off the cargo boat and dumped by means of a dinghy on an isolated stretch of the foreshore. Then, by some means or other, it's transported to the cellars of 'The Admiral'. To make the risk worth while the profits would have to be fairly high. This means storing the spirit in bulk. Now, as you probably know, all licensed premises are liable to inspection at any time, by the local Excise Officer. How then are they to conceal the illicit spirit without the Excise man finding out? How would you set about minimizing the risk, Meredith?"

"I should unload the bulk of the stuff at places which are not under Excise supervision."

"Exactly," agreed the Superintendent. "*In our case, the isolated garages!*"

Meredith let out a whistle.

"I see, sir! I see what you're driving at now! You mean that No. 4 collects the stuff in some way from 'The Admiral' and then dumps it at certain garages on its route?"

Thompson nodded.

"Small quantities could then be retained on the hotel premises without risk of discovery. Then when the stock runs low, Rose gets an S.O.S. and the lorry picks up a further small quantity from one of the garages and delivers it at 'The Admiral.' Rather a clever scheme."

"Brilliant!" agreed Meredith. "Brilliant, sir! And how do you suggest the lorry takes in the spirit from the hotel?"

"Well, suppose they're smuggling French brandy. It's put up in small kegs. What's to prevent them from slipping a couple of kegs into the cab of the lorry? After all, Prince and Bettle have got a perfectly genuine excuse for stopping outside the place. It's my idea that they only take in the spirit when an actual load of petrol is being discharged."

"Then it's strange they don't put in an advance-order like any other place," objected Meredith. "That would make it seem more genuine than ever. Instead of which they apparently have a standing arrangement with Bettle and Prince for the lorry to call whenever there's a surplus on board."

"Certainly a curious point," acknowledged the Superintendent. "But remember, so far, we haven't got down to details of their scheme. To continue, Meredith. We must now suppose that the call at the Stanley Hall and the two calls, noted by you, at the Lothwaite, were made for the purpose of taking in bottles of French brandy—let's say half a dozen at a time. Wick and the others probably open up the kegs and decant the stuff into bottles. How does that explanation strike you?"

"Well, it gives us the probable meaning of Prince's curious remark which I overheard that morning, sir."

"Namely?"

"'We thought we might have something to take in.' Prince was referring, of course, to the brandy."

"Yes, I see that. Go on."

"On the other hand I didn't see the stuff being put on to the lorry last Saturday morning at the Lothwaite. Prince disappeared with Wick into the office. But when he came out, I swear he hadn't anything in the nature of a bottle about his person. Not *one* bottle, sir, let alone half a dozen!"

"Umph! Awkward. Very awkward. Are we on the wrong track again, Meredith?"

"There's another point, sir," went on Meredith, ignoring the Superintendent's leading question. "If No. 4 is picking up the brandy and conveying it in small quantities to 'The Admiral' in Whitehaven, why did it call at the Stanley Hall on its homeward run? Surely that would heighten the risk of discovery? The men would have to conceal the stuff somehow when they got back to the depot."

"Awkward," repeated the Superintendent glumly. "Very awkward."

"And again, sir. No. 4 called at the Lothwaite on Saturday morning. But the lorry didn't call on 'The Admiral Hotel' until to-day. Surely the obvious thing to do would be to call on the two places in the *same* day? The spirit would then be aboard the lorry only for a short time."

"In other words, Meredith—my theory doesn't hold water!"

"No—I wouldn't say that … yet, sir. I'm merely taking a review of the known facts and trying to fit them in with the new supposition. For example, where does Ormsby-Wright enter into this smuggling scheme?"

Thompson laughed.

"This time I have got an answer for you, Inspector. I mentioned before that Ormsby-Wright has got his finger in a good many pies. For all we know he may own 'The Admiral Hotel'. I'll go further than that. I'm going to suppose that he owns all the hotels which are served by the Nonock lorry. You recall— there were six licensed premises sporting Nonock pumps? That means he would have a chance of getting rid of exactly six times the amount of smuggled spirit. With a consequent increase in illegal profit."

"That's a point we should investigate, at once. Don't you agree, sir?"

"Most decidedly," was the Superintendent's emphatic answer. "See what the result is of our final observation campaign to-morrow. Have the Lothwaite watched day and night as I suggested. Then on Wednesday, start investigations over in the coast towns. Concentrating, of course, on those six hotels."

"Right, sir."

But Tuesday turned out to be a blank day. No. 4 went out with five advance-orders totalling a capacity load, and did not call at any other pump *en route*. On Wednesday, therefore, Meredith arranged for two plain-clothes constables to keep alternate watches on the Lothwaite, whilst he, himself, set out for Whitehaven.

Thompson had given him the address of Maltman, the White-haven Excise official. But on calling at his office in Turnpike Road, he learnt from his assistant that Maltman was out at Hensign-ham supervising a brew of beer. Armed with the address of the brewery, Meredith set out at once for the suburb. It did not take him long to run the Bee's Head Brewery to earth. It was situtated on the fringe of a newly developed building estate, which fronted on to the Whitehaven–Egremont road. Meredith saw at a glance that it was not a big place—a few tall brick buildings, surrounded by one or two long, corrugated-iron sheds, the whole enclosed by a high brick wall. An inquiry at the main office sufficed to bring Maltman from his job. After Meredith had introduced himself and briefly stated his business, Maltman suggested a retirement to his own office.

"I have the loan of one," he explained, "while I'm working in the brewery."

Here he produced cigarettes, and as soon as they were comfortably settled, Meredith fired off his questions.

"I want some information, Mr. Maltman, about 'The Admiral Hotel'. You know the place?"

"Naturally, Inspector."

"Then you can probably tell me who owns it?"

Maltman laughed. "Well, that's simple enough. It's owned by this brewery. It's one of their tied houses."

Meredith glanced up sharply.

"A tied house. I see. And who owns the brewery?"

"Well, the shares are held by a number of directors; but if you mean who is the largest shareholder, then that, of course, would be the Chairman of the Board."

"And the Chairman?"

"I daresay you've heard of him, Inspector. He lives out your way. A fellow named Ormsby-Wright."

Hardly able to conceal his interest and excitement, Meredith leaned forward eagerly.

"Ormsby-Wright! You're sure about that?"

"Certain. He's got his money in all sorts of business concerns. You may have heard of the Nonock Petroleum Company?"

"I have," replied Meredith drily. "And I understand he owns that as well. So 'The Admiral Hotel' belongs to Ormsby-Wright? Are there any more tied houses attached to this brewery?"

"Yes—five. Two more besides 'The Admiral' in Whitehaven, two in Workington and one in Maryport."

"Half a minute," exclaimed the Inspector. "I've got a list here." With an impatient hand he drew out his list of Nonock customers. "Now, Mr. Maltman, can I have the names of those five other places?"

"Certainly. There's the 'Dragon's Head' and 'Isle of Man' in Whitehaven—then in Workington there's the 'Station Hotel' and the 'Blue Anchor'."

"The first in Merrydew Street and the second in Trueman's Yard," put in Meredith, elated. Maltman looked up in surprise. "Go on, Mr. Maltman! Go on!"

"Then there's the Maryport place——"

"'The White Hart,'" cut in Meredith. "In Seaview Road. Am I right, sir?"

"Absolutely, Inspector. You seem to know more about these places than I do!"

"Well, I know something about them now, all right!" was Meredith's triumphant return. "Thanks to you. But perhaps I ought to explain why I'm interested in these hotels. If the police suspicions are correct, then it's more in your province than in ours. Listen, Mr. Maltman."

And in a couple of minutes Meredith had outlined the Superintendent's theory about the brandy smuggling. Maltman's eyes grew rounder and rounder as the Inspector proceeded ... incredulity gave way to doubt and doubt to a very lively interest.

"Well, I'll be blowed!" was his comment when the Inspector had concluded. "So you think Ormsby-Wright's a wrong 'un, do you? Maybe you're right. Though from what I know of the man he's straight enough. Reserved, mind you. A bit of the Pierpont Morgan touch about his methods. You know, Inspector—'What

I says goes, and don't you forget it!' That sort of attitude. But for all his high-handed ways I believe he's generally liked here."

"Know anything about the managers of the tied houses?"

"Only in a general sort of way. Never heard anything against them, if that's what you mean."

"Who engaged them?"

"Ormsby-Wright, of course. He keeps the administrative side of the brewery pretty well in his own hands."

Meredith noted this point. It was suggestive.

"What's your opinion as to the possibility of smuggling along this coast?"

Maltman shrugged his shoulders and threw out his hands, with a non-committal gesture.

"Well, frankly, Inspector, I don't think it could be done. There's a pretty efficient coast-guard patrol along this stretch of the shore. A clever crew might bring it off once, but as a regular practice, I should say it's out of the question."

"You supervise 'The Admiral' premises, I suppose?" Maltman nodded. "Ever come across anything suspicious?"

"Never!"

"Well, Mr. Maltman," said the Inspector, rising. "I won't keep you away from that brew any longer. But I should be obliged if you'd keep a strict eye on those tied houses in the meantime. If you can do it without advertising the fact, so much the better." He held out his hand. "Thanks, I may look you up again later."

It was with a feeling of triumph and satisfaction that the Inspector drove back to Keswick. Here, at last, was real honest progress! The two concerns which had come under police suspicion were owned by the same man. That in itself was of enormous significance. So the boss, referred to by Bettle, was Ormsby-Wright, after all! And the investigations into a petrol fraud had been so much wasted time and energy. There was absolutely no doubt now that No. 4's call at "The Admiral" on Monday afternoon was a prearranged visit. In all probability, the lorry called there *every* Monday afternoon. Meredith wondered if the other five tied houses were served with the same regularity. He would certainly have to get all six places under constant observation. If kegs of brandy, or the like, were being dumped in the lorry from any of these premises, it was certain that the trick would be discovered sooner or later. And once establish the fact that Ormsby-Wright and Co. were dealing in illegal spirit, it should prove a simple matter to find out how they were doing it, and to run the various members of the gang to earth.

And that done—what then? Meredith made a wry grimace. What a fool he was! Absorbed in his later investigations, he had all but forgotten Clayton's murder. There was still that problem to solve. The major problem, in fact.

A great deal of his previous optimism evaporated at the thought. He realized, with a pang of hopelessness, that he still had a long way to go.

CHAPTER XVII

THE MUSLIN BAG

FOUR days passed without anything new coming to light. No. 4 had behaved with exemplary frankness. No calls had been made at any of the six public houses, nor had any contact been made with the Derwent, Lothwaite, Filsam or Stanley Hall garages. Meredith now had every one of these places under observation. The Lothwaite was being watched day and night. Extra precautions were also being taken by the coast-guards and every likely landing-place had been specially ear-marked and a man put on duty at night.

The Inspector was disturbed. Did it mean that the gang had got wind of the police suspicions and were lying low for a time? It was quite possible that one of the numerous watchers had been spotted and the news flashed round among the members. If that were so, good-bye to any chance of clearing up the mysteries or arresting the murderer of Clayton. Despite the springtime weather, Meredith remained in an obstinate mood of depression.

Then on Monday morning there came news!

At his office Meredith found Constable Gratorex waiting for him, note-book in hand, success written all over his cheerful, rubicund features. The Inspector waved him into a chair and sat down at his desk.

"Well, Constable—out with it!"

"It's the Lothwaite, sir. I was on duty there last night from eleven o'clock. I've got something to report."

Meredith drew a sheet of paper toward him and unscrewed his fountain-pen.

"Right."

Flicking open his note-book, Constable Gratorex began to deliver the report in his best court-room manner.

"At twelve-twenty-two a.m. on Monday morning the party under observation came out of the cottage adjoining the garage. He appeared to have something bulky in his arms. Moving round to the back of the buildings, he entered the wood in which I was secreted. Thinking his actions suspicious, I decided to follow him. This I did. There was a bright moon and when he entered a small clearing I saw that he was carrying an oil-drum. I followed him for a matter of four hundred yards up the slope. Arriving at a deep gully formed by a beck, the party stooped and set down the drum. Taking advantage of the noise made by the beck, I crept forward to within some ten yards of where the party was standing. He then disappeared down the side of the gully, enabling me to take up a position in some bramble bushes at the top of the bank. The party then unstoppered the oil-drum and poured the contents into the beck. After that the party returned with the empty oil-drum to the cottage. There was nothing further to report during the remainder of my watch."

"Very clear and concise," was Meredith's comment when Gratorex had concluded. "You had no doubt that it was Wick?"

"No, sir. None at all."

"Any idea as to what was emptied from the drum?"

"No, sir. When Wick was safe back in the cottage I cut up through the wood again and took a look into the beck. But although I made a close examination with my torch I found nothing in the way of a clue."

"The beck was flowing fast at that point?"

"Very, sir. In spate after Saturday's rain."

"Then anything thrown in at that point would soon be carried away," observed Meredith. "How big was the drum?"

"I should say it held about four gallons, sir."

"Who's on duty at the Lothwaite to-night?"

"I am, sir."

"Very well. I shall join you there at eleven o'clock."

Meredith, with his usual efficiency, was there to the tick. Gratorex had just taken over from Peters, who was working the shifts with him. In reply to the Inspector's whispered query, Peters stated that, so far, nothing untoward had taken place. He had seen the lorry pass on its homeward run about five-thirty.

"Right. That's all."

The man melted away into the shadows.

Then for more than an hour nothing happened. The night was intensely still, abnormally warm for the time of year, and moonlit. Meredith could just discern the outline of the constable's features in the faint glow dispersed by the lighted petrol-pumps below. At midnight these flicked out, and save for a single light burning in one of the cottage windows the place was in darkness. Ten minutes later this light, too, went out. Meredith held his breath. Did it mean that Wick was now in bed or was he——?

He felt the constable's hand on his arm.

"Look, sir!" came the tense whisper. "There he is again. Heading for the beck, too, by the look of it!"

"Quietly does it," hissed Meredith. "We'll follow him up as close as we dare. Come on!"

With infinite caution they set off through the larch trees, preceded by the dimly discernible figure of the loaded man. By the manner in which he laboured up the slope, Meredith guessed that the oil-drum was pretty weighty. Gratorex was right. It looked as if it would hold just about four gallons of—what? Oil? Meredith smiled. Hardly that. A man doesn't empty four gallons of oil into a beck. All day he had been puzzling over the contents of that drum. Petrol? Brandy? Nothing plausible had suggested itself.

He was suddenly aware that Wick had reached the edge of the gully and set down his burden.

"Stay here," was his whispered order. "No need for both of us to go forward."

He waited a few seconds until Wick had disappeared into the gully then rapidly worked his way forward until he reached the bramble bushes. There, safely concealed, he watched.

Everything happened again just as Gratorex had reported. Wick unstoppered the drum, tipped it up and waited until the contents were completely emptied into the beck. Then, shouldering the drum, he climbed up the bank, passing some five yards away from Meredith, and set off at a swinging pace down through the wood. The moment he was well out of sight, Meredith, shielding his torch with his cap, made a careful examination of the beck. He then realized Wick's cleverness. If his intention had been to rid himself of something incriminating, he could not have chosen a better spot. The beck, at that point, dropped sheer for twelve feet or more into a regular "Devil's Punchbowl". It was into this seething mass of water that Wick had emptied the drum. If, therefore, its liquid contents contained any incriminating sediment, which might not be immediately washed away, it would be necessary to divert the flow of the beck before this sediment could be examined.

As he was staring down into this foaming pool, Meredith was struck by a sudden thought. Had he been wrong in his surmise that the drum did not contain brandy? He recalled the exemplary behaviour of No. 4 during the last few days. What if the gang *had* got wind of the police activities? Wouldn't their first thought be to rid themselves of any incriminating evidence? In brief—wasn't Wick pouring the smuggled brandy into the beck?

He sniffed. There was no suggestion of any odour and the smell of spirits was notoriously strong. But if the drum had not contained brandy—then what?

A hiss cut short his speculations. Gratorex, on top of the bank, was beckoning wildly. In a flash Meredith had climbed out of the gully and dropped down into the bramble bushes beside the constable.

"What the devil——?"

"He's coming back again," was the whispered reply.

Gratorex was right. In less than a minute Wick reappeared with the oil-drum and repeated the entire process of a few moments before. Once the coast was clear, Meredith, for the second time, scrambled down the bank and sniffed at the water. Then he let out an exclamation of surprise. Surely there was a faint odour on the air this time? A curious odour, rather like baked bread. Was it brandy, perhaps? Or if not brandy, some other sort of spirit?

He signalled to the constable.

"Can you smell anything, Gratorex?"

The constable sniffed in turn, then nodded.

"Smells like a brewery, sir—doesn't it?"

"A brewery?"

"Yes, sir. Maltings."

"Maltings! Maltings!" thought Meredith, his brain a whirl of swift conjectures. Where exactly did maltings enter into the picture? Surely malting was a brewing operation? And what had brewing operations to do with smuggled brandy? Then suddenly, in a single illuminating flash, he saw the explanation and uttered a smothered cry of triumph. "Man alive! I believe you've hit it! A bull's-eye! If you haven't, I'm a Dutchman! I'll eat my hat! I'm willing to wager every penny I possess that——"

Meredith suddenly realized that he was in the presence of a subordinate. He gave vent to an ashamed chuckle.

"Sorry, Gratorex. Only I've got an idea. I forgot that you haven't the faintest notion of what I'm talking about. Well, you needn't hang about *here* any longer. You can go off duty and get some sleep. Understand?"

"Very good, sir," was the delighted reply.

Back at Greystoke Road, Meredith crept in between the sheets, without waking his wife, and lay thinking.

He had got it at last! He knew now what Ormsby-Wright was up to!

He had, so to speak, walked through a pitch-black tunnel and emerged into blinding sunlight. Now the whole case, like a smiling stretch of countryside, lay spread out before him. One or two necessary tests, he felt, and this part of his job was at an end. Why hadn't he thought of it before? But that was what one always asked when, after a long and arduous struggle, the solution of a problem appeared. There were still details of the *modus operandi* to clear up, but even as he put his mind to thinking about them the shadows smoked up in his brain and he slid into the toils of a profound sleep.

But next morning early found the Inspector over at White-haven. There, in his Turnpike Road office, Meredith had a long talk with Maltman. It was, as he realized, the most vital inter-view which he had held since the opening of the dual-case. But this time there were to be no depressing disappointments. He left Maltman's office with a broad grin on his face, certain now that the end of the journey was in sight.

Back at Whitehaven police station, he put through a call to Carlisle. In a few moments the Superintendent was at the phone. After he had made his report and modestly accepted his superior's congratulations, Meredith made a request.

"I want a night watch kept on the Stanley Hall and Filsam now, sir. We've only got them covered during the day at the moment. You see what I'm after?"

"Perfectly. Righto, Meredith. I'll see that it's done. The men will be on duty to-night. Anything more?"

"Not at the moment, sir—thanks."

Leaving Whitehaven, Meredith drove off along the Cockermouth road until he came to the Filsam. He found the broad-shouldered proprietor "de-carbing" a client's engine.

"Good morning," said Meredith affably. "I wonder if you could spare me a moment?"

The man straightened up, wiped his hands on an oily rag and declared himself at the gentleman's service.

"The fact of the matter is," began Meredith glibly, "I've heard the land behind your garage here is for sale. I'm on the look-out for a small dairy farm, as it happens, and I wondered if this place would suit."

The man looked surprised.

"It's the first I've heard about it! Mr. Transome farms the land at the back here. There must have been some mistake, sir."

"No, really, I don't think so. The agent mentioned your place as a landmark. At any rate, now I am here, perhaps I could use that gate of yours behind the garage and take a look round?"

"Certainly, sir, if you like. But I'm sure Mr. Transome isn't selling."

After thanking the proprietor, Meredith passed out through the little wicket gate into the meadows beyond. A single glance brought to light what he was looking for. Close under a stone wall, which divided one meadow from another, was a shallow, swift-flowing beck. In pretence of taking stock of the property, Meredith strolled down to the edge of the stream and began to work up it to a point where it disappeared under a low stone arch beneath the main road. The bank at this spot was muddy and clearly defined in the soft soil were numbers of large footprints. Casting his eye back to the wicket gate, Meredith could trace a faint line of muddied grass, suggestive of the fact that somebody had been passing to and fro between the garage and the bank of the stream. But although he peered under the arch he could unearth no clue as to the reason for these visits. That, he suspected, was another thing. Suspicions and proof were poles apart—but for all that he returned to the garage in a highly satisfied state of mind. He wondered if the constable concealed in the derelict barn had taken note of his movements. He glanced across at the ventilation hole and smiled. If the constable didn't incorporate this visit in his nightly report he'd be for it!

After thanking the proprietor, he mounted his motor-cycle, passed through Cockermouth, and in a short time drew up outside the Stanley Hall. The wizened, white-haired little man came forward and demanded in a querulous voice what Meredith wanted. The Inspector adopted the same tactics and fifteen minutes later he was in possession of yet one more incriminating fact. A similar beck passed under the road, close to the garage, and again there was a defined track leading from the rear of the premises to the bank of the stream. This time, however, on account of the shaly nature of the soil, there were no footmarks.

For all that, Meredith was in a happy mood. Three isolated garages, three nearby becks, with, doubtless, three men emptying oil-drums into the water at the dead of night. And before he reached Keswick he had added a fourth to the list—the Derwent. In this case he had no need to dismount and pursue an inquiry. The beck was perfectly evident from the road, running parallel with it for some distance, before vanishing, like magic, underground. And at the point where the stream disappeared the bank was churned up with the marks of human footprints. Was Higgins back at work again? was Meredith's passing thought. Well, he was having the place covered that night, so by to-morrow he might know the answer to that question.

Back in his office he found Gratorex waiting.

"Got those measurements, Constable?"

"Yes, sir. Width six feet. Length five feet. Depth four feet. Approx., that is, sir. We've allowed about six inches on the width and length for a good clearance."

"Quite good enough for our purpose," was Meredith's comment. "You'd better come with me up to Wilkinson's Yard."

Meredith, who knew his way about the builder's premises, made straight tracks for the carpenters' workshop.

"Mr. Root about?"

"Down in the timber-shed, sir," said one of the apprentices.

Meredith found the old man rooting about under a pile of elm boards. After a few exchanges about local topics, the Inspector got down to the matter in hand.

"Now, Mr. Root, I want you to make me a box-frame to these measurements. Width six feet. Length five feet. Depth three feet six inches. It needn't be——"

"Excuse me, sir," cut in the constable quickly. "You've made a mistake. The depth was four feet."

Meredith cast a withering glance at his subordinate.

"Don't be a fool, Gratorex! We don't want the damned thing to show, do we?" He turned to the carpenter. "You've got that, Mr. Root? Good. I want it within an hour. No need for a cabinet-maker's job. Just knock it up out of any old stuff."

"Oh, and by the way," he added as he was leaving the yard, "I want you to nail four strips of lead round the base."

His next visit was to Burry and Sons, the big drapers in Main Street, where he purchased a large square of muslin. After lunch, accompanied by Gratorex, he returned to Wilkinson's Yard, where Root was just driving the last nails into the box-frame. Meredith unpacked his parcel of muslin.

"Now, Mr. Root—I want you to tack this muslin securely over the top of your box-frame. Not stretched, mind you—but so that the stuff sags a bit in the middle. Understand?"

The carpenter nodded and in a few minutes the job was complete. Paying the man for his work, Meredith and the constable then carried the contraption to a closed Ford van, which was waiting at the gates of the builder's yard. Once it was loaded, Meredith instructed the driver to stop on the road about half a mile beyond Braithwaite Station.

"Then I want you to help the constable here," he concluded. "Just take your orders from him. And, don't forget ... no chattering!"

The lad grinned and he and Gratorex drove off in the direction of Braithwaite.

At six o'clock reports came in from the Filsam and Stanley Hall watchers. No. 4 had coupled up with both places. The Filsam delivery had been run out in eight minutes—the Stanley Hall in seventeen. Meredith grinned. He was no longer interested in these time factors. He felt certain now that they had little bearing on the case. That the lorry had called at these two isolated garages was, of course, significant. It meant that his previous fears were groundless. The gang had not got wind of the police investigations. They were obligingly carrying on with the good work and supplying him with further incriminating data.

If his anticipations were correct, No. 4 was due to call, on the morrow, at one or more of the six tied houses owned by the Bee's Head Brewery.

After a long phone talk with the Superintendent during the afternoon, instructions had been sent to the coast-guard stations to relax their watch on the ear-marked points along the fore-shore. Thompson apologized for the trouble he had caused them, but the smuggling scare had proved to be an error of judgement. The police were now working along different lines.

Early the next morning Meredith set off on the combination for the Lothwaite.

Parking on the roadside about half a mile from the garage, he dismounted, climbed the fence and plunged into the larch wood. He had proceeded only a short distance when Gratorex appeared, coming to meet him.

"All O.K., Constable?"

"Yes, sir. He turned up shortly after midnight. Made three journeys this time, as I explained on the phone this morning."

"And you got the gadget out of the water soon after he'd made the third journey?"

"Yes, sir. And hid it in some bushes, according to your instructions."

"Good."

In ten minutes they had reached the spot where Gratorex had dumped the box-frame and covered it with a mackintosh sheet. Meredith drew aside the sheet, knelt down and closely examined the muslin pocket. Then, with extreme care, he ripped the muslin off the top of the box-frame, bunched the four corners together and tied them with a piece of string.

"Looks like a tea-bag, eh, Gratorex?"

The constable grinned broadly.

"Any luck, sir?"

"Well, the bag doesn't contain tea, if that's what you mean! You'd better remove the frame and hide it deeper in the wood. I don't want to scare the bird away from the net. As soon as Peters turns up, you can go off duty for the day. Return as usual at eleven to-night."

Holding the bag carefully, Meredith returned through the wood to the point where he had parked the motor-cycle. Then, after he had safely deposited the bag in the side-car, he sped on past the Lothwaite toward Whitehaven.

Mr. Maltman, warned of his approach by phone, was waiting for him in his Turnpike Road office. When he saw Meredith entering with the muslin bag he burst out laughing.

"Strange and wonderful are the ways of the minions of the law!" he exclaimed. "What the deuce have you got there, Inspector? The body in the bag?"

Meredith responded to his amusement with a grin.

"No—not this time. I'm hoping that it contains the confirmation of that theory we were discussing yesterday."

"You mean—?" Meredith gave a meaning nod.

"Then, for heaven's sake," was Maltman's excited demand, "undo the knot and let's have a peep. But wait a minute—before you do that, you might tell me where the bag came from and what it's got to do with the case. No need to keep me in the dark, is there? I mean official caution and all that?"

"Nothing of the kind, Mr. Maltman. I'll tell you about it now. Do you mind if I smoke a pipe?"

"I'll join you," answered Maltman, still curiously eyeing the bag. "Try some of my brand and help the British Empire."

With both their pipes pulling sweetly, Meredith settled down to recite the history of the muslin bag.

"It's like this, Mr. Maltman. I explained to you yesterday how we observed that fellow at the Lothwaite garage emptying something into the beck. You remember I asked you what liquid had an odour of baked bread? Your answer more or less satisfied me that I was on the right track. But I wanted to go further than that. I wanted to get absolute proof. In the process we were discussing you pointed out that a considerable sediment would be present in the liquid residue. Well, I set out to get hold of a sample of that sediment. I couldn't collect it from the bed of the stream, for obvious reasons. For one thing, Wick was emptying the stuff into a 'devil's punchbowl', so that it was impossible to see anything through the water. Secondly, although the hollow bowl caused by the waterfall was nearly four feet deep, the force of the water was so great that any sediment would soon be forced out and dispersed downstream. You follow me?"

"Perfectly."

"So all I did was to have the 'punchbowl' measured up and a box-frame made to fit roughly inside it. I covered the top with this muslin, in such a way that it formed a sort of strainer. I arranged for the top of the box-frame to be about six inches under water. The result of this was that when Wick went to empty his oil-drum last night, he emptied it slap into the muslin sieve."

Maltman looked at the Inspector with admiration.

"Neat, Mr. Meredith. Very neat. But didn't Wick notice the gadget?"

"Not a bit of it! The churned-up surface of the pool made it impossible. Remember, there was a twelve foot waterfall above the bowl."

"And the result?" asked Maltman, whose curiosity had now reached boiling point. "Did you catch any of the sediment?"

"Take a look here," was Meredith's answer, as he untied the bag and spread out the muslin square on the carpet. "What do you make of *that*, Mr. Maltman?"

The Excise official dropped on to his hands and knees and began to sniff at the brownish residue, which had collected in a little heap toward the centre of the muslin.

Then he looked up.

"We're right," he said shortly. "No mistake about it!"

He gathered some of the sediment into his hand, examined it, then rubbed it over with his fingers.

"If there was any doubt about it yesterday," he went on impressively, "then this settles it, Inspector. It's the residue of alcoholic distillation right enough! I've seen enough of the stuff in my time to be sure about it. That 'baked bread' odour supplied us with a clue, but the nature of the sediment sets the seal on it! If you wanted confirmation of your theory—then you're quite right. It's here! Caught in this muslin! If you want a second opinion——?"

Meredith shook his head.

"No need, Mr. Maltman. Your opinion fits in too neatly with the other facts of the case."

"Which means, Inspector?"

Meredith gave a triumphant chuckle.

"That Mr. Ormsby-Wright and his minions have been caught by the short hairs! That's my opinion, anyway." Then: "Illicit stills!" he exclaimed after an electric silence. "Why the devil didn't I think of it before? But there—that's always the way. It's so darned easy to be wise *after* the event!"

CHAPTER XVIII

MEREDITH GOES TO EARTH

MEREDITH'S report to Carlisle fetched the Superintendent over to Keswick early the next morning. The new slant on the case needed carefully going into, and the two men settled down to a long discussion of ways and means. Although, as the Superintendent pointed out, they were now in a position to arrest Wick on suspicion of being engaged in illicit spirit-making, it was his idea that the arrest should be postponed. As he put it, "We don't want to raise a red flag to warn the rest of the gang." Meredith was of a like opinion.

"We've now got undeniable proof of the nature of their racket," he said, "but I'd like to unearth one of the stills. Once find out where the stills are hidden and we ought to catch 'em red-handed, sir."

Thompson nodded.

"Can you tell what spirit they're making from the nature of the residue?"

"Maltman's making an analysis of the stuff this morning, sir, and phoning through the result. He has an idea it's whisky."

"Then I wonder how the deuce they're planting the stuff on the public? Any ideas?"

"None, sir. That's one of the first things we've got to find out. And the other problem to be solved is how exactly the lorry picks up the stuff and delivers it at the pubs."

"Well, we ought to get a line on that. You've got those four garages under day and night observation."

"I think the idea you put up when we were working on the lines of a smuggling racket is the probable one, sir."

"You mean small kegs? Yes—it strikes me as the only feasible method. Well, Meredith, what's your next move going to be?

The Chief still wants to be posted up to date, so if you've got any world-shaking scheme up your sleeve you'd better trot it out."

"I'm going to make a thorough search of one of the garages," was Meredith's prompt answer.

"Can you manage that without giving the game away?"

"Take a look at this, sir," replied Meredith, handing the Superintendent a copy of the mid-weekly *Cumberland News*. "You see, I've blue-pencilled an advert under the 'Weekly Car Mart' section."

"You mean this—'Second-hand Rover saloon for sale. Good condition. Only done 6,000. Bargain price. Trial run by appointment. Apply Higgins, Derwent Garage, Braithwaite.'"

"That's it. I've rung up a friend of mine in Ambleside and got him to write a letter to say he's interested in the car. He's trying to fix an appointment with Higgins for to-morrow afternoon at three. At Ambleside, of course. And as our friend is now running the place single-handed, it looks as if we shall have an hour or two in which to make our search without fear of interruption."

"Good, Inspector. Well, I won't keep you longer. I've——"

"Just a minute, sir," interposed Meredith as the phone bell started ringing. "This may be Maltman." He lifted the receiver. "Yes—speaking. ... I see. Very kind of you, Mr. Maltman. No—nothing further at the moment. But I shall probably be worrying you again a little later on. Thanks. Good-bye." He turned to the Superintendent. "Maltman has made that analysis. It's just as he thought. Whisky, sir."

"One more fact in our pocket," observed the Superintendent, as he made ready to go. "Let me know the result of your investigations at the Derwent. I'll expect your call about six to-morrow evening."

More news came in the next day. The constables on night duty at the Filsam and the Stanley Hall both reported suspicious behaviour on the part of the proprietors. In each case the men had been seen crossing to the nearby becks and emptying something into the water. They both thought the men had been carrying large oil-drums, though they wouldn't swear to this fact.

Meredith was delighted. Here was more incriminating evidence to back up his suspicions. But to balance up his satisfaction came negative reports from the day watchers. Although No. 4 had coupled up with the Filsam, the constable secreted in the barn had seen nothing in the nature of small kegs or casks being loaded on to the lorry. On the other hand, the proprietor—whose name Meredith had discovered was Wilkins—had acted in the same curious way as Wick. On the approach of the lorry he had disappeared into his cottage, emerging some ten minutes later after Prince had coupled up with the pump. He had then signalled with his hand and Prince had, at once, turned off the valve. That this coincidence was significant Meredith no longer doubted. But it was beyond him to find an explanation for the men's peculiar behaviour.

At twelve-thirty his friend, Mr. Barrow, rang up from Ambleside. It was all fixed up. Higgins had promised to be over at his house at three o'clock that afternoon. A study of his map enabled Meredith to gauge roughly the amount of time he would have at his disposal at the Derwent. He reckoned that Higgins would set out about two-fifteen and return, at the earliest, at four-thirty. After warning Railton to be ready with the combination at one-thirty, Meredith set off for Greystoke Road and an early lunch.

On his way back to the station, however, he was detained by one of those incidents, which trivial in themselves, cannot be ignored by a member of the Force. Rounding the corner of Grey-stoke Road, he was aware of a sudden shout of alarm, followed by an appalling crash of broken glass. From a side-turning, only a few yards up the street, there debouched a crowd of excited youngsters. The apparent ring-leader of this juvenile gang, intent only on putting as great a distance as possible between himself and the broken glass, rushed straight into the arms of the Inspector.

"Now then, sonny," said Meredith, shooting out a hand and detaining the lad. "What's all this about? Throwing stones, eh?"

The boy whimpered out an unconvincing denial and attempted to break away from the Inspector's grip. As he urged his squirming captive toward the side-turning, Meredith demanded his name.

"Andy Pearson," snivelled the lad. "An' it weren't my fault as it happened. We was only playing gunmen."

"Gunmen, eh?" Meredith looked into the boy's face and could scarcely restrain his laughter. The small, pinched features were almost obliterated by a dirty green felt hat pulled well down over one ear. The upper lip was adorned with a false moustache, and round the boy's neck was suspended a cap-pistol on a long string. Thrust into a leather belt round his waist was a huge wooden knife, the tip of which had been painted a lurid scarlet. This fiercesome get-up contrasted comically with the lad's obvious timidity at being in the hands of the law.

Meredith, after placating the enraged householder whose window had been broken and taking down the lad's address, delivered himself of a stern homily. Once freed, the boy departed at great speed, with the Inspector's threat of a parental retribution hanging over his head. Meredith, who knew Pearson, felt sure that the young culprit would be suitably dealt with at home.

Then, annoyed by the delay, he bid the householder good day, and hurried off to the police station.

At Portinscale, Meredith instructed Railton to take the left fork in the village, instead of continuing along the Braithwaite road. About a hundred yards up the turning he signalled the constable to stop. Then, lounging casually against a cottage fence, he waited.

He did not have to wait long. Shortly after two o'clock a blue Rover saloon swung round the bend by the post office and vanished in the direction of Keswick. Quick as its passage had been, Meredith had not failed to recognize the man at the wheel.

"Come on, Railton. Step on it! We can't afford to waste time!"

The constable dutifully "stepped on it", and in a few minutes the combination drew up outside the Derwent. A rapid survey of the place left no doubt in the Inspector's mind that it was deserted. The garage doors were shut and locked and a notice pinned on to them: "Closed until 5 o'clock."

"This way," snapped Meredith. "We'll try the cottage first. I've an idea we shan't find what we're looking for in the garage itself. Too public, Railton."

With the constable close on his heels, the Inspector strode up the path and tried the handle of the front-door. As he anticipated, it was locked. The windows, too, were closed and fastened. Skirting round the path to the back of the cottage, he then tried the back door and the two windows of the scullery. This time luck was with him. One of the windows, although shut, was not fastened with an indoor catch. With the aid of a penknife it was the work of moments to slide down the sash and, in a short time, both he and the constable were standing in the stone-floored scullery.

Meredith realized that he had not been inside the building since the tragic night when Clayton's body had been carried in from the lean-to and laid out on the sofa. He was surprised to find the place so untidy. Mrs. Swinley was evidently adequate rather than efficient. The tiny sitting-room was littered with all sorts of odds and ends—old newspapers, odd garments, hats, coats, books and business letters. There was scarcely a clear space in which to sit down. The same chaos was repeated in the upper rooms, where Meredith set about making a methodical search of every nook and cranny. But at the end of twenty minutes he felt sure that the distilling apparatus was not concealed in the upper part of the house. He even sent the constable up a rickety pair of steps to see what lay beyond a trap-door in one of the bedroom ceilings. But there was nothing under the rafters save an old tin bath, a broken gramophone, and a number of empty packing-cases.

"Now for the sitting-room," said Meredith briskly, when the constable had safely negotiated the flimsy ladder.

An even more meticulous examination followed on the ground floor. Instructing Railton to move the table on one side, Meredith rolled back the threadbare carpet and went over every inch of the stone floor on his hands and knees. But there was no sign of a trap. The cement between the stones was unbroken, and no single slab appeared to be in any way loose. Replacing the carpet and table, their next move was to inspect the fireplace. It was of an old-fashioned design, with a high mantel-shelf, the three sides of the recess framed in enormous oak beams. An ordinary kitchen-range had been fitted into the recess with the usual damper and flue-pipe arrangements at the back. But despite Meredith's exhaustive examination, the fireplace failed to yield a single clue.

"Now for these cupboards," said the Inspector, pointing to the two large, built-in cupboards which flanked the hearth. "You take the right. I'll take the left."

The handle of the left cupboard, though stiff, yielded to a little pressure, and a glance sufficed to show that every shelf was loaded with crockery and other ordinary domestic utensils. But scarcely had Meredith shut the door when an exclamation of surprise switched his attention over to Railton.

"Won't budge, sir. Feels as if it's jammed," he said, struggling with the door of the other cupboard.

"Here, let's take a look."

Meredith examined the handle and lock closely.

"Naturally it won't budge," was his immediate verdict. "It's locked! No key here, either. Looks as if we'll have to do a little amateur housebreaking, Railton. Have you got that length of wire and those hooks?" The constable nodded. "Then hurry up and get to work. We can't afford to waste time!"

Railton, who had studied the niceties of lock-picking in his leisure hours, drew out an array of implements and got down to the job. In less than five minutes there was a sharp click as the lock turned over. Meredith caught hold of the handle and pulled the door open.

Then he swore roundly. Although he had refused to be carried away on a wave of optimism, the locked door had decidedly stimulated his hopes. He had expected to find something, a clue perhaps that would point the way to other more valuable clues. Instead there was nothing. Literally nothing! The cupboard was empty!

But hardly had he swallowed his disappointment when a new thought struck him and his hopes rapidly revived. Why was the cupboard empty? He cast his eye round the room at the litter of hats and coats and newspapers.

"You'd think Higgins could have done with cupboard space, wouldn't you, Railton? Yet, look here—bare as a bleached bone! There's something odd here or I'm a Dutchman. Let's have a look at the flooring."

Dropping on to his hands and knees, he began sounding the stone floor of the cupboard with a poker he had snatched up from the hearth. Then, with a gleam of triumph in his eye, he looked up at the constable.

"Listen hard, Railton. And then tell me what you think of it?"

He rapped first on the stone in front of the range and then again inside the cupboard.

"A different note, sir," was Railton's verdict. "The floor of the cupboard's hollow!"

"Out of the mouths of babes!" grinned Meredith. "I thought the same thing myself. But there can't be a trap-door of any sort because these two slabs here in the cupboard project out into the room."

"I don't quite see—" began Railton, puzzled.

"Well, look here, man!" said Meredith impatiently.

"There's a wooden sill across the base of the cupboard that the door shuts on to. And you couldn't lift either of the stones without first removing this sill, could you?"

"Perhaps they do remove it," was Railton's lugubrious reply. "Let's heave on it, sir!"

Half-heartedly Meredith lent the constable a hand. To his intense amazement, without the exercise of the slightest effort, the wooden sill came away in their hands. Although evidently nailed securely into position, it had only been lightly jammed between the two uprights of the door-frame.

"Good heavens, Railton. Take a look at that!"

He was pointing to that part of the two stone slabs which had previously been concealed by the sill. A wide crack ran across them.

"Then they don't project out as we thought, sir."

"Of course not! Come on, out with that penknife of yours. I've an idea that we can prise up the whole of the cupboard floor.

Got it? Good. Now shove it underneath. Steady! Easy does it!"
Then with an exclamation of triumph: "There you are, Railton—
what did I say? A trap-door! Come on, man, don't stand there
gaping. Get out your torch and let's investigate!"

Drawing back the two loosened slabs, Meredith grabbed the
constable's torch and shone it down into the hollowed space
under the cupboard. Against the back wall of the shaft he noted
the dim outlines of a cat-ladder. Wasting no time, calling on
Railton to follow, he got his feet on to the upper rungs and
began to descend. In a few seconds his feet encountered solid
ground again and he found himself looking down a low horizontal shaft, which he judged to be driven directly under the
garage. For the time being, however, he left the exploration
of this tunnel, to devote his attentions to an unusual object
recessed in the left wall of the vertical shaft. Noticing an electric
switch at the foot of the ladder, he clicked it on. Immediately
the well in which he was standing and the whole length of the
tunnel itself was flooded with light.

"Electrics!" ejaculated the constable, who had now arrived
on terra firma. "They've made it cosy enough, sir!"

Meredith nodded.

"Not only cosy, Railton, but efficient. Take a squint at this."

"Good Lord, sir—what's that?"

"That, if I'm not mistaken, is what the *Encyclopædia Britannica*
calls a 'Coffey's still'. It's a patent still for making whisky. I mugged
it all up in the public library yesterday evening. It's pretty obvious
that money's been no object. You couldn't make a piece of apparatus like that *under* a thousand. Looks as if our investigations are
more or less at an end, Constable."

"What about that shaft, sir?"

"Yes—I'm coming to that in a minute. First of all let's take a look
at the still. Does its position suggest anything to you, Railton?"

The constable shook his head.

"You know," went on the Inspector admiringly, "they really have made a very neat job of this racket. You may not know it, but during the process of distillation you've got to get rid of the fumes—to say nothing of smoke if you're distilling over an open fire. So they've done the sensible thing and shoved this contraption bang under the sitting-room fireplace. Clever, eh? No extra chimney needed."

The constable was suitably impressed.

"And what about that aquarium up there, sir? What's that?"

"That aquarium, as you call it, is probably the collecting chamber. You can see it's half full of spirit now. Yes. There's the intake pipe from the analysing column and the outlet pipe runs along the wall of the tunnel."

Railton, who had crossed over to look at the tank in question, observed: "It looks more like water to me than whisky."

"It would. Newly distilled spirit is colourless. It only takes on colour after it's matured. Now let's follow this outlet pipe. It interests me far more than that still, Railton."

Bent almost double, for the horizontal shaft was not much over four feet high, Meredith and the constable set off to track down the termination of the pipe. As they proceeded on their back-aching way the Inspector's admiration grew apace. Everything about this subterranean plant had been most beautifully thought out and constructed. The sides of the tunnel were riveted with cement and the ceiling formed by a series of broad stone slabs. The tiny metal pipe dropped in a gradual decline from the glass container beside the still, until about thirty feet up the tunnel, where it ran into a second glass tank.

"What on earth's the idea of this second container?" demanded Meredith, puzzled.

"Sort of storage tank, maybe, sir. At any rate, we can straighten up now. The roof's a good seven feet high at this spot." Suddenly the constable threw out his arm. "What in the name of thunder is that, sir? Another blooming gadget!"

Meredith took a couple of rapid paces forward and bent down to examine the object which had caught Railton's attention. It was a small piece of machinery, firmly bedded on concrete and evidently wired for electric power. It stood some two yards beyond the second container, linked to it by means of another small-bore metal pipe, which, passing through the machine, continued for a short distance up the shaft and then abruptly disappeared into the face of a blank wall. It was obvious at a glance that this wall completely terminated the shaft.

For a moment Meredith stood stock-still, contemplating these perplexing factors, then with a sharp cry of realization he bent double and raced back up the shaft. Whipping out his flexible steel rule, he began to measure up the length of the tunnel from the base of the vertical shaft to the wall through which the pipe so mysteriously vanished. This done, he jotted down the result in his note-book and called on the constable to follow him.

In a couple of shakes he had gained the top of the cat-ladder, where he perched, for a moment, staring out through the cupboard door into the room.

"Now then, Railton," he called down, "I'm going to hold out my arm in what I consider to be the direction of that shaft. I want you to stand directly below me and correct me if I'm wrong. Ready?"

"Right, sir."

Meredith flung out his arm.

"Well?"

After an upward glance, the constable stared down the lighted vista of the shaft, then back again at the Inspector's rigid limb.

"A few degrees left, sir. Not much. Whoa! That's it."

"So?" thought Meredith, following the line of his out-stretched arm across the sitting-room, out through one of the front windows, across the garden to the corner of the garage building. He glanced at his watch. Ten minutes to four. Unless anything unforeseen occurred, Higgins would not return for another forty minutes, at least. Time enough, he felt, in which to prove his supposition up to the hilt.

He looked down on to the head of the waiting constable.

"Look here, Railton—I've got to take another measurement. In the meantime, I want you to draw off a sample of that spirit. I shoved a medicine bottle into my pocket. Here it is—catch!"

Leaning over the little well, he dropped the bottle neatly into the constable's hands.

"There's probably a tap in that container. I didn't notice at the time. As soon as you've done that, turn off the light down there, get these stones back into place and re-fix the false sill. Then get to work with your fancy bits of wire and relock the cupboard door. After that, if I'm not back, join me outside."

The moment he had delivered these instructions Meredith fixed his eye on the flue-pipe of the office stove, brought the centre frame of the casement in line with it and began to measure up along this imaginary line. The distance from the cupboard to the skirting-board under the window proved to be a little over twelve feet. Adding to this another foot to include the thickness of the cottage walls, he clambered out through the open window in the scullery and ran round to the front of the house. Again he took a line of sight. Standing directly in front of the centre frame of the casement, he now brought the trunk of an apple-tree, which he had previously marked down in the room as being a point on his imaginary line, into alignment with the flue-pipe projecting from the garage roof. Keeping the trunk always in front of the pipe, he then measured up from under the window to the foot of the tree. Fourteen feet. He made a note of it. He next strode through the wicket gate, which gave on to the cinder track dividing the side of the garage from the garden wall. Taking up his position at a point somewhere below the flue-pipe, he then brought the trunk into line with the middle of the casement. Then, working toward the trunk, he measured up between the wall of the garage and the apple-tree. This time he noted down ten feet.

He was now faced with a problem. How was he to project his imaginary line through the corner of the building and take the necessary measurements? If only he had a ladder! Surely it was within the bounds of possibility that there was a ladder lying about somewhere on the premises? With one eye on his watch, Meredith made a rapid search of the cottage back-garden and the rear of the garage itself. Luck was with him. Lying flat on the ground, half overgrown with rank grass, was a short and rickety fruit ladder. It was a matter of seconds to rush it round to the front of the garage and set it up against the coping. In no time, perched on the top rung, he had brought the flue-pipe, the apple-tree and the casement into line again. Then, climbing up on to the flat roof, allowing a foot for the overhang of the coping at each arm of the angle, he took the necessary measurement. Before descending, he placed his tweed cap on the edge of the coping, thus forming a fourth point along his imaginary line. The rest was simple. Backing out into the road, he brought one of the petrol pumps into alignment with the cap and the flue-pipe, and, with his heart in his mouth, began to take his final measurement. His previous measurements had accounted for forty-five of the tunnel's fifty-seven feet. He had, therefore, exactly twelve feet to play with. And if the distance from the rear of the pump to the base of the wall beneath his cap proved to be within a foot or so of twelve feet—well ... so much the worse for Messrs. Bettle and Prince!

It was one of the most intensely exciting moments of his career when Meredith laid out his flexible rule for the final reading. And when his anticipation gave way to complete realization he experienced that sort of thrill which comes only once or twice in a man's lifetime. His supposition was right! *The underground shaft terminated at a point some three feet behind the Nonock pump!* And that three feet would be occupied by one half of the underground petrol-tank! Which meant that the small-bore pipe from the still disappeared not into a blank cement wall, as he supposed, but through the cemented side of the petrol-tank itself! He now saw with absolute clarity the explanation for those confusing and spurious deliveries of petrol. The whole purpose of the bulk-wagon became apparent. What a fool he was not to have thought of it before! It was all Meredith could do to restrain his laughter. There he was again! Belittling himself because the problem appeared simple when the solution was in his hand. Naturally it did!

But he had not time to stand there juggling with the niceties of logic. He must fetch his cap from the coping and replace the ladder precisely where he had found it. He had only just finished covering up his tracks when the constable's portly form projected through the scullery window.

"Hurry up and close that sash," he called across. "It's just on four-thirty!"

"Coming, sir!" was the constable's cheery answer.

"Got that sample?" demanded Meredith as he was joined by his breathless subordinate.

"Yes, sir."

"Then let's get going, while the going's good. It's about time our friend turned up. We'd look a couple of prize idiots if he caught us here! Buckle into it! Start that engine."

The combination broke into a deep roar and shot off swiftly in the direction of Portinscale. And when some two hundred yards up the road a big Rover saloon swung round the corner, sped by and vanished up the road, Meredith broke into a chuckle.

"My Lord, sir!" exclaimed Railton, leaning over and shouting into the Inspector's ear. "That was a close shave!"

"It was," replied Meredith tersely. Then: "Railton," he added sternly, "your breath smells of whisky! Am I to infer that——?"

"Well, sir," began the constable with obvious reluctance.

"You did?" demanded Meredith.

The constable nodded.

"Just a nip, sir, by way of investigation. And, by jingo, it's got a kick in it! A kick in it like a mule!"

Meredith threw back his head and roared with laughter.

CHAPTER XIX

PIPES

AFTER his customary high tea at Greystoke Road, Meredith returned in a thoroughly agreeable mood to the police station. Punctually at six o'clock he put through his call to Carlisle and in a few moments was in touch with Superintendent Thompson. He then gave a concise, though graphic, résumé of his afternoon's activities; a report which, to judge by the warmth of his congratulations, evidently more than satisfied his superior.

"That's great news, Inspector. It looks as if the end of the case is in sight. Your next move, of course, is a re-examination of that bulk-wagon? Can you get that done to-night?"

"I'm hoping to, sir. I'll arrange with the Penrith station to run Dancy out to the depot with the keys."

"And what about that sample of the spirit?" was Thompson's next query.

"I sent it off at once to Maltman with a request for an immediate analysis. His report may give us an idea as to how the stuff is being planted on the public. Meredith laughed. "According to Railton, sir, I should imagine the stuff is somewhere round the region of a hundred over proof! But quite apart from his unofficial investigation, it's pretty obvious that the strength would have to be broken down. Then again, there's the matter of its maturity. The distillate is, as you probably know, sir, colourless. It doesn't take on the proper amber colour until it's been well matured in the wood. They must either store it somewhere until it's fit for use, or else add the colouration by artificial means. But I'm looking to Maltman for the necessary technical information."

"Quite right," agreed the Superintendent. "It's always best to get in an expert where possible. I suggest that you should concentrate on 'The Admiral', or one of the other five hotels, the moment you've cleared up your investigations of the lorry and the garages. But before you do that I think it advisable you should come over here early to-morrow morning and put in a verbal report to the Chief Constable. You know how keen he is on the personal touch in these matters."

"Right, sir. Nothing more?"

"No, Meredith. That's all. Let's say ten-thirty here to-morrow."

The moment the Superintendent had rung off, Meredith got through to Penrith and arranged for a police sidecar to bring Dancy out to the depot. He was to be there at seven o'clock with the necessary keys. Collecting Railton from the outer office, where Meredith had instructed him to be ready, the two men climbed into the combination and set off through the rain-fresh air to meet the yard-man.

Dancy and the Penrith constable were already waiting outside the depot gates. Not wanting the yard-man to be present during his vital investigations of the bulk-wagon, Meredith tactfully suggested that it would be as well if he and the Penrith constable kept watch on the road. Dancy then handed over the keys and Meredith, accompanied by Railton, unlocked the big corrugated-iron doors and entered the yard. Familiarity with the lay-out of the place enabled the Inspector to make straight tracks for the garage, and in a short time he and Railton were examining the lorry behind carefully fastened doors.

"Now then, Railton," said the Inspector brusquely, "I'll hold that torch, while you get down to work. We'll deal with this wooden box first. Can you pick the padlock all right?"

"I'll have a shot at it, sir. It shouldn't prove difficult."

After a brief inspection of the lock Railton drew out his array of little wires and got down to work. Now that he was nearing the final confirmation of his theory, Meredith was keyed-up to an intense pitch of anxiety. Everything depended on certain peculiarities of the feed-pipe and, despite an undercurrent of optimism, the Inspector dreaded that these peculiarities might prove to be absent. The constable's drawn-out operations roused him to a frenzy of impatience.

Then suddenly there came a welcome click and, with an exclamation of content, Railton thrust back the spring of the lock and drew it from the staple.

"Here, hold this," ordered Meredith eagerly, pushing the torch into the constable's hand.

Without wasting breath on further explanation, he pushed back the long lid and peered into the narrow trough. Side by side on the floor of the box lay two wire-and-canvas feed-pipes. Pulling out the one nearest to hand, Meredith up-ended it, snatched the torch from the puzzled constable and shone it directly into the mouth of the pipe. Then he let out a muffled oath. Here, at any rate, was nothing startling or confirmatory in the way of a clue. The pipe was exactly as one would have expected to find it. There was nothing unusual in its appearance or construction.

With a quickening pulse, Meredith realized that all his hopes were now centred on the second of the feed-pipes. If that failed him he was, once more, up against a hopeless blank wall.

But this time he was not to suffer disappointment. He plunged the rays of the torch up the inside of the tube and saw, in a flash, that his profoundest desires had been realized. He had imagined that pipe endowed with certain peculiarities and here, before his eyes, were those peculiarities made manifest. He swung round on Railton, who had been following his superior's action with a look of perplexity.

"Got it, Railton!" was his excited observation. "No mistake this time!" Then noting the blank look on the constable's face, he added in more sober tones: "Take a look at this pipe. Notice anything curious about its design?"

Railton craned over and examined it carefully.

Then: "Good heavens, sir!" he exclaimed. "There's a——!"

"Precisely," was Meredith's incisive comment. "Just as I thought there would be." He dumped the two pipes back into the box. "Now let's leave that for the moment and have a look at these discharge valves."

Followed by the constable, he moved round to the rear of the bulk-wagon and indicated the locked metal box which encased the outlet pipes.

"Can you manage this one as well, Railton?"

The constable thought that it should prove as simple a matter as the first padlock and, in less than a minute, the box was open and the three valves revealed.

Meredith was now in a mood of exhilaration and an examination of the three discharge pipes only served to heighten this mood. Everything was just as he had anticipated. Where before he *thought* his theory correct, he now *knew* it was. And the difference between these two mental states was the difference between failure and success.

Success, save for one small point. A point which, in the light of his sanguine mood, he had no doubt could be instantly cleared up. But for all that, it was not until he had made an exhaustive examination, not only of No. 4, but of the remaining five bolt-wagons, that Meredith finally hit on the answer to the problem. But by the time Railton had replaced the padlocks and covered up all traces of their search, he knew that, as far as the lorry was concerned, his investigations were at an end.

Inside ten minutes, after handing over the keys to Dancy and thanking him for his co-operation, Meredith and the constable were speeding back to Keswick.

Early the next morning the Inspector set out for Carlisle, and after an exhilarating drive through the balmy springtime air, he reached that historical, old, walled city just as the clocks were striking ten. Half an hour later a constable entered the Superintendent's office and said that the Chief Constable was ready to receive them.

When they were comfortably settled round the room Colonel Hardwick lit one of his inevitable Henry Clay's and signed for Meredith to go ahead with his report.

"Where do you want me to begin, sir?" was Meredith's respectful query.

The Chief Constable smiled.

"I have a predeliction for beginning at the beginning, Inspector, and then pursuing a story until I come to the end. Suppose you adopt that procedure now, eh?"

"In that case, sir, I'd better go back to Constable Gratorex's discovery at the Lothwaite because it was his report which first put me on to the track of a solution. You remember, sir, that up till that time we had an idea that the gang were engaged in the fraudulent sale of petrol. Well, this was all right as far as it went, but it didn't go far enough. In fact, all my investigations along that line seemed to end in a blank wall. There was no secret tank on the lorry capable of holding 200 gallons. There was no conceivable way of the lorry delivering short on its genuine orders. Yet we were up against the fact that amounts varying from two to four hundred gallons were apparently being delivered at certain garages on No. 4's route. The Superintendent then put forward an alternative theory. It was his idea that brandy or some other spirit was being smuggled into these coastal hotels which sported a Nonock pump. But as licensed premises are liable to Excise supervision, he thought that the brandy was being planted out on certain of the garages by means of the bulk-wagon." Meredith turned to the Superintendent. "That was your idea, sir?"

"It was," agreed Thompson. "And we embellished it with the further theory that the lorry was also used to convey small quantities of the brandy, probably in bottles, back to the coastal hotels. But go on, Inspector, you're telling the story."

Meredith turned back to the Chief Constable.

"Well, sir, we were up against one or two nasty snags. To begin with, we couldn't see how the brandy was dumped on the lorry from the hotels. We had the places under observation, but none of our men noticed anything suspicious about No. 4's calls at these particular places. We imagined it would be handled in small kegs. But as our men didn't spot anything in the shape of a keg, we had to search around for another explanation. Then again—nothing passed back out of the garages to the hotels. And to cap it all the expert opinion was that smuggling along that part of the coast would be extremely difficult, not to say impossible. The only bit of progress we made by following up this theory was that all the hotels were owned by the Bee's Head Brewery—and that Ormsby-Wright owned the brewery!"

The Chief gave vent to an exclamation of surprise. His interest deepened.

"Then I received Gratorex's report," went on Meredith. "He'd seen Wick, the proprietor of the Lothwaite, emptying something out of an oil-drum into the beck. I naturally went into the matter and the upshot of it was that I discovered the true nature of the racket. Perhaps the Superintendent has explained how I arrived at that conclusion, sir?"

The Chief Constable shook his head.

"I should have told you, Inspector—I've been up in London for the past week. Only came back late last night. In consequence,

I'm not exactly up to date in the affair. So you'd better let me have the details."

Thus prompted, Meredith went on to describe his experiment with the box-frame, the collecting of the tell-tale sediment and Maltman's analysis of the residue. He then explained how he had discovered a beck in the near neighbourhood of each of the four suspected garages and how he now had conclusive evidence that illicit distilling was being carried on by the proprietors of these four places.

"You knew, of course, sir, that we had found out about this illicit whisky-making?"

"Just the bare fact, Meredith. No details, naturally. The Superintendent rang through on my return last night."

"Well, sir, once we had established this fact the rest was fairly easy. I faked a means to get Higgins away from the Derwent and made a methodical search of the premises. In the floor of a locked and empty cupboard I found a cleverly concealed trapdoor. Beneath this I found the still—the whole apparatus for large-scale distilling operations."

Meredith then went on to describe the salient points about the subterranean distillery, the type of still in use, its proximity to the sitting-room chimney, the strange tunnel driven out from the vertical shaft and the small-bore pipe which ran along the cement wall. When he had created a graphic picture of the place, he switched over to his interpretation of the various peculiarities which he had noticed during his search.

"One thing puzzled me at once. At some distance from the still I found a second glass container. I couldn't see the point of conveying the whisky from one underground point to another. At least, sir, not until I noticed the electric drum-pump a couple of yards away."

"A drum-pump!" exclaimed the Chief. "What on earth for, Meredith?"

"To pump the spirit up through the petrol tank, sir."

"But why spoil excellent spirit by pumping it into a tank full of petrol?"

"Not into—but *through* the tank, sir. The pipe passed through the side of the petrol tank and then curved up into the mouth of the countersunk intake pipe behind the Nonock pump!"

"Good Heavens! I see now what you're hinting at. The lorry received the spirit while it was discharging the petrol?"

"Exactly, sir. Mind you, I haven't actually been able to set eyes on this section of the spirit-pipe, but I'm dead certain that when we can make the necessary examination, we shall find it there right enough."

"In other words, Meredith, you've picked up the footprints on the other side of the stream? Is that it?"

"Very neatly put, sir," laughed the Inspector. "That's exactly what I did do. Last night I made a second examination of the bulk-wagon. Inside the feed-pipe I found a second small-bore pipe, coinciding exactly with the diameter of the pipe which passed in through the side of the Derwent's petrol tank. Finally to clinch the whole business, I discovered a similar pipe inside the centre of the three discharge valves at the rear of the lorry. This was fitted with a curiously designed union nut, obviously made so as to prevent any vestige of the petrol getting into the spirit. I imagine that the section which emerges into the mouth of the garage intake pipe is fitted with a similar union. I'm not an expert on engineering matters, but it looked to me as if a very simple operation would enable the lorry-men to connect up the small-bore pipe, whilst to all apparent purposes they were just coupling up the petrol feed-pipe. Essential, of course, since they depended on this genuine link with the garages to cover up the hidden link inside the bigger pipe." Meredith paused and looked across at the Chief. "I hope I've made all this clear, sir?"

"Startlingly so!" was Colonel Hardwick's smiling reply. "One of the neatest criminal arrangements I've ever come across. But don't let me interrupt, Inspector. You'd traced the whisky as far as the discharge valves at the rear of the bulk-wagon. Then where did it go?"

"Well, sir, as far as I could see there was only one place where it could go. But for the life of me I couldn't see exactly how they wangled it. Mr. Weymouth, the Penrith Weights and Measures official, had already proved to us that the tank itself was in order. It had been certified to contain 1,000 gallons and according to his calculations it couldn't contain *more* than 1,000. So I naturally ignored the tank and concentrated on the bodywork and chassis. Then I made my final discovery. I grant you, sir, I haven't yet been able to prove my supposition up to the hilt, but I think you'll agree with me that I'm on to what might be called a 'probable certainty'. I don't know if you're familiar with the design of the Nonock bulk-wagons, sir?"

The Chief shook his head.

"Hardly in my province, Meredith. But I daresay I'll catch hold of your explanation all right. At any rate, go slowly and I'll try!"

"It's like this, sir," went on Meredith. "The tank itself is circular. It's rather like a slice out of an enormous tree trunk."

"A large cylinder, in fact," put in the Chief.

"The very word I was looking for! Well, on the bulk-wagons the base of this cylinder projects through the floor." Catching the puzzled expression on the face of both the Chief Constable and the Superintendent, Meredith went on hastily.

"Let me explain like this, sir. Imagine a long, narrow picture frame with a long, narrow tin fitting into it in such a way that the majority of the tin is above the frame. Then to keep that tin steady two long narrow wedges are fixed on either side of it."

"Go on," prompted the Chief Constable.

"Well, in the case of the lorry, these two long, narrow wedges are, as you can imagine, pretty big. They run the length of the tank and are made of stout wood reinforced with a series of iron brackets. At first glance I naturally thought they would be solid. The weight of the tank obviously called for a pretty strong sort of support. Well, sir, to cut a long story short I found that on all the other lorries, save No. 4, these wedges *were* solid. Solid wedges of wood cut out in one piece. But in the case of No. 4 there was no doubt left in my mind that they were hollow. When I rapped them I got quite a different note. And thinking things over I came to the conclusion that these wedges were ostensibly of wood, whilst actually they had been constructed of metal with a thin veneer of wood over the outer surface. I further argued that when the whisky-pipe had passed through the centre discharge valve it divided, passed through the two sides of the tank and discharged the spirit into the hollow wedges! About as neat an arrangement as one could wish for!"

"Perfect!" exclaimed the Chief Constable with a delighted chuckle. "The very simplicity of the scheme was its chief safe-guard against discovery. The only thing which perplexes me is why the trick was not found out at the depot. Surely there are *some* honest men in the Nonock company?"

"I think you're right about that, sir. Ormsby-Wright wouldn't be such a fool as to let too many into his secret. In my opinion there's only Rose, Bettle and Prince who are in the know. The rest work with petrol only!"

"Then how do they manage it?"

"Like this, sir. At every point where that small-bore pipe could be seen, it was boxed in and locked and the key held by the lorry-men. Take the garage intake-pipe first. It's protected by a metal cap and the cap is secured to the pipe by a padlock. The Nonock men hold the key. The feed-pipe itself is kept in a wooden box, again secured by a padlock and again Bettle and Prince held the key. Finally, the discharge valves are encased in a locked metal box and, once more, the key is in possession of the lorry-men. This is the normal arrangement, sir. It applies to the men on *all* the bulk-wagons, and as each driver and his mate are responsible for their own bulk-wagon, it stands to reason that the trick couldn't come to light."

"Well, Inspector," said the Chief Constable, rising and glancing at his watch, "it's been a most interesting half-hour. I'm pleased, very pleased with the progress you've made in the case. We're in a position now to make a wholesale arrest, but I've a strong feeling that it wouldn't be in the best of our interests to do so. And for two very good reasons. First we've still got to find out how the whisky is being taken in by the pubs and how it is being planted on the public. Both very necessary investigations if we're to lay our hands on the proprietors of the hotels. Secondly—there's the murder case—the major case, of course. I understand that you've come to a standstill in that direction?"

Meredith nodded glumly.

"True enough, sir—unfortunately."

"Well, I'm not going to lay down any hard and fast rules for your procedure. I'm going to leave the *modus operandi* to you. You've got the details of the case at your finger-tips. I haven't.

But I'll just say this—I want results! Don't let your satisfaction at the solution of the first problem cool your ardours in pursuit of the second. Talk things over with the Superintendent and keep me posted up to date with your progress in the case. That's all, gentlemen. Thank you."

"ONE thing's certain, Inspector. They're not selling the distilled spirit directly to the public. There must be an intermediary process."

Meredith and Maltman were seated in the latter's office at Turnpike Road. They were busy trying to evolve a theory as to how Ormsby-Wright was planting his illicit whisky on the public. Maltman had made an overnight analysis of the sample which Meredith had sent him and they were now trying to base their theory on the facts deduced from the results of this analysis.

"What makes you think that?" asked Meredith.

"Well, the distillate is somewhere round the region of sixty-five over proof. Do you know anything about the maturing and blending of whisky?" Meredith shook his head. "The matured spirit generally varies from genuine proof to ten over proof. The distillate is broken down, matured in sherry casks to get rid of the fusel oil and when ready for consumption, stored in bond. It's usually bottled and labelled in bond and then distributed to the retailers. So we can be certain that this illicit stuff is broken down with water before it goes over the counters of the pubs."

"*If* it goes over the counters," put in Meredith cautiously. "We're only assuming that the Bee's Head tied houses are mixed up in the racket. We don't know. It's possible the stuff is being sold privately. Say to shady night clubs, or even private individuals."

"Quite," acknowledged Maltman. "But that doesn't alter the fact that it's got to be broken down. No man would be such a fool as to sell spirit at sixty-five over proof, when by simply adding the requisite amount of water he could make the stuff go four or five times as far. Then again—what about the maturing? Any man with a palate could detect raw spirit at the first sip. To say nothing of the colouring. The distillate is opaque. Matured spirit is amber. So they've either got to let it mature in the normal way or else add some form of colouring matter. In other words—somewhere or other this illicit spirit is going through another process before it's being handed on to the public. The question remains, how is it being done and where?"

"Exactly. Any ideas yourself, Mr. Maltman?"

"Well," began Maltman slowly. "I see a way in which it *could* be done. I lay awake until the small hours last night, trying to unravel this particular knot. In the end I was left with two possible explanations."

"And the first?" asked Meredith.

"Yours," replied Maltman shortly. "Sale by private treaty, as it were. Suppose Ormsby-Wright gets the lorry to dump the raw spirit at one of his tied houses. There it's secretly broken down with water, coloured, probably with caramel, bottled and labelled and then secretly sold to private individuals at about twice the cost of manufacture. As you know, the duty on a 12s. 6d. bottle of whisky is 8s. 4d. So I reckon that if our friend sold the stuff at 3s. 6d. a bottle he'd net a handsome profit for himself and more than satisfy his customer at the same time. Of course, there are snags in this scheme."

"The labelling, for example," suggested Meredith. "What about that?"

"Well, if it was for private consumption that wouldn't matter. Nor would it enter in if the stuff were being sold at night clubs. There's no need to produce the bottle every time you sell a whisky and soda is there? On the other hand it would be quite easy to print off labels of a recognized brand and stick 'em on the bottles. The only danger in that scheme would be if some connoisseur cottoned on to the fraud and lodged a complaint with the genuine firm."

"Such an obvious danger," put in Meredith, "that it looks as if the scheme would be knocked on the head at the start."

"That's my opinion," went on Maltman. "Now let's come to my second theory. Suppose the raw spirit is dumped at the tied houses, broken down to somewhere between genuine proof and ten over proof, and then blended with a recognized brand. The chances of the fraud being detected then are pretty remote. See the point? One bottle of genuine whisky is made to net the profit of two!"

Meredith whistled.

"I see what you mean! The seal on a genuine bottle is broken and half the whisky decanted into a second bottle, also bearing the label of a recognized brand. The deficit in each bottle is then made up with the diluted raw spirit and two bottles of genuine whisky are sold over the counter instead of one!"

Maltman nodded. He was obviously pleased with the Inspector's acute interest in his suggestion.

"Think of the profit!" he went on emphatically. "Just think of it! At a guess I should say that the illicit stuff could be turned out at about ninepence a quart bottle. Say a shilling to cover the overhead charges. In other words, on every two bottles of the half-and-half spirit sold, Ormsby-Wright nets a clear 11s. 6d., plus the normal profit made by the retailer on two quart bottles of genuine whisky. Man! It's a colossal scheme! All those tied houses do a roaring counter trade, to say nothing of what they do in the off-licence department. The Bee's Head places probably retail the stuff to half the private houses in the district! To say nothing of Working Men's Clubs, Public Functions and Dances. I wouldn't dare make a guess at his yearly profits from the ramp. They must be staggering!"

Meredith grinned affably at the thinly disguised note of admiration in Maltman's voice. It was obvious that the Excise Officer was carried away by the subtle manner in which the spirit duty was being evaded. It appealed, no doubt, to the professional side of his nature.

"Hang the profits, Maltman! I'm not concerned in how much Ormsby-Wright makes out of this racket. I want to know exactly how he does it. You suggest a secret blending and bottling department in one of the tied houses?"

"Or in all of them," cut in Maltman quickly.

"All of them if you like. But the question remains, have you ever had a hint of these illegal operations when you were making your usual tour of inspection of the premises? You haven't, eh? Just as I thought. Yet you still persist in your theory?"

"I do. You must remember that I'm more concerned with checking-up the stock in hand rather than nosing around for an illicit bottling department."

"And your checking-up always tallied with the proprietor's books, of course?"

"Naturally. The man wouldn't be such a fool as to show more stock than he had taken out, under our supervision, from bond. He'd keep the extra spirit hidden away until it was needed and then pop it over the counters to the public."

"What about his sale returns?"

"Nothing doing, Inspector. An Excise official has no entry to a publican's books. It's his duty to keep a check on the actual stock and premises. Nothing more."

"Suppose your supposition is right. What action would you suggest that we take?"

Maltman considered the point carefully for a moment, toying with the pens and pencils on his desk. Then he looked up and suggested:

"Why not buy a bottle of whisky from 'The Admiral'? We could then compare it with a genuine bottle of the same brand bought at a safe place. If on analysis we can prove that the blend has been tampered with—well, that's all we need know, isn't it?"

"A sure test, you think?"

"Not absolutely," admitted Maltman. "Blends of the same brand vary. But the difference in this case would be too marked to leave us much in doubt."

Meredith nodded.

"That would certainly take us part of the way but not the whole road. We'd still have to prove that the stuff was being tampered with on the premises."

Maltman laughed and looked across at the Inspector with a knowing look in his twinkling eyes.

"In other words—a search of the premises! All right, Inspector. I'm game—if that's what you're after. When shall it be?"

"To-day?"

"Good enough. We'll tackle 'The Admiral'. I'm about due to take a look round there, so our appearance won't start a panic. Are you known in this district? You're not? Good! Then you're being trained up to the job of Excise official. I'm showing you the ropes. You're a bit old for an apprentice but we'll let that pass. Shall we say two-thirty outside 'The Admiral'?"

"Splendid! I want to have a word with the local Superintendent, then I'll get some lunch and meet you outside the pub." Meredith rose and grabbed up his hat from Maltman's untidy desk. "And if we don't find something startling it won't be for the want of trying!"

And after the exchange of a few bantering remarks he jumped on to the saddle of his motor-cycle and headed for the Whitehaven police station.

At two-thirty, after an excellent lunch, Meredith turned into the top of Queen Ann Street and sauntered toward the imposing façade of the old-fashioned hotel. Maltman was already waiting for him under the glass awning of the entrance to the saloon-bar.

"We'll have to go in through the hotel," he explained. "It's after closing-time. Let me do the talking in case Beltinge—that's the proprietor—asks any awkward questions. I don't think he will, but be on your guard."

The Inspector nodded and the two men passed into the dark and dingy reception-hall. Maltman, who knew his way about, turned down a long panelled corridor and rapped smartly on a door labelled "Office". A wheezy voice bade them enter.

Mr. Beltinge was seated in an arm-chair before a roaring fire with a sheaf of papers on his lap. He was a moon-faced, unhealthy, stout individual with long, drooping moustaches and tiny black eyes. On seeing Maltman he rose cumbersomely from his chair and extended a podgy hand.

"Afternoon, Mr. Maltman. A pleasant surprise this! I was wondering when you were going to take it into your head to look us up again. Take a pew, won't you?" He cast an inquiring glance at Meredith. "And you too, sir."

Maltman shook his head.

"We really haven't got time to spare, thanks all the same, Mr. Beltinge. I'd like to do the round straight away, if it's all the same to you. Let me introduce Mr. Johnson to you. He's working in with me for a time. Learning up the practical side of the Excise business."

"Pleased to meet you," wheezed Beltinge. "You'll excuse all this litter, but I'm behind-hand with my books. Sorry you can't stay for a chat, but I know what busy chaps you officials are! Do you want me to come round with you, Mr. Maltman?"

"No thanks. There's really no need. Just a routine inspection. If you'll give me the usual details of your stock and all the rest of it, we'll just wander round on our own."

Beltinge waved a plump hand toward the scattered papers. "Good! Suits me fine! And I reckon you know your way about the old place better than I do, Mr. Maltman." He rummaged in his desk and produced the necessary invoices. These he handed to Maltman, together with a labelled bunch of keys.

"There we are, gentlemen," he said with a husky chuckle. "And I hope you find everything in order."

"Sure of that," returned Maltman affably. "But England expects and all the rest of it! Well, see you later, Mr. Beltinge."

The moment the door was closed Maltman caught the Inspector by the arm and walked him rapidly down the corridor. "We'd better snap into it," he explained. "We daren't take too long, else we shall rouse the blighter's suspicions. This way!"

Unlocking a stout oak door, Maltman switched on an electric light and they plunged down a long flight of stone steps into the dry coolness of the cellars. Meredith made out long rows of fat barrels ranged along the walls, bins full of straw-hooded wine bottles and piles of beer crates stacked high in one corner.

"We won't waste time here," suggested Maltman. "This is the main cellar. I doubt if they'd tamper with the walls here—too conspicuous."

He crossed the cellar, passed through a stone arch and vanished into a second, smaller cellar which lay beyond. Acutely excited, under his cloak of official calm, Meredith followed. He saw at a glance that this second cellar was full of barrels. All manner of barrels—ranging from tiny kegs to enormous, iron-hooped casks. The air was redolent with the pungent odour of beer. High up in the left wall was a small grille, through which streamed a pale wash of April sunlight.

Meredith seized on this at once.

"Where does that give on to? Any idea, Maltman?"

The garage yard, I imagine. Here, steady this barrel while I take a look." With surprising agility Maltman sprang on to the top of an up-ended cask, caught hold of the bars of the grille and pulled himself up until his eyes were level with the opening. "I'm right," he announced. "This wall flanks the end of the yard. I can see straight out into Jackson's Mews. We're just about under the lock-up garages."

"And the Nonock pump? Can you see that?"

"Yes. It's about eighteen to twenty feet from this grille."

"Good!" exclaimed Meredith. "So if the spirit is being passed into the secret vault via the petrol pump, the entrance must be somewhere in this particular wall?"

"Looks like it," agreed Maltman as he regained terra firma. "Suppose we start one at each end and run the tape over it."

Without wasting a moment they got down to work.

Except for three or four large casks firmly fixed on trestles the wall was blank. It presented no buttresses or recesses, but stretched from one side of the cellar to the other, an unbroken, whitewashed wall of stone. But Meredith refused to be disheartened by its apparent solidity. Snatching up a spigot from the floor he began, with his usual thoroughness, to sound every inch of the surface. For ten minutes he and Maltman continued with this task until every stone in the wall had been meticulously tested. But the result was nil. Every stone seemed to be tightly cemented in place and there was no suggestion of hollowness in the whole length of the wall.

"Well, that's that!" observed Maltman, unable to keep the disappointment out of his voice. "What now?"

"The floor," replied Meredith tersely. "There might be a trap leading to a shaft driven under the wall. That would account for its apparent solidity, anyway. If there is a trap I think we can rely on it being this side of the cellar. They wouldn't want to make that shaft longer than was absolutely essential. Suppose we test a strip eight feet wide? That should tell us if we're on the right track or not."

"Right!" said Maltman incisively. "Let's jump to it!"

Another ten minutes of frantic tapping and listening followed. But the result was the same. Everything was normal. There was no trap in the floor—not even the slightest suggestion of hollowness.

"Confound it," exclaimed Meredith. "I'm sure there's an opening here somewhere. It *might* run out of the main cellar, of course, with a right-angled shaft to bring it to the rear of the Nonock pump. But this seems the obvious place. Twenty feet from the pump! We *must* be right, Maltman!"

"Doesn't look as if we are, for all that," commented the excise official. "We've been over every inch of that wall and along this strip of the flooring. And there's not——"

"Hold on!" exclaimed Meredith, clipping his fingers. "You've given me an idea. You say that we've been over *every inch* of that wall?"

"Well, we have!"

Meredith shook his head.

"That's just where you're wrong. We haven't! What about those barrels? There's a circular spot behind each of those casks that we haven't tested. "Come on, Maltman, help me to drag these trestles away from the wall. I shan't be satisfied with our test until we've had a look behind the barrels."

Seizing hold of the first trestle they tugged with all their might. The trestle refused to budge.

"Good heavens," cried Maltman. "They're fixed. Look, they're clamped on to the stone!"

"And the barrels are clamped on to the trestles," added Meredith. "Surely that isn't usual, Maltman?"

"Extraordinary," said Maltman in puzzled tones. "I can't quite see——"

But wasting no time on further speculation he suddenly strode down the line of casks, sounding them with the toe of his boot.

"Three full—one empty," was his report.

"Which is the empty one?" asked Meredith.

"This one. The third from your end. But I still don't see——"

But Meredith made no attempt to enlighten the mystified official. He was already kneeling in front of the empty cask tugging at the circular end into which the wooden spigot had been driven. Suddenly the whole end of the barrel gave way and Meredith all but fell backwards on to the floor of the cellar.

Maltman took an excited step forward and peered into the yawning hole.

"But, good heavens!" was his excited observation, "there's no——"

"Exactly," snapped Meredith. "There's no back to the barrel. Just as I anticipated. And I'll tell you why there isn't any back to the barrel—because this particular cask is the entrance to that shaft we were looking for. Clever, eh?"

"You mean?" stuttered the amazed Maltman.

"I mean that if we crawl through this barrel we shall eventually find outselves in that secret blending and bottling department. No wonder we got no reaction from the wall itself. We shouldn't. The vault probably lies behind a good thick slab of mother earth. Our friends weren't taking any chances. At any rate, don't let's stand here theorizing. We've only got to crawl through that barrel to make certain." Meredith glanced at his watch. "We've been down here for about twenty-five minutes. Is it safe to stay any longer?"

Maltman, after a quick consideration of the point, thought that it was. At his suggestion, however, Meredith was to crawl through the barrel, whilst he, Maltman, fitted the false end into place. Then if anybody should come down into the cellar the Excise man would merely be about his official duties. If Beltinge turned up, Maltman would be ready with an explanation to account for Meredith's absence.

This line of action decided on, Meredith, with a joking remark about obstacle races, crawled on all-fours into the cask and disappeared into the hole which had been driven through the wall. No sooner was he well inside when Meredith heard Maltman refixing the false lid and the last vestiges of light were swallowed up by complete darkness. Groping for his torch, he clicked it on and directed the rays down the narrow, arch-shaped tunnel which ran away in front of him. Although it was very airless and uncomfortable in the shaft, the cement floor was dry and the bricked arch which supported the earth comparatively clean. On his hands and knees Meredith made rapid progress to where he had already noticed a slight bend in the tunnel. Turning this corner, he came suddenly on the very thing he was looking for! The shaft continued for about another eight feet and then terminated in a small, square vault!

Gaining this vault, he was able to straighten up and take stock of his surroundings. A single glance sufficed to show that he had reached, as it were, the very nerve-centre of the racket. The little cellar was chock full of whisky bottles, some full, some empty, some labelled, some ready for labelling. Crates filled with capped and sealed bottles lay piled one on top of the other along one wall. In a corner stood a small table on which were stacked little bundles of labels and boxes of metal caps. A pot of gum, one or two wire-brushes for cleaning the bottles, several squares of wash-leather, two or three glass funnels, a couple of graduated beakers and a large tank full of water completed the apparatus. Above the tank was a tap, obviously connected up in some secret way with the water-main which supplied the hotel. From the right wall projected a short length of small-bore metal pipe, which curved down into a glass container half-full of raw spirit. Meredith saw at a glance that the principle in action here was the same as that he had seen at the Derwent. It was evident that the small-bore pipe passed through the cement side of the petrol tank and thus up into the mouth of the countersunk intake in the yard above. If he had had any doubts as to how this end of the business was being managed, now they no longer existed. Maltman's second theory was right. It meant that genuine whisky was being blended with the diluted products of the illicit stills and sold as *bona fide* stuff over the counters of the public house above.

All the unused labels bore the wording and trade marks of recognized brands. The empty, unlabelled bottles were similar in shape and size to those favoured by certain genuine whisky distilleries. What could be simpler? thought Meredith. With a good supply of labels, bottles and illicit liquor, the ramp could be carried on wholesale. And if the other five tied houses belonging to Ormsby-Wright were fitted up in the same way, the profits from the racket must be enormous.

Only waiting long enough to verify the contents of the glass container, Meredith crawled into the shaft and worked his way back as fast as he could to the barrel. Once inside it, he stopped dead and listened. There were no voices. Only the sound of Maltman's measured footsteps passing up and down the stone floor. Softly he tapped on the end of the cask.

"Right," came Maltman's low answer. "It's all O.K."

Meredith felt him tugging at the false end of the barrel and the next minute the Inspector was standing upright in the cellar.

"Well?" demanded Maltman, excitedly.

"It's the goods right enough," was Meredith's quick answer. "Tell you about it later."

"I was right?" Meredith nodded. "I thought as much. Now we'd better leg it as quick as we can back to old Beltinge's office. We've been down here just three-quarters of an hour. He may smell a rat. Come on, Inspector."

Together they raced up the cellar steps and, at a more demure pace, passed down the panelled corridor to the proprietor's office.

Beltinge greeted them with an expansive smile and held out his hand for the keys and invoices.

"Well, Mr. Maltman—everything in order? No complaints, I take it?"

"Nairy a one, Mr. Beltinge."

"That's good. Would either of you gentlemen care to join me in a spot of Scotch?"

Maltman and Meredith exchanged glances.

"Well, speaking for myself, I'm not averse to the suggestion. What about you, Johnson?"

"Every time," replied Meredith with a broad grin.

"Good stuff this," said Maltman when he had set down his glass.

"It is that, Mr. Maltman. We only stock the best brands, as you know. Inferior quality spirit never pays in the long run. My customers want the best and I see that they get it."

"And a very sound business motto it is!" commented Maltman. Then, thrusting out his hand:

"Well, we won't keep you from your figures. You look as if you're snowed under with work."

"See you some time, I expect, Mr. Maltman." Beltinge turned his moon-face in Meredith's direction. "And you, too, sir, if you haven't left the district. Drop in any time you like. There's always an odd spot locked away in the cupboard, you know."

"Thanks," said Meredith. "I daresay we shall meet again all right. Good day, Mr. Beltinge."

Once out of sight of the Admiral, Maltman turned on the Inspector and burst out laughing.

"Poor devil! The irony of your last remark was entirely wasted on him. I reckon he'd sleep ill o' nights if he so much as guessed what you were hinting at. But tell me—what exactly did you find, Inspector? I'm dying to hear."

When Meredith had concluded his story, Maltman whistled.

"So you've now got 'em by the short hairs, eh? Looks to me as if the case is at an end."

"It is," agreed Meredith. "*That* case."

"Is there another?"

"You're forgetting that a man named Clayton was found murdered in his garage on the night of March twenty-third. What about that little packet of trouble?" Meredith sighed. "If only I could find a stepping-stone across the stream. Known facts on both sides with nothing to link them together. That's the situation. And between you and me, I don't think we ever *shall* find that stepping-stone, Maltman. The scent's grown cold."

CHAPTER XXI

RECONSTRUCTION OF THE CRIME

WHEN Meredith had put in his report to Thompson that evening a late phone call came through from Carlisle bidding him attend a conference at headquarters the following morning. He wondered what was in the air. Did it mean that the Chief had decided on the gang's immediate arrest, in the belief that Clayton's murderer would never be run to earth? The crime had been committed over a month ago, and, except for a few unconnected clues, Meredith was no nearer a solution of the mystery. He *believed* that Prince and Bettle were mixed up in the affair. But he could not prove it. He *believed* that the motive for the murder was rooted in the gang's determination to silence a man who might turn King's Evidence. But again there was no proof. Facts without proof. That was the situation in a nutshell.

It was with a mixed feeling of trepidation and curiosity, therefore, that Meredith knocked on the door of the Chief Constable's office the next morning. Was he to be congratulated in bringing one half of the case to a successful conclusion? Or was he to be hauled over the coals for his inability to lay his hands on the murderer?

Colonel Hardwick's first words dispelled his uneasiness. The Chief, seated at his desk behind the inevitable blue haze of cigar-smoke, beamed all over his face as the Inspector entered.

"This is great news, Meredith. I can't tell you how pleased I was to get your report last night. I didn't expect you to get a conclusive result so quickly. Anyhow, sit down and put on a pipe. You too, Thompson. We've got one or two rather tricky problems to discuss and my time's unfortunately limited."

"First of all, Inspector, about this man, Ormsby-Wright. I'm having him shadowed. We can't afford to let him slip through our fingers, because it's pretty evident that he's the brain and boss of the racket. And once he'd got wind of our investigations, he'd be certain to nip across the Channel and bury himself in some ungodly corner of Europe. According to the report which came in yesterday, he's still living in his house at Penrith. Going about his usual business in a perfectly normal sort of way. Obviously unsuspicious of our attentions. So far so good. The question remains, how long do we dare hold up the arrests, in order to give you time to complete your investigations of the murder case? As our future actions hinge on this point, suppose we run over the various facts which you have discovered and see if we've missed anything. Agreeable, Meredith?"

"Perfectly, sir."

"Very well, then—let's see what we know." The Chief picked up a few sheets of paper from his desk and slipped on his reading glasses. I spent yesterday evening tabulating your isolated bits of evidence. The result runs briefly like this. (1) *On the night of the crime No. 4 bulk-wagon called at the Derwent. It delivered petrol on its inward journey instead, as one would expect, on the outward. Why? It arrived after dark at the Derwent owing to engine-trouble. Was this engine-trouble faked so that the roads might be reasonably clear of traffic returning from the football match at Cockermouth? After leaving the Derwent we have conclusive proof that No. 4 parked for a few moments up a side-turning. Why? We know that the lorry could not have parked long up the side-turning because just before eight o'clock on the night of the crime a man named Burns saw the lorry speeding through Threlkeld on its homeward run to the depot.* So much for the lorry. Now for the next point. (2) *The hose-pipe. We know that the length of hose attached to the exhaust of Clayton's car came from the rubbish dump behind the Nonock depot. Care had been taken to conceal this fact and to suggest that the length had been cut from a hose-pipe hanging in an outhouse at the Derwent. The boot-blacking clue. Are we to infer, therefore, that the murderer was employed by the Nonock Company?* (3) *The broken glass. A very puzzling factor. Are we to dismiss it as irrelevant or try to find some connection between the broken glass and the crime?* Now what do *you* think about this, Meredith?"

Meredith pondered the question for a moment before making reply. He was not anxious to commit himself to an opinion, for the simple reason that the clue—if, indeed, it *was* a clue—had puzzled him quite as much as it had puzzled his Chief.

"Well, sir," he vouchsafed at length, "you've set me a bit of a poser. I certainly found the glass at a spot where the lorry, in all probability, parked, but it's beyond me to say if it has any actual bearing on the case. Dr. Burney had an idea that it might have been the shattered remains of some piece of chemical apparatus. Such as a test-tube or small flask or a retort. But I can't see what chemical apparatus has to do with the crime."

"Well, let's see if we can't forge a link," suggested the Chief. "Consider how Clayton met his death. He was asphyxiated by the inhalation of carbon-monoxide fumes. Are those facts in any way suggestive? What do you say, Thompson?"

The Superintendent smoked for a minute in silence.

Then: "I think I can see a way in which we could connect the glass with the crime, sir."

"You do. Good. Then let's hear it."

"Your marshalling of the facts has just put the idea into my head, sir. Chemical apparatus. Carbon monoxide. Isn't it possible that the gas had been manufactured by the murderer and the incriminating apparatus afterwards destroyed?"

"But why, Thompson? Why manufacture the carbon monoxide by chemical means when there was a perfectly good source of the poison in the exhaust of Clayton's car?"

Thompson shook his head.

"I can't answer that one, sir, I'm afraid."

"Well, we won't dismiss the idea. Suppose we look up carbon monoxide in the encyclopædia there, Meredith. On the shelf just above your head. Got it? Now turn to the Cs, and read out what it says about the stuff."

"*Carbon monoxide*," began Meredith, when he had found the required reference. "*Formerly known as carbonic acid. A gas formed during the combustion of——*"

"You can cut that," broke in the Chief with an impatient gesture. "All we want to know is how it is formed chemically."

Meredith ran his finger rapidly down the paragraph.

"Here we are, sir! *It is prepared in the laboratory by the action of concentrated sulphuric acid on oxalic acid.*"

"Good enough," commented the Chief. "Now, suppose the murderer did prepare the gas in this way. He'd probably have two small flasks. One containing sulphuric and the other oxalic acid. By pouring the contents of one flask into the other he'd get off carbon monoxide, which could be led off through a rubber tube terminating in a face-piece—say the kind used by dentists. He would then be in a position to asphyxiate his victim without having to resort to the exhaust-fumes of the car. But, if he did do this, I can't for the life of me see why."

"There's another point," broke in Thompson.

"Wouldn't the grass show some sort of stain where you found the broken glass, Meredith?"

"Not necessarily, sir," replied Meredith. "The murderer might have emptied the residue of the acids into a drain. He'd probably realize the danger of leaving a clue like that behind him."

"Now, gentlemen," cautioned the Chief Constable, "don't let's wander off up side tracks. We're going to assume that the murderer manufactured that carbon monoxide. What we want to know is, why did he go to all that trouble when there was a perfectly good flow of gas coming from the exhaust? Did he imagine that the car might not start up at the critical moment? Was the apparatus merely a second string to his bow? Or had he some mysterious reason for gassing Clayton first and sitting him in the car afterwards? But before we go into that question, suppose we consider the rest of the known facts. The fourth point on my list is marked—*Trional*. The keystone of the whole case, as I see it. For if Clayton hadn't been drugged, we shouldn't have felt so certain that he'd been murdered. Now the drug had to be administered in such a way that Clayton's suspicions weren't aroused. This, I think, is a strong argument in favour of the Bettle–Prince solution. They were both well-known to Clayton. From Major Rickshaw's evidence, we must suppose that the men were in the office when Clayton served him with petrol. I think we can assume that Clayton returned to the office, was offered a drink of whisky from a pocket-flask and engaged in conversation until the veronal took effect. So much for the drug.

"My fifth and last point is the motive for the crime. Now I've been over the case again and again in an attempt to shake my original theory. But for all that, I've found myself unable to supply a more feasible motive. I still hold to my original opinion—Clayton was murdered because the gang valued his silence at a higher price than his life." The Chief pushed aside his papers, capped them with a paperweight and sprawled back in his chair. "Well, there we are. Those are the known facts. Any questions?"

Meredith nodded. "About that chemical apparatus, sir. You don't think it possible that the murderer thought to gain time by using it instead of the exhaust?"

"I don't quite see how you mean, Inspector."

"This way, sir. If Prince and Bettle *did* murder Clayton, then the first thing which concerned them was the establishing of an alibi. They had to prove that they were back in the depot at a time which would have made it impossible for them to have committed the crime. In other words—they had to juggle with time in such a way as to make it look as if they left the Derwent *earlier* than they actually did. If you've no objection, sir, I'd like to tabulate the various events which took place on that Saturday night. Chronologically, I mean."

"Yes, do, Inspector. I'm still a trifle hazy about the all-important time-factor."

At the end of five minutes Meredith had made out a neatly written time-table, which he handed over to the Chief. It ran as follows:

5.45. *Lorry leaves the Lothwaite.*

6 o'clock (circa). *Braithwaite postman stops at Derwent.*

6.20 (circa). *Driver and fireman see lorry parked on roadside near Jenkin Hill.*

7.20. *Major Rickshaw and wife draw up for petrol at the Derwent. Served by Clayton. Lorry standing by pumps.*

7.35. *Freddie Hogg cycles past Derwent. Sees Clayton standing in garage entrance. Lorry gone.*

7.55. *Frank Burns sees lorry passing at high speed through Threlkeld.*

8.35. *Lorry arrives back at depot.*

"I think that makes it quite clear, sir," said Meredith when Colonel Hardwick had studied the paper. "You can see at a glance that we've got the lorry's movements pretty well pinned down. We know that it must have left the Derwent at some time between 7.20 and 7.35. And we can fairly safely say that before

7.35 it was parked up that side-turning—otherwise Freddie Hogg would have met it on his way back from the Keswick cinema."

The Chief agreed. "So far so good, Inspector; but how do these facts combine with the chemical apparatus supposition? I don't quite see what you're leading up to?"

"This, sir," explained Meredith. "My first theory was that Prince returned to the Derwent directly after Hogg had gone by, leaving Bettle up the side-turning with the parked lorry. I then reckoned it would take about forty-five minutes for Prince to administer the drug, wait for it to take effect, place Clayton in the car, start the engine and get back to the waiting lorry. This meant that the lorry would not set off for the depot until eight-twenty, arriving there about nine-thirty. But since we learnt from Dancy that the lorry actually arrived at the depot at eight-thirty-five, I immediately dismissed this reconstruction of the crime as impossible. But suppose Prince took advantage of the chemical apparatus? Suppose both Prince *and* Bettle returned to the garage, and that while Bettle held Clayton, Prince clapped the nozzle of the apparatus over Clayton's face and gassed him? He would be dead inside five minutes at the most. They then carry him to the car, sit him upright in the seat, start the engine and race back to the bulk-wagon. Say eight minutes to do the double journey between the lorry and the garage. Five minutes to actually commit the murder. Five minutes to arrange their victim in the car and start the engine. In all eighteen minutes. They would then start on their homeward run at about seven-fifty. And since we know that they arrived at the depot at eight-thirty-five, it means they covered the nineteen odd miles in forty-five minutes. The question is, could an empty bulk-wagon keep up an average of"—Meredith made a quick mental calculation—"some twenty-five miles per hour? What do you think, sir?"

The Chief considered the point for a moment.

Then: "Frankly," he said, "I don't think it could. The road, if I remember rightly, twists and turns a good bit. It was dark, too, and there are one or two nasty gradients on the run. What do you say, Thompson?"

"I'm of the same opinion," answered the Superintendent.

"And quite apart from the time factor, Inspector, you've omitted one important fact—the trional. What about that?"

Meredith clicked his fingers in annoyance.

"Confound it, sir! I'd completely forgotten about the drugging! It looks as if I've wandered up another of those damned *cul-de-sacs*!"

"Not so fast!" returned the Superintendent with a laugh. "I don't think there's any need to get disheartened ... yet. Your new theory has set me thinking along another line. Let's reconsider that time-table of yours. When you look into it, aren't you struck by one very significant fact?"

Meredith appeared puzzled. "I don't quite see——?"

"I'll explain," cut in Thompson. "You know roughly the time the lorry left the garage. You know exactly the time it arrived at the depot. But you haven't the faintest idea as to the time it *arrived at the Derwent*! You see, what I am leading up to? Isn't it possible that the murder was committed *before* the lorry left the garage?"

"Before!" exclaimed the Chief Constable, astonished.

"Before!" echoed Meredith, bewildered. "But that's impossible! What about Hogg's evidence? He saw Clayton standing in the garage after the lorry had left."

"Admittedly. Did he speak to Clayton?"

"He called out 'Good night.'"

"And did Clayton answer?"

"Yes. He waved his hand."

"Exactly!" snapped Thompson triumphantly. "But he didn't *speak*! See what I mean? How are we to know for certain that the man Hogg saw at seven-thirty-five *was* Clayton? I suggest that he thought it was Clayton and that in reality it was Prince disguised to look like Clayton!"

"And the idea, Thompson?"

"Simple, sir," replied the Superintendent. "A gaining of time. As you pointed out just now, Inspector, Bettle and Prince had to suggest that they left the garage earlier than they did. Well, I uphold that they left the garage at the stated time. When they told you that they left at seven-thirty, they were speaking the truth. They did leave at that hour. But when they left, *Clayton was already dead and seated in the car*."

"But what about Major Rickshaw's evidence?" objected Meredith. "He swears that Clayton served him with petrol at seven-twenty. Surely the drug couldn't have been administered, the murder committed and the victim placed in the car inside a matter of ten minutes?"

"Quite. But if Hogg was deceived, why not Rickshaw? He didn't know Clayton personally. He saw a man who looked like Clayton and since he expected to be served by Clayton, he didn't trouble to think twice about it."

"In that case—?" demanded the Chief.

"In that case, sir, Bettle and Prince had almost unlimited time in which to commit the murder. We don't know the exact time they arrived at the Derwent. At six-twenty the train-driver saw them parked at Jenkin Hill, but after that we really know nothing at all about their movements. But suppose, for the sake of argument, we assume that they arrived at the Derwent at six-forty-five."

"Quite a reasonable assumption," commented the Chief. "Go on, Thompson."

"Well, sir, I see it something like this. No. 4 draws up at the garage. Prince connects with the pump, whilst Bettle retires with Clayton to the office. There he suggests a drink to keep out the cold. He produces the doped whisky from his hip-pocket. Clayton takes a good swig and Bettle pretends to follow suit. Prince, in the meantime, keeps a good look-out, whilst Bettle holds Clayton in conversation. At the end of twenty minutes the drug takes effect. The time now is about seven-five. Bettle signals to Prince, who hastily disguises himself as Clayton by means of a false moustache, felt hat and buff dungarees. He'd have these ready in the cab of the lorry of course. In the office they produce the carbon monoxide apparatus and asphyxiate Clayton. But the job is only just completed when Major Rickshaw draws up and orders a couple of gallons of petrol. Prince, on the alert, is already outside waiting to serve him. Shortly after seven-twenty Rickshaw drives off. The coast being clear, the two men hurriedly carry the dead man to the lean-to. Higgins has already fixed the hose-pipe over the exhaust, planted the mackintosh and the twine and locked the garage door. The key is hidden in a prearranged place. The murderers place the dead man at the wheel, clap the mackintosh over his head, stick the end of the pipe underneath it and tie the twine round his neck. Retaining the key, but leaving the door unlocked, Bettle pours the chemical residue down the drain, climbs up on to the lorry and drives off, whilst Prince hangs about in the lighted entrance to the garage. This part of their programme is all-important. It's essential that Clayton should appear alive and well *after* the lorry had left for Penrith. So Bettle parks up that side-turning, without lights, and waits until he sees somebody pass the end of the lane. Freddie Hogg, as it happens, on his way home from the Keswick cinema. The time now is seven-thirty-five. Hogg cycles by the garage, sees Prince and imagines him to be Clayton.

"Prince, aware that Hogg has taken a good look at him, waits until he is out of sight, then rushes to the shed and starts up the engine of Clayton's car. He closes the doors and races along the road to where Bettle, who has now smashed the flasks with a stone, is waiting with the lorry. Time, say seven-forty. The coast being clear, the lorry backs out on to the main road and speeds off on its homeward run. It arrives at the depot at eight-thirty-five—all perfectly normal, of course, since the stated time of their departure from the garage was seven-thirty. That's my reconstruction of the crime, sir. I don't know whether you'll agree with it or not. But it does, at any rate, incorporate and explain away nearly all the known facts."

The Chief Constable sat immobile for a moment drumming the rims of his reading-glasses against the desk. It was obvious that he was adjusting his mind so as to view the case from this entirely new angle.

At length he looked up and observed: "Impersonation, eh? Well, it's certainly a feasible explanation. You agree, Inspector?"

Meredith gave an emphatic nod.

"I do, sir. Wholeheartedly!"

"Still, it's very dangerous," went on the Chief in measured tones, "to accept a theory just because it fits so many of the known facts. You'll acknowledge that yourself, Thompson. On the other hand, it certainly opens up a new line of investigation. If we follow up these new assumptions, there's always a chance that we shall find proof to uphold them."

"I agree there, sir," put in Thompson. "For example—the disguise. Prince must have got rid of this incriminating evidence somehow. We might find out how he did it—*if* he did it."

"A job for you, Meredith," said the Chief, glancing at his watch. "Well, gentlemen, I can't discuss the matter more fully at the moment. I've an appointment at eleven. So I'll leave you two to thrash matters out on your own account. I feel strongly now that the arrests ought to be held up, pending further investigations. We'll keep an eye on Ormsby-Wright, also on the four garages and the six tied houses. In the meantime, we'd better arrange for the rest of the hotels to be searched. Maltman will probably help us there. Now that he knows what to look for, I think it would be best for him to play a lone hand, Inspector. There's less chance of arousing suspicion if he takes in these places as part of his usual round. From now on you'd better concentrate on the murder case. You'll find plenty of new lines to follow up if you use the Superintendent's theory as the basis for fresh inquiries. Keep in touch with us here. And remember what I said before—I want results. Good morning, gentlemen."

Back in Thompson's office the two men threw off a good deal of their official restraint and plunged into a lively discussion of the new viewpoint.

"I admit," said Thompson, "that there was an element of chance in their scheme. Prince's wait at the garage, for instance. If Hogg hadn't turned up so soon after the lorry had driven off, it might have been ages before another witness came along. They couldn't have waited for much over twenty minutes without arriving suspiciously late at the depot. Still, it was Saturday night, and it was odds on that the necessary witness would come along."

"There's another point, sir," put in Meredith, who had been over this identical point before. "They hoped that a suicide verdict would be brought in at the inquest. After all, that was their strong suit. If the jury brought in suicide then we shouldn't have pushed our investigations any further. Only unfortunately, like most criminals, they made one or two little slips in staging the scene. Clayton's clean hands, for example, and that waiting meal."

"Luckily for us," smiled Thompson. "Well, Meredith, it looks as if you'll have to try and find out if either Prince or Bettle bought a suit of buff dungarees about five weeks ago. Or you might go round the local theatrical costumiers and wig people to see if you can trace the sale of that moustache. I doubt if he could have manufactured it himself. On the other hand, he may have taken the precaution of ordering it from London or Blackpool or some other big town. Same with the clothes. I doubt if Prince would be such a fool as to get the things locally. Still, it's worth making inquiries. Then, there's the purchase of the acids. A forlorn hope, I'm afraid, as they probably originated from Ormsby-Wright. It looks as if you're in for a colossal job, Inspector!"

Meredith pulled a long face.

"Universal would fit the case better, sir! I'd rather look for that proverbial needle in a haystack!"

Thompson laughed.

"Well, I wish you luck of it!"

"Thanks, sir," replied Meredith grimly. "I'll need it all right. Nothing more?"

"Not at the moment. I shall want a usual nightly report."

"Right, sir. Then I'll be up and doing."

"What?" laughed the Superintendent. "The labours of Hercules?"

Meredith scowled.

"Hardly. He knew exactly what he was up against. I don't! I'm like a chap that's spoiling for a fight but doesn't know where to look for an opponent!"

CHAPTER XXII

CIRCUMSTANTIAL EVIDENCE

BACK in Keswick, however, surrounded by the familiar objects in his office, a great deal of Meredith's pessimism evaporated. After all, was he up against such a monumental task as Thompson suggested? He might, of course, make a long and methodical round of the local shops in the hope of pinning down the purchases. But that was not the sole line of investigation. There was another, which on the face of it, appeared to afford a greater chance of result. Prince must have bought the necessary clothes and make-up for the impersonation. Meredith didn't deny that. On the other hand, Prince was also faced with the necessity of getting rid of the disguise after the murder had been committed. To find out exactly how he managed this was a formidable but not an impossible task, surely?

Meredith's first action was to consider the details of Clayton's appearance when Luke Perryman had made his tragic discovery. Crossing over to a cupboard, he unlocked it and laid out the exhibits on his desk. The blue lounge suit and the various articles of underwear did not concern him. These would be entirely concealed by the suit of dungarees. What then was he left with? Brown brogue shoes, grey worsted socks, a suit of buff dungarees opening at the neck with a zip fastener and a green felt hat. Both the dungarees and the hat were decidedly the worse for wear—the former blotched with oil and grime, the band of the latter sweat-stained. To this he had to add the moustache—that small, characteristic moustache, which Major Rickshaw had graphically described as a "Hitler".

Both Prince and Bettle wore peaked caps and butcher-blue overalls, with the name of the company emblazoned on the lapels of their collars. This was their regulation attire. It meant, therefore, that Prince would have to discard his overalls and cap, and exchange them for the buff dungarees and the green felt hat. That was all. A transformation, even with the addition of the moustache, that would take only a few seconds. A point, Meredith felt, strongly in favour of Thompson's argument.

Dungarees. Hat. Moustache. Buff. Green felt. Hitler.

Again and again these facts circled round in his mind. Dungarees … Hat … Moustache … round and round without cessation.

Then, suddenly Meredith started. A sharp exclamation sprang involuntarily from his lips. Was there anything in it? Was it a clue or pure coincidence? But surely? A green felt hat! A Hitler moustache!

Scarcely able to restrain his excitement and impatience, he snatched up his cap, buttoned on his cape and strode out into the street. At the end of five minutes' brisk walk he turned into the gate of a small, semi-detached cottage and knocked on the door. After the lapse of a few seconds, an unkempt, poorly-dressed woman thrust her head out of an upper window and demanded in a stentorian voice to know who it was.

"Police," said Meredith curtly. "I want a word with you, Mrs. Pearson."

The woman's tones, at once, grew more conciliatory, and, after effusive apologies, she drew in her head and came down-stairs to open the door. Once in the steamy warmth of the Pearsons' kitchen-parlour, Meredith got down to the job in hand. He knew from long experience that a certain officiousness was all to the good when questioning a woman of Mrs. Pearson's type and mentality. Not that she appeared in any way hostile. She seemed to be trembling, in fact, with a fervent eagerness to propitiate the law.

"It's about that lad of yours," began Meredith sternly.

Mrs. Pearson looked startled.

"You don't come here to tell me that he's got himself into more trouble, Inspector?"

"No, not this time. It's about that window-breaking affair some time back. You remember?"

"I do!" was Mrs. Pearson's emphatic reply. "And I don't doubt that the lad does, too. His dad gave him a good welting such as he deserved. I hope there's to be no further fuss over it, sir."

"It's not that," explained Meredith. "It's about a green felt hat and a false moustache."

Again Mrs. Pearson looked startled.

"You're not accusing my boy of stealing that hat, are you?"

"I have my suspicions," was Meredith's cryptic answer.

"Then you're wrong," said Mrs. Pearson with a sudden flash of spirit. "Andy may be a bad boy but he never was a thief! You'll not make me believe that! He told me where he got that hat, Inspector. He never took it. He found it accidental like, when he was playing up the beck near Portinscale."

"Found it!" Meredith could scarcely conceal his elation. "When was that?"

"Maybe a month ago. Maybe more. I can't remember rightly. But Andy might be able to tell you."

"Very well," said Meredith. "I'll have to talk to Master Andy. What time does he come out of school?"

"Sounds like him coming up the path now," observed Mrs. Pearson. "That's his whistle right enough."

Mrs. Pearson's supposition proved right, for the next instant the door was flung open and Andy burst into the room, calling out that he was hungry and was his dinner ready? On seeing the Inspector, he stopped dead. His self-confidence oozed out of him like air out of a pricked balloon. He just stood on the mat shuffling his feet, casting uneasy eyes in Meredith's direction, evidently wondering which of his sins he was about to answer for.

"Well, sonny," grinned Meredith. "Been behaving yourself?" The boy nodded and gulped. "No more window-breaking?"

"No, sir," came the husky assurance.

"Now I want you to answer one or two questions. And I want the truth, mind you! First of all, where did you get that green hat you were wearing when I caught you breaking the window. Remember the one I mean?"

The boy nodded. "Aye—that's my gunman's hat, that is. Found it, I did, sir."

"Where?"

"By the Portinscale bridge, sir, when me and Jim Turner was playing pirates."

"And the moustache?"

"It was inside the hat, sir, when I picked it up."

Meredith could have cried aloud with joy! So the two objects *were* connected! If he wasn't on the right track this time, he'd eat his *own* hat, peak and all! Just managing to keep the elation out of his voice, he went on:

"Find anything else, sonny?"

"Yessir. It's in there."

"Then let's have a look."

The boy crossed to the dresser, opened a drawer and took out a small object, which he placed in Meredith's outstretched hand. One glance sufficed to convince the Inspector that he had not wasted his time in coming to interview Master Andy Pearson! If the hat and the moustache had been a pure matter of coincidence, this, at any rate, was more than sufficient to dispel the idea. A spanner! A blue spanner! Blue, the colour of the Nonock bulk-wagons! The colour of all the fittings and equipment connected with the firm. But why a spanner?

"And where did you pick this up exactly?"

"Inside the hat too, sir. Rolled in the hat."

"Rolled in it!"

Meredith almost shouted. A green felt hat, wrapped round a blue spanner and a Hitler moustache, picked up by Andy Pearson beside the Portinscale bridge. In a flash Meredith saw the whole thing. The swift-flowing beck under the bridge, the speeding bolt-wagon on its way back to Penrith, Prince leaning out of the cab and hurling——!

In a furore of impatience he turned to the bewildered boy.

"Now look here, sonny—I want you to come out with me to Portinscale bridge and show me exactly where you found that hat. Understand?" He swung round on Mrs. Pearson. "I'll get him back in time to have his dinner before he returns to school. Come on, my lad."

Half-running, the boy followed Meredith to the police garage, where the Inspector wheeled out the combination and dumped his excited young passenger in the side-car. A swift run brought them to a point near Portinscale, where the old stone bridge seemed to hump itself sulkily over the shallow, fast-flowing beck, with its feet planted on either bank.

"Now then," said Meredith, "which side of the beck did you find it?"

"Just down there, sir," replied Andy, pointing to where a path meandered along the left bank of the stream. "Over that stile."

When they had crossed the stile into the meadow, Meredith allowed the boy to take the lead. After a moment's hesitation he seemed to make up his mind about the exact spot and started off at a sudden trot down the slope of the meadow. Reaching the edge of the bank, about some fifteen feet from the bridge, he stopped dead and pointed down into a thick fringe of rushes which lined both sides of the swirling waterway.

"Just here, sir."

"Sure?"

The boy nodded eagerly.

"There's the stones what Jim Turner and me laid on the mud afore we could reach the hat."

"And the hat was lying?"

"Right on the edge of the reeds, sir. Nearly in the water."

"Good. Now can you remember when you and Jim Turner found that hat?"

"Sunday it was. 'Cause Jim had his best suit on. He got in hot water for it when he got back home, sir!"

"Last Sunday?"

The boy shook his head decisively.

"Long time afore that. Jest after my birthday."

"Your birthday, eh? When's that?"

"Nineteenth of March, sir."

"Right. Now we'll go back." Once on their way, Meredith asked, "Have you still got that hat and moustache?" The boy nodded and looked a trifle disconcerted. "It's all right, sonny," Meredith assured him, "I only want to borrow them for a time. I'll let you have 'em back."

"You see," explained Andy, "it's my gunman's hat. I'm chief of the gang and I couldn't go about without a hat."

"Quite," said Meredith, amused, as they drew up at the Pearsons' gate. Then slipping a shilling into the boy's somewhat grubby palm, he added: "Now don't you tell anybody I gave you that. You can buy something at the toy shop, see?"

There was no doubt that Andy was quick to seize the point, and after Meredith had collected the hat and the moustache, he jumped on to his bike and drove back to the police station.

Once in his office he placed the two hats side by side on his desk and realized, with a thrill of satisfaction, that they were practically identical. Although Prince had probably bought a new hat he had evidently gone to the troubling of soiling the felt and pulling it out of shape. Inside the crown, as Meredith had anticipated, there was no hint as to the maker's or retailer's name. If there had been a label then Prince had taken care to rip it off before throwing it from the lorry. Not that Meredith attached much importance to the tracing of the sale. There no longer seemed any need for that! Here, on the direct route between the Derwent and the Nonock depot, was a discarded green felt hat, wrapped round a false moustache and a heavy blue spanner. It was now perfectly obvious that Prince had intended to sink these objects in mid-stream as the bulk wagon passed over Portinscale bridge. Unfortunately, he had misjudged the distance and the weighted hat had fallen on the edge of the reeds instead of in the water. Andy Pearson said that he had picked it up on the Sunday following his birthday. His birthday fell on the 19th of March, which meant that the boys had made their discovery on the 24th. And the crime had been committed on the night of the 23rd! So much for the hat.

Meredith now switched his attention over to the moustache. It was neatly made, of dark hair and designed to pinch on to the nostrils by means of two tiny metal clips. Standing before a mirror, the Inspector tried fixing it into position. He reckoned that Prince could have dealt with this part of his disguise in a couple of seconds. The moustache fitted neatly and securely into place and the result was astoundingly life-like. That it had been made by an expert was evident, but, as in the case of the hat, there was not the slightest clue to suggest where Prince had made his purchase. So much for the moustache.

Meredith was left with the dungarees. Had Prince thrown these from the lorry together with the hat? Or had he considered the article too bulky to be safely disposed of in this rather slip-shod manner? Had he seized on the only obvious alternative and burnt them? Meredith dealt with the two methods in the order in which they had occurred to him.

First—their disposal from the cab of the lorry. Wasn't it possible that Prince had hung on to the dungarees and disposed of them later on during the homeward run? He might have marked down a spot some time before the murder had been committed where he considered the dungarees would be safe from discovery. A wayside pond perhaps. An isolated clump of gorse or brambles. There were hundreds of possibilities. He might even have retained the incriminating bundle until he reached the depot and smuggled it out without Dancy's knowledge and perhaps hidden it in some innocent person's dustbin. The more Meredith pondered the question, the more clearly he realized the hopelessness of the task which lay ahead of him. It would mean an exhaustive search of every inch of the roadside between the Derwent and the depot, coupled with a somewhat belated notice in the Penrith papers for information concerning an old suit of buff dungarees. And if Prince *had* dumped the bundle in a dustbin the chances were that this priceless bit of evidence had been destroyed weeks ago in the municipal incinerators! Meredith sighed. Could the police hope for a conviction on the evidence of the hat, the moustache and the blue spanner alone? Certainly, combined with other bits of circumstantial evidence, there was ample justification for arrest. But what about those twelve "good men and true" who would be called upon to bring in the verdict?

Meredith felt certain that those dungarees would have to be found. But what if they had been destroyed?

This brought him to his second point. Had Prince smuggled the dungarees out of the depot unnoticed and later burnt them? To do this he would need time and privacy and a reasonable chance of being uninterrupted. This naturally suggested his lodgings or, if he were married, his rooms or cottage. It would further call for some means of walking out of the depot with the dungarees, without arousing Dancy's curiosity. Rose, of course, didn't enter in, because he was mixed up with the racket and almost certainly had knowledge of the murder. Meredith decided that his first move should be a visit to Dancy at 24 Eamont Villas. He glanced at his watch. One forty-five. He could not get a private interview with the yard-man, therefore, until some time after six. In the meantime how had he best fill in the intervening hours? First another examination of the spot where Andy Pearson had found the hat, then a slow journey to Penrith, ear-marking probable localities where the dungarees might be concealed.

He returned to Greystoke Road, therefore, and after a hasty lunch drove out to Portinscale bridge. There he made a lengthy and exhaustive search not only of the banks of the river, but, clad in waders, of the bed of the river itself. But all to no account. There was no sign of the missing dungarees. He did not dismiss the possibility that the bundle might have been carried downstream by the swiftly-flowing waters, but until he had explored all other avenues of investigation, he determined to leave this part of the search in abeyance.

Then followed a long and annoying reconnoitre of the full nineteen miles of roadside between the Derwent and the depot. Again and again Meredith drew up, made a quick survey of a likely hiding-place and jotted down its position in his notebook. It was not until six o'clock that he drew level with the depot and passed on his spasmodic journey to Penrith.

At six-thirty he turned into the end of Careleton Street and drew up before number 24 Eamont Villas. As luck would have it, Dancy had just returned from work and was sitting over his tea in his shirt-sleeves. On seeing the Inspector, he made a sign for his wife to retire into the kitchen and waved Meredith to a chair.

"More trouble, Inspector?"

Meredith laughed genially.

"You're like all the rest of them, Mr. Dancy! They all suspect that my appearance heralds trouble! In this case I can assure you there's no cause for alarm. I'm after my usual quarry—information. Nothing more. Can I go ahead?"

"Do," said Dancy, putting on his pipe and tilting his chair back from the table.

"About that Saturday night once again. I want you to cast your mind back to when Prince and Bettle left the depot after they had garaged No. 4. Were either of them carrying anything under their arms? A brown paper parcel for example?"

Dancy sucked meditatively at his pipe. Then he shook his head.

"No—they had nothing of that nature with 'em as far as I can remember. Mind you, it's over a month ago. I may be wrong, Inspector."

"Think again. You feel sure that they were carrying nothing."

"Well," corrected Dancy, "nothing unusual that is. Such as a parcel or the like."

"Then they were carrying *something*," snapped out Meredith eagerly.

"Of course they were," replied Dancy stolidly. "Their dinner-baskets. But there wasn't anything queer about that, was there?"

Meredith hastened to reassure the yard-man.

"No. I quite see that, Mr. Dancy. Tell me—how big are these dinner-baskets?"

Dancy illustrated their approximate size.

"About like that, I reckon.'

"Large enough to take a rolled-up boiler-suit, for example?"

"Easy," said Dancy with a puzzled look. "But I don't quite——"

"I suppose you didn't see either Bettle or Prince stuffing anything like a coat or a boiler-suit into them on that particular Saturday night?"

"They may have done," answered Dancy judicially. "But if they did, I didn't see 'em!"

Satisfied that he had got all possible information from Dancy, Meredith thanked him, called out "good night" to his wife and let himself out into Careleton Street.

It was obvious that his next move was to pay a visit to Prince's and Bettle's lodgings. According to their signed depositions they were housed by a Mrs. Arkwright at 9 Brockman's Row, Penrith.

He realized, however, that he'd have to postpone his visit to Mrs. Arkwright until the following morning. He didn't want the lorry-men drifting in whilst he was in the middle of a cross-examination. He, therefore, returned direct to Keswick, where he got through to Thompson and reported on the progress of his investigations.

Shortly after ten-thirty the next day, however, he turned out of the Penrith High Street and found his way to number 9 Brockman's Row. In answer to his knock the door was opened by a stout, genial looking woman of about forty. Ascertaining that this was Mrs. Arkwright herself, Meredith explained that he was a police inspector. He believed Mrs. Arkwright could supply him with certain important information. Would she be good enough to do so?

Much impressed by the solemnity of the Inspector's voice, she ushered him into an airless, sunless little drawing-room full of ferns and aspidistras. Seating herself on the extreme edge of an elaborately upholstered sofa she faced Meredith with a look of defiant respectability. It was rather as if she was saying: "There may be trouble somewhere but I'm quite sure it has nothing to do with *me*!" Virtue was rampant in the very attitude of her somewhat portly person.

"Now, Mrs. Arkwright," began Meredith, "I understand that a gentleman by the name of Mr. Prince lodges with you here?"

"That's right, sir," replied the landlady promptly. "Him and Mr. Bettle. They share the room across the passage there and the bedroom over this. I hope Mr. Prince hasn't got himself into trouble?"

"Oh, nothing to speak of," was Meredith's light answer. "How long have these two gentlemen been with you?"

"About three years now, sir."

"Ever had any cause for complaint?"

Mrs. Arkwright hesitated a moment, glanced across uneasily at the Inspector and finally elected to remain silent.

"Now don't you worry, Mrs. Arkwright," Meredith reassured her. "Anything you may care to tell me will be treated in the strictest confidence. You needn't answer my questions unless you want to."

"Well, sir, I don't like to talk about the private doings of my gentlemen. After all, this is their home if you see how I mean?"

"Quite. I appreciate your feelings."

"But since you promise not to let things go any further I don't mind telling you that I'm fair worried by that Mr. Prince. It's the drink, see? He doesn't seem able to keep away from the public house."

"And he sometimes returns home at night—er—rather the worse for wear, eh? Is that it?"

Mrs. Arkwright nodded.

"And of late it's got worse, sir. Once or twice I've been fair frightened, what with him and Mr. Bettle argufying and knocking things about in their room. Mind you, it's Mr. Prince that makes all the bother. Mr. Bettle would be quiet enough if it wasn't for Mr. Prince."

"When did things seem to take a turn for the worse, Mrs. Arkwright?"

"Ever since about a month ago, sir. It all started of a Saturday night. If it hadn't been for Mr. Bettle I don't know how Mr. Prince would have got home that night. Blind drunk he was, sir. Shocking! We had to more or less drag him upstairs to his bed."

"You couldn't be more precise on the date, I suppose?"

Mrs. Arkwright thought over this point for a minute.

"Well, it was the week-end afore Annie—that's my sister-in-law, sir—came over from Troutbeck on a visit. Let's see now, that would be about the end of March."

"The 30th or 31st?" suggested Meredith.

"That would be about it, sir, because her boy was a talking about what he'd be up to on April Fool's day."

"So the night you and Mr. Bettle had to see Mr. Prince upstairs must have been the 23rd."

"I suppose it was about then."

"Now could I have a look at this room of theirs?"

"Well, I haven't cleared out the grate and so on yet, but if you——"

"Never mind that," answered Meredith with a laugh. "I'm a family man. I know that everything can't always be ship-shape in a house by ten-thirty. Go ahead, Mrs. Arkwright."

"Perhaps you'd follow me, sir."

Meredith did so and found himself in an unpretentious, plainly-furnished room with a big sash-window giving on to the street. Two wicker arm-chairs were set on either side of an old-fashioned grate, whilst in the centre of the room stood an ordinary kitchen table camouflaged with a red plush table-cloth.

"I can see that your gentlemen are made comfortable enough," was Meredith's tactful observation. "By the way, Mrs. Arkwright, what time do you have to clear up the room on Sunday morning? Earlier than during the week, I take it?"

"Gracious, no sir! Mr. Bettle and Mr. Prince never so much as stir from their beds until just on opening time. I always take them up a cup of tea about nine. So there's no cause for me to worry about this room until eleven or later."

"Now I'm going to ask you a rather peculiar question," said Meredith slowly. "On Sunday, March 24th, did you find anything out of the ordinary among the ashes when you cleared out this grate? That was the Sunday, remember, after Mr. Prince had come home so bad. Well, Mrs. Arkwright?"

"It's funny you should ask that, sir."

"Why?" demanded Meredith sharply.

"Because that was the very morning when I found a half-crown among the cinders under the grate."

"A what?" exclaimed Meredith.

"A half-crown, sir. How it got there I can't say. One of the gentlemen must have dropped it on to the hearth and it had rolled under the grate out of sight. Course I spoke to Mr. Prince about it and he said that it was his right enough, but how it got there he couldn't for the life of him say."

"I suppose," said Meredith, drawing something out of his pocket and holding it out for the landlady's inspection, "that you didn't find anything like that, eh?"

Mrs. Arkwright's eyes seemed to start out of her head. She seemed scarcely able to credit the evidence of her own senses. Twice she tried to give expression to her astonishment and merely succeeded in producing a muffled croak. Then finally she managed to gasp out:

"But where did you get hold of it, sir? I threw it away in the ash-bin! And what made you think that I found it that morning in the cinders along with the half-crown?"

Controlling his exuberance, Meredith hastened to calm the bewildered woman.

"It's all right, Mrs. Arkwright. I'm not a magician. This isn't the one you picked up out of the ashes. This is another one like it. Do you know what it is?"

Mrs. Arkwright shook her head, obviously relieved to hear that she had not been the victim of some form of sorcery.

"And I didn't at the time, sir."

"It's a 'zip' fastener," said Meredith. "Ever seen one before?"

"How silly of me! Of course I have, now I come to think of it. Mrs. Grath next door but one has got a hand-bag that opens with one of them things. Fancy me not thinking of it at the time!"

"Did you tell Mr. Prince about this other discovery?"

"No, sir. I didn't think it was anything of value. I only mentioned the half-crown."

"I take it that you handed the half-crown back to Mr. Prince?"

"Yes, sir."

"You found nothing in the nature of a piece of charred cloth among the ashes?" Mrs. Arkwright shook her head. "What did you do with the fastener?"

"As I said before, sir, I threw it away in the ashbin."

"Which, of course, has been cleared more than once since that date, Mrs. Arkwright?"

The landlady looked surprised. "Oh, no, sir! I don't empty my ashes into the ordinary rubbish bin. I always shoot them into a separate bin."

"Why do you do that?"

"Well, sir, to be honest with you, I make a bit of money that way. Not much—but every little helps in these hard times, as you'll admit."

"You mean you sell the ashes?"

Mrs. Arkwright nodded. "To Mr. Parsons, my next-door neighbour. He's got an allotment out near the football ground and he likes the ash for his soil. I think he's sifting the ash, sir, and using the clinkers for a path he's making. If you really want to know what he does with them you'd better see him yourself, Inspector."

"I think I will, Mrs. Arkwright—thanks. Which side of you does he live?"

"At number 8, sir."

Armed with this further information, Meredith thanked the landlady for her help and warned her, on no account, to make any mention of his visit. Then, thrilled and immensely pleased with the progress he was making, Meredith stepped out into the street and knocked on the door of number 8. In answer to his inquiry, he learnt that Mr. Parsons was to be found at Messrs. Loveday and White's, the ironmongers in Duke Street. And as he did not return to his dinner until one o'clock, Meredith decided to get in touch with him at the shop.

A brisk walk brought him to the ironmongers. On asking for Mr. Parsons, he was told by an assistant that he was over in the store at the rear of the premises, checking in a new consignment of stock. Meredith, thereupon, pointed out that his business was rather urgent and suggested that he might see Mr. Parsons in the store. The assistant agreed and piloted the Inspector through a series of narrow shelf-lined passages, which eventually opened out into the main stock-room. As soon as the assistant had left,

Meredith introduced himself to the storeman and got down to tin-tacks.

"I won't bother you with the exact reasons for this visit," explained Meredith glibly. "Suffice it to say that it's a serious matter—a very serious matter, Mr. Parsons. And I want your co-operation."

Briefly Meredith set out the information concerning the ashes, which he had learnt from Mrs. Arkwright. This done, he concluded with a request that Parsons should accompany him there and then to the allotment. A word to the manager evinced the necessary permission for the store-man's absence, and the two men set off at a smart pace for the football ground. Arriving at the allotments, Parsons guided the Inspector through a maze of tiny intersecting paths, until they reached a fair-sized patch of ground, which the store-man proudly indicated as being his own. Meredith noticed, at once, that this particular allotment was all but encompassed by a newly-laid ash path. That the work was not quite completed clearly indicated that the clinker had only recently been dumped there. A fact to which Parsons immediately testified.

"As a matter of fact, sir, I only brought the stuff out a couple of days ago. I borrowed a hand-cart from the shop and brought all the clinker out in one journey."

"This is all sifted stuff, I take it?" Parsons nodded. "And you use a fairly fine-meshed sieve?" The man agreed. "So if anything like this," added Meredith, producing the zip fastener which he had detached from Clayton's dungarees, "was among the ash it would remain with the clinker?"

"Yes, sir."

"You didn't notice a strip of metal like this, I suppose, when you were doing the sifting?" Parsons shook his head. He was quite certain he hadn't. "Then we can pretty well assume that if the fastener *was* among the clinker you had from Mrs. Arkwright, it's now lying somewhere on this new path of yours?"

"I should say so, sir."

"Do you mind if I look? It may mean disturbing the surface a bit with a rake or a hoe, but I'm afraid it's a job that's got to be done, Mr. Parsons. Sorry!"

Although it was obvious that the thought of having to disturb the carefully rolled surface of his new path was not exactly pleasing to Parsons, he gave in with a good grace to Meredith's request. Unlocking a small wooden shack, he produced a rake and a hoe and, in a few moments, the two men were hard at work. Starting from the opposite ends of the incompleted rectangle, which encompassed the allotment, Meredith and the store-man hacked up and sifted through every inch of the clinker. To Meredith the moment was one of the most crucial importance. As he saw it, the most critical piece of investigation in the whole of the murder case. Find that second zip fastener and the chain of evidence against Bettle and Prince was complete. Which of the two men actually administered the carbon monoxide it was impossible to say, and if Thompson's theory was right, it really didn't matter. For if Prince had administered the fumes, then Bettle must have held the victim while the dastardly job was being done. They were both equally culpable of murder.

But the question remained—was he going to find that final scrap of evidence among the cinders? As foot by foot they covered the rolled surface of the path, Meredith's heart sank. Another eight feet or so and he and Parsons would be back to back. With feverish impatience, yet with commendable care, the Inspector dug his hoe, again and again, into the compressed clinkers, loosening them and raking them over. Behind him he heard the scratch of Parsons' rake, now perilously near and every second approaching.

Then, just when he had abandoned all hope and given himself up to despair, there came a sudden, sharp exclamation from his co-worker. Meredith swung round. The store-man was craning over, staring at something which gleamed near the toe of his right boot.

"Good heavens!" cried Meredith. "You've found it! No mistake about it, Mr. Parsons! Here, let's have a look at it. Quick!"

Leaning down, he snatched up the thin, flexible bit of metal and examined it closely. A single glance was enough. Parsons' find was identical with the fastener which he had ripped from Clayton's dungarees! It meant that the conclusive proof he had so hankered after was now in his grasp. Literally in his grasp—for with a cry of satisfaction his fingers closed about that commonplace, innocent trifle. A rusted, tarnished scrap of metal which, in all probability, was destined to slip the hangman's noose round the necks of two unsuspecting men!

So much for that! The second case, like the first, was now at an end! It only remained to make the necessary arrests and set the great wheel of justice in motion and the work of the police would be over and done with. The closing chapters of the crimes would be written by the relentless hands of judge and jury—a relentlessness tempered with all the fairness and common sense of British justice.

After thanking the bewildered Mr. Parsons for his assistance, Meredith found his way to the Penrith police station, where he had parked the combination. Mounting the saddle, he drove post-haste back to Keswick.

One thing, in the midst of so much that was now startlingly clear, remained to puzzle him. That Prince had burnt the dungarees in the sitting-room grate at Mrs. Arkwright's was now certain. That in his haste and excitement he had overlooked the damning fact that the fastener would not be destroyed with the dungarees was equally certain. As Meredith saw it, he had stuffed the rolled suit into his dinner-basket before he reached the depot. Then, unnoticed by Dancy, he had conveyed this dangerous clue to his lodgings. There, the moment it was safe, probably after Mrs. Arkwright had cleared away the men's supper, he had thrust the dungarees on to the flames and waited until they were entirely destroyed. Satisfied on this point, he and Bettle had then retired to a nearby pub and drowned their fears in a drinking bout, Prince returning to Brockman's Row entirely incapacitated. From that day to this he had evidently resorted to alcohol as a means to keep up his courage, in the light of what he had done. Bettle, of a more phlegmatic nature, had apparently taken things more calmly. Meredith imagined that he would be far more callous and less imaginative than his companion in crime.

And the one thing which still puzzled him?

The half-crown. Why the half-crown? Was it coincidence that it had tumbled from one of the men's pockets and rolled under the grate along with the metal fastener? Had it happened when one of the murderers was leaning over the fire during the destruction of the dungarees? If so, it was a lucky accident from the police point of view. Meredith was quick to realize that but for the half-crown Mrs. Arkwright would have been unable to fix the date of Prince's drinking bout and the finding of the "zip" fastener with such exactitude. A fact which he considered all-important. But somehow he could not think that the half-crown had got among the ashes by accident. It was almost certain that had it slipped from one of the men's pockets they would have heard it drop on to the hearth. What then were the alternative explanations? Meredith could see only one that was within the bounds of feasibility. The half-crown must have been in the pocket of the dungarees. But why? The dungarees were part of a disguise, not a normal part of Prince's attire. What reason would he have for slipping a half-crown into his pocket whilst he was actually wearing those dungarees? Was there any reason?

Meredith ran through the series of events which had taken place during the impersonation. First of all Major Rickshaw and his wife had drawn up at the pumps and——

The combination swerved violently, narrowly missing a farm-cart which was drawn into the side of the road. Fool, thought Meredith. Blind fool! Major Rickshaw had pulled up at the Derwent for petrol. Prince, disguised as Clayton, had served the pump. Rickshaw had paid for two gallons of one shilling and threepenny petrol with a half-crown. Prince had slipped it into his pocket *and forgotten it*! There was the explanation right enough. Meredith recalled his interview with the Major. He remembered asking particularly about the denomination of the coins he had handed over and Rickshaw had aired his faith in cheap petrol and spoken about the half-crown. So his visit to 9 Brockman's Row had provided him with two damning clues instead of one! It set the seal on the lorry-men's fate. From that moment the lives of Prince and Bettle were doomed! The net had finally closed round them—a fine-meshed, entangling net of circumstantial evidence.

That the murder was a cold-blooded, premeditated affair Meredith could not deny, yet now that success had crowned his efforts, he could not help feeling something akin to pity for the men he had brought to justice. It was his first unaided murder investigation and his humaneness recoiled from the consequences of his success. Then he thought of Clayton, about to turn over a new leaf; Lily Reade stricken with the news of her fiancé's death. Instinctively his jaw tightened and his hands gripped more fiercely on to the handle-bars of his bike. He had only done his duty. Life and property had to be protected. It was right, without any vestige of doubt, that Bettle and Prince should hang!

CHAPTER XXIII

THE LAST ROUND-UP

MEREDITH'S final discoveries at Penrith virtually brought his investigations to an end. After he had put in a report to Carlisle, he was summoned to attend a final conference over at headquarters on the following day. There he learnt that Maltman had succeeded in running to earth the secret labelling and bottling departments in the other five tied houses. In each case the same method had been utilized as in force at 'The Admiral.' A false cask gave entrance to a shaft driven through the cellar wall to a point more or less directly beneath the Nonock pump. Each of these hidden vaults was crammed with whisky bottles and the necessary apparatus for labelling and diluting the raw spirit.

It only remained, therefore, to organize a wholesale arrest of the miscreants. The Chief had drawn up a comprehensive list of the men for whom warrants were to be issued. First, on two charges, there came Ormsby-Wright. He was to be indicted both for the murder of Clayton, a crime which he had almost certainly instigated, and the running of illicit stills for the purpose of defrauding the Excise authorities. Then, of course, came Bettle and Prince on the major charge, Higgins as an accessory both before and after the fact and for being in possession of apparatus for the distilling of illicit liquor. Wick and the proprietors of the Stanley Hall and Filsam Garages for illicit distilling. Finally there were the proprietors of the six tied houses who had passed out the illicit liquor over the counters of their premises. Coionel Hardwick also anticipated that there might be further arrests when the machinations of the gang had been more fully gone into. In the case of Rose, the manager of the Nonock depot, although at the moment there was no definite case made out against him, he was to be detained on suspicion as being a party to the fraud. It was generally felt that evidence would be forthcoming in the cross-examination of the other prisoners which would definitely incriminate him.

The Chief Constable then turned to the manner in which the arrests were to be carried out.

To prevent any member of the gang from communicating a warning, the arrests were to be made simultaneously. Watches were to be synchronized, so that there would not even be an opportunity for a phone call to be sent out. The Chief had decided that, since they could no longer procrastinate, these plans were to be put into operation at midnight on the morrow. Two plain-clothes constables were to be detailed to each of the four garages and the six tied houses. Two more men were to attend to Rose at his private address. Thompson was to make his own arrangements for dealing with Ormsby-Wright at his Penrith house, whilst Meredith, with the help of a sergeant and two constables, was to tackle Bettle and Prince at Brockman's Row. Once the arrests had been made, the prisoners were to be conveyed to headquarters at Carlisle. In the case of the three garages which so far had not been fully investigated, an immediate search of the premises was to follow the arrests. As the Chief pointed out, material evidence was naturally needed to back up each of the individual charges. For the same reason, with Dancy's help, a further search was to be made of Rose's office. His books and private papers were then to be gone through in the hope of finding material which would give conclusive details of the illicit organization.

At the conclusion of his orders the Chief Constable inquired of Thompson and Meredith if they had any other points for discussion.

The Superintendent took advantage of the offer.

"There is just one thing, sir. I suppose we are quite safe in our assumption that the other lorry-men are not connected with the racket?"

"No," acknowledged the Chief. "We're not! But that's a risk we've got to take. If there is a case to be made out against any of these men, it's bound to come to light when the gang is broken up. Personally, I'm inclined to believe that only Prince and Bettle are incriminated. For two very sound reasons. Inquiries have been made since we last met and we have definitely ascertained that Ormsby-Wright owns just that one group of tied houses in the coastal towns. And since they're a vital factor in his scheme, it follows that the other lorries are used solely for the delivery of petrol. And again—when you made your examination of the bulk-wagons, Meredith, you found that only No. 4 was fitted with a false tank."

"That's true enough, sir! Besides, a limited personnel is always an advantage in a criminal organization—don't you agree, sir?"

The Chief intimated that he did and, after further details had been gone into, the conference broke up.

And as the Chief Constable had arranged, so it came about. At midnight on the following day the various arrests were made. In every case, save one, the culprits were in bed and entirely unsuspicious.

In Meredith's case, there was nothing dramatic in the arrest of the murderers. According to instruction, Mrs. Arkwright had left the front door of No. 9 unlocked. Followed by Sergeant Matthews, Railton and another constable, Meredith crept upstairs. Flinging open the door of the bedroom, he switched on the lights, roused the two men and told them to get into their clothes. Realizing that the game was up, the prisoners came quietly. A search of the room brought further incriminating evidence to light. In a drawer Meredith found two half-empty bottles of acid. Although the labels had been scratched off, analysis proved that the bottles contained concentrated sulphuric and oxalic acid respectively, convincing proof that Superintendent Thompson's reconstruction of the crime was correct.

The other arrests were carried out in the same efficient and unobtrusive manner. Thompson alone ran headlong into melodrama.

At eleven-thirty, according to plan, he and his men posted themselves in the grounds of Brackenside, preparatory to making the arrest at midnight. There was a single light burning in an upper window when they arrived on the scene. From the man who had been shadowing Ormsby-Wright they learnt that he was in, and that the light was coming from his bedroom window. Thompson decided, therefore, to post a man at every door and french window on the ground floor, for even if Ormsby-Wright was in bed by midnight, it was pretty obvious that he wouldn't be asleep. Thompson and a Sergeant were to ring the front door bell. If Ormsby-Wright answered in person they were to arrest him on the spot. If it was answered by a maid or manservant, they were to rush the stairs and make direct for his bedroom.

At ten minutes to twelve the light went out. The men took up their positions. On the stroke of midnight Thompson rang the front door bell. After a considerable pause, the door was opened by a maid-servant in her night attire. On seeing the two men she gave a scream before they were able to warn her and, apparently in the hubbub that followed, she, feminine-like, threw a faint. Thompson and the Sergeant, having previously worked out the exact location of the wanted man's bedroom, took the stairs two at a time and rushed straight for the door. Then they struck an unexpected snag. To their immense chagrin, the door was locked! Thompson thereupon hammered and demanded entry in the name of the law, but although the light was switched on Ormsby-Wright made no effort to comply with his request. The two men then got their shoulders to the door and after a series of violent efforts succeeded in breaking in an upper panel. Then came the tragedy!

Even as Thompson was reaching through the splintered woodwork to turn the key on the inside there came a deafening report. It is hardly necessary to tell what they found. Ormsby-Wright stretched out over the bed, a smoking revolver in his hand and blood oozing from a fatal head-wound. He was dead before they reached him. Warned by the approach of the police that the game was up, he had seen that there was only one way out of the predicament, and taken it.

Ormsby-Wright's suicide provided conclusive proof of his own guilt, and the various books, accounts and personal memoranda found in his private safe were more than sufficient to convict the other members of the notorious gang, Rose included. That he had incited Bettle and Prince to do away with Clayton was certain. Both the murderers upheld this point, though it did nothing to divert the ends of justice. Bettle and Prince paid the extreme penalty. Higgins was sentenced to fifteen years' penal servitude. It was Higgins who had fixed the hose to the exhaust of Clayton's car, locked the lean-to and hidden the key in a pre-arranged place. He had then left for the Beacon at Penrith to establish his cast-iron alibi.

For the rest there is little to be said. The racket had been going on for seven years and it was estimated that Ormsby-Wright had netted a cool fifty thousand pounds during that period. The rest of the gang received sentences ranging from two to four years. Prince, Bettle and Rose were all known to each other before they came North and Ormsby-Wright had engaged them for the specific purpose of running the liquor racket. The proprietors of the tied houses were of a similar kidney and a share of the handsome profits had ensured their silence. At the trial of Bettle and Prince it came out that Thompson's theory as to how the murder was committed was right in every detail, whilst Inspector Meredith's statement as to how the racket was being managed received a like confirmation.

Inspector Meredith? Well, that is hardly correct. Superintendent Meredith would meet the case better—a co-worker with Thompson at Carlisle headquarters! A well-merited promotion!

THE END